Unraveled

[a novel about a meltdown]

by Alda Sigmundsdóttir

ENSKA TEXTASMIÐJAN

Cover design: Erlingur Páll Ingvarsson

Cover photo: Annie Atkins

ISBN-13: 978-9979-72-311-0

CONTENTS

CHAPTER ONE

Before she found the earring, there had been no cause for Frida Lowe to doubt her husband's fidelity. It had never even occurred to her that he might be unfaithful. It wasn't his style. Sure, he was suave, sophisticated, attractive and successful, but he wasn't the philandering type.

Anyway, he worked too much.

They were on their way out to a party. Damien, freshly spritzed with cologne, was pacing back and forth at the foot of the stairs, waiting for his wife.

"Frida!" He called, a hint of annoyance in his voice.

"Coming!" she called out, her voice light as a girl's. "Two minutes!"

He was always punctual; she never was. He was British; she was Icelandic. That explained it, she reasoned to herself. At least as far as she was concerned. Icelanders always did things late, or at the last minute.

Quickly she finished assembling things into her clutch. She pulled on a pair of slingback pumps, and with a critical glance at herself in the mirror – her hair was never quite right, too wispy around the temples – headed out of the bedroom.

At the top of the stairs she hesitated. The light was on in Damien's study. He would want her to turn it off. Quickly she strode down the hall and pushed open the door. The illumination was coming from the floor lamp next to his desk.

Heading over there, a glittering object on the floor caught her eye. She bent down and picked it up. It was a woman's earring – a clip-on, shaped like a drop, with an emerald green stone surrounded by smaller stones, set on a faux-antique background. An earring that you would most likely not wear with casual clothes, thus an earring that was not likely to belong to Kristín, their middle-aged housekeeper.

And it was not hers.

"Frida!" His voice again, clipped and irritated.

"Coming!" she called back. She slipped the earring into the pocket of her jacket and swiftly turned out the light.

"We're already late," Damien said irritably as she came down the stairs. She threw a cashmere shawl loosely around her shoulders and pulled on beige kid gloves that matched her tailored cream-colored skirt and jacket. Stepping outside, Damien held Frida's elbow for support as she gingerly made her way down the steps in her heels. Jonni, the driver, waited in the Range Rover out on the street in their reserved parking spot, watching them approach. They made a stunning couple. Damien in his impeccable Armani suit, Frida in her crisp cream-colored skirt and jacket, blonde hair cascading in soft waves down her back. As always, she'd taken special care with her appearance. Damien liked for her to look nice. It made him proud.

He was unusually quiet on the drive to the party. Frida glanced at him, thoughts churning. An earring. Not hers. She put her hand in her pocket and ran her fingers over it, feeling the rough surface of the stones.

Her stomach clenched and she felt pressure in her head. *How dare he!*

She was taken aback by the violence of the emotion and drew a deep breath, trying to will her heart to stop pounding and her nerves to calm down.

Within minutes, they pulled up outside a stately residence on Ægissída, across from the sea. Jonni got out of the car and opened the door for Frida – something that always made her uncomfortable. For Damien it was normal, but it seemed so out of place in Iceland's egalitarian society. Also, it made her feel like a fraud. She had left twelve years earlier as Frida Jóhannsdóttir, the scrawny, invisible kid who never invited anyone to her house, and returned as Frida Lowe, wife of Damien Lowe, Her Majesty's Ambassador to Iceland – a woman of means and stature. And now her car door was being opened by someone who could easily have been in her class in grade school, and whom she probably would have avoided and feared because that's how she was in grade school: always avoiding everyone out of fear.

They strode up to the house and took their place by the door, tall and erect like two statues, still and perfect.

Canada's Ambassador to Iceland, George Rogers, martini in hand, thick moustache glistening, threw open the front door. From behind him wafted the sound of talk, glassware and laughter.

"Damien!" His eyes were swimming, "Hello old chap! Do come in – ah Frida," dropping his voice, "you fox! Stunning as always." He winked, bowed his head, took her hand, raised his eyes, kissed it wetly.

She gave him her most gracious smile. "Hello, George."

"Well don't just stand there, come in. We've all been waiting for you."

He scurried off in front of them. *Like a rat in a hole.*

Her breath caught in her throat. Thoughts like that had begun to accost her lately, lunging at her – disturbing and utterly unacceptable.

Glancing in a mirror in the vestibule, her grim expression took her by surprise; this was not the right look for the occasion. She rearranged her features into a mask of gentle contentment, then slipped her hand through her husband's arm and walked inside.

The light from the crystal chandelier was blinding. Out of the whiteness appeared the face of George's wife Patricia, standing next to her husband. Her jaw was clenched and her eyes hard. Yet she smiled.

"Frida! Damien – how lovely to see you."

"Hello Patricia. How *are* you."

"Dinner is almost ready. We were starting to wonder if you would *ever* get here." Smile. Underlying resentment in the voice.

Suddenly Frida had a vision of Patricia standing before her with her face black and disfigured, hair like soot-grey pipe cleaners, vomiting obscenities.

She put her hand to her forehead and breathed deeply.

What is wrong with me?

Damien's smooth, caramel voice. "Patricia, we do apologize. Something came up just as we were leaving the house."

"Oh, that's all right!" Incongruous laughter; jarring, disturbing.

Frida smiled sweetly; Damien took her arm and led her away, joining another group of ambassadorial couples – Germany and Denmark. Denmark were new, like Frida and Damien had been five months earlier.

"Hello Frida." Heike, wife of the German Ambassador, leaning sideways and speaking in a low, conspiratorial tone. Already Heike had latched on to Frida as an ally. Her eyes were filled with unwanted camaraderie; they told Frida that she'd witnessed the scene just now and she would join forces with her, she would savor their delicious alliance and denounce Patricia later, licking her fingertips when nobody was looking.

Frida felt nauseous, then a surge of panic, as though someone had heard her thinking, like she was completely transparent and they had seen into her, *seen what was happening....*

Damien again, to the rescue: "Mr. and Mrs. Pedersen, may I introduce my wife Frida?" His hand rested lightly on her waist. "Frida, this is the new Danish Ambassador to Iceland, Carl, and his wife Annelise."

"Pleasure." The shaking of hands.

"I understand you're Icelandic and that you've come home now?" Carl seemed genuine enough; his eyes twinkled, his expression was kind.

"Yes, that's right."

"How many years were you away?"

Frida glanced at Damien and smiled. Everyone saw. He grinned back at her. They saw that, too. He reached out and pressed her hand. She could almost hear them sigh. "Twelve, isn't it, Frida?"

"Twelve." She turned back to Carl and nodded. "It goes by so fast."

"Doesn't it?"

"I'm very much looking forward to being here for New

Year's this year," Damien continued, "Frida has been telling me about the spectacular Icelandic New Year's celebrations for years."

Exclamations of concurrence from the group.

"So you've not been here for New Year's Eve?" inquired German Ambassador Rainer with a raised eyebrow, his head twitching curiously. His hands around his champagne flute were red and swollen; there was dirt beneath his fingernails.

"No, never. We've always been somewhere else over Christmas."

"Our children have come over every New Year's since we've been here. Even though they're adults, they still love it!" said Heike, ebullient. Then she glanced guiltily at Frida and looked away.

Frida straightened her back and raised her chin. Already there would have been speculation among the wives as to why she and Damien were childless. Surely whispered rumors were already in circulation – which one of them, she wondered, was infertile?

Patricia's shrill voice and clapping palms cut through the air. "Can I ask you to take your seats, please?"

Ornate tableware; cards in small holders on which names were written. Frida to sit next to Patricia who was at the head of the table, Carl on her left. On the far end of the table, on the opposite side, was Damien. Frida gazed at her husband, keeping her expression resolutely soft, watching him leaning over to hear something George was saying. Attractive, charismatic, sophisticated, with his smooth skin, excellent sense of style and immaculate grooming. For one moment she felt a twinge of something elusive, a mixture of attraction and desire, yet also sadness.

When had their marriage become such a charade?

The kitchen door swung open and a woman in a black skirt and vest entered, holding a bottle of wine with a white napkin wrapped around the neck. She made her way clockwise around the table, pouring white wine into the smaller of two wine glasses, first serving the ladies, then the men. A moment later the door swung open again and a young girl followed, holding three plates of smoked salmon. She began to distribute them, starting with Patricia, then going clockwise around. Patricia sat like stone with her elbows propped on the table, staring straight ahead. Her eyes looked ravaged.

The men were talking.

"How the two smaller banks plan to refinance themselves is anybody's guess."

"Their equity is too low."

"It's been low for a while now. That's why Landsbanki – the National Bank – launched that online bank in the UK – what's it called again?"

"Icesave."

"They were having trouble borrowing. Financial markets have been nervous about the Icelandic banks for years."

"No wonder. A banking system that inflates so quickly – and becomes far bigger than the country's economy … just think what could happen if credit lines began to dry up."

"It's already happening. Things are shaky in America right now, with the mortgage crisis."

"What a bloody mess that is …"

"There's no telling where it might end."

"Gentlemen, the unraveling has begun. Mark my words."

The girl placed a plate in front of Frida. On it was a little salmon-pink rosette with a leaf of curly lettuce and dab of horseradish mayonnaise, artfully arranged.

Patricia sat frozen at the end of the table.

Mustn't pick up fork until she does!

"Well, dig in everyone!" George. Jolly George and his happy absence of etiquette.

The conversation continued. "Try telling that to the Icelanders, though, and they become irate. They're adamant that there's no cause for concern."

"Of course they would say that. No one wants a run on the banks."

"They're living in a bubble. The denial here is astonishing."

Frida dropped her fork with a clatter. The talking stopped; all eyes fell on her. She kept her eyes to her plate. Something terrible was welling up inside her; what was happening?

Conversation resumed. Frida glanced at Patricia. Her eyes were fixed in a stare on some faraway point. Her mouth was moving, chewing her smoked salmon ever so slowly. There was a dab of mayonnaise at the corner of her mouth. Everyone had finished, except her. She put her fork down, chewed, stared ahead, like a robot. The kitchen door swung open and the girl came out. Beginning to gather the plates now. People were talking. Frida's sensibilities were heightened to a point of bursting – around her everything was normal, and yet it was not. It felt like everything was in loud, excruciatingly slow motion.

The girl put her hand out to take Patricia's plate. Wham! In a flash Patricia's hand clamped down on her wrist, pulling her down. Her knuckles were white.

"*Not. Finished.*" she hissed through clenched teeth into the girl's ear, intoning each word.

The girl straightened up abruptly. Patricia yanked her back down.

"Next time, you serve the guests first and begin with the women. Do you understand?"

The girl straightened up again and with one swift motion shook her wrist free. Then she turned and walked quickly into the kitchen, the door swing-swinging behind her.

There was a hush at the table.

"What …?" said George, open-mouthed, breaking off as soon as he saw his wife.

Patricia waved one hand in the air. "You know what they say: it's so hard to get decent help," she said with strained mockery, dabbing at the corner of her mouth with her napkin.

How dare you?

Frida opened her mouth to speak, but felt her mind grow thick and muddled, her vision blur. She tried to stand, putting her hands on the table for support, but her arms were made of rubber and then

everything went black.

She came to on the sofa in the living room.

Their heads arranged in a circle above her, staring down. Except Damien, who sat next to her and held her hand.

"Open a window, open a windooww," cried George, frantically waving one arm.

Frida rose up on one elbow. Her head felt groggy, her tongue like cotton wool inside her mouth. "What happened?"

"You fainted!" exclaimed George. "Just like that!"

Frida closed her eyes. Her head was spinning, and she feared standing up, that her legs would not support her. She turned her head slowly towards Damien.

"We should go," she murmured.

He nodded gravely and brought her hand to his lips for a moment, looking into her eyes with deep concern. Then stood up and reached into his jacket pocket. "I'll just call my driver," he said, pulling out his cellphone.

~~

Fifteen minutes later the Range Rover coasted quietly past the Tjörnin lake once more.

"You engineered that one well," Damien said calmly, looking out of the window, as though he were speaking to the trees in Hljómskálagardur park.

"You think I did it on purpose," said Frida, speaking to the Idnó theatre on the other side.

Damien leaned forward and spoke to the driver. "Can you turn on the radio, please."

"Certainly." The sound of a radio host with a caramel-smooth voice came on.

"You don't want to believe me," she said, turning her head.

Silence.

"What do you take me for?" Her voice was beginning to sound shrill.

Silence.

She turned her head back to the window. It was no use. He would say nothing in front of the driver.

~~

Inside the vestibule, as Damien shut the door, Frida put her hand in her pocket and pulled out the earring. She held it in her open palm, arm extended.

Damien, his demeanor icy, glanced at the earring, and then at her. She thought she saw a slight … something in his manner, a fraction of a second in which he was startled or taken aback, but she couldn't be sure.

"What's that?" he said, the calm of his voice designed to antagonize, or at least that's how it seemed to her.

"It's an earring."

"I can see that."

"What was it doing in your study?"

His steel-gray eyes met hers. They were infuriatingly neutral. "How should I know?"

"It's your study. You should know."

He shrugged. "I've never seen that thing before. Are you sure it isn't yours?"

"Would I be asking you if it was?"

"Well maybe it belongs to Kristín."

"It's something you'd wear with a formal gown. As far as I'm aware, Kristín hasn't been dressing in formal gowns at work."

"Just what are you accusing me of?"

Frida felt her conviction slip away. Somehow Damien had the power to wipe out all her thoughts and leave her tongue-tied. As though he petrified her mind with his antagonism. *When* had she become so weak? Or had she always been like this, and was she only just starting to see it now?

"I'm not accusing you of anything. I'm just asking a question," she said feebly.

"It feels more like I'm being cross-examined. If you think this earring is some indication or proof that I'm having an affair, Frida, then you're even more of a silly girl than I thought." He paused. "I'm not having an affair, and I don't know anything about that earring. I don't know how it got into my study, if that is indeed where it was. I just don't know."

He met her eyes again for a brief moment, then nodded his head once for emphasis and stepped into the hallway.

Frida was left standing in the vestibule, holding the earring. She felt like an idiot. No doubt there was a perfectly logical explanation as to why the earring had been on Damien's floor. And yet, deep inside of her there was a nagging sense of something akin to doubt.

She made a mental note to ask Kristín about the earring the next time she saw her.

~~

"I can't find anything wrong with you," said the doctor, sitting across the desk from her. His name was Jónas. He didn't look like a doctor, more like a rugby player, in his casual jeans and shirt open at the neck. Also his nose had clearly been broken. On his lips an involuntary smile refused to depart. She got the feeling he wanted to undress her.

"Blood's normal, except that your haemoglobin is low – which isn't anything iron supplements won't cure. Brain scan was normal. Everything checks out, at least physically."

"At least physically?" She repeated, leaning back in the chair and crossing her legs. A hint of a smile flickered on her lips.

He leaned forward. "Have you been under much stress lately?"

"Probably."

"Your condition could be stress-related."

She nodded, keeping her eyes on him.

"My guess is that you need to make some life adjustments."

His voice was surprisingly soft. If she made the slightest move right now, she thought, she could seduce him.

It had been at least three months since she'd had sex with her husband.

Her mind circled back to the earring.

"Maybe this is a wake-up call."

She nodded again, her eyes fixed on his face.

~~

Frida walked quickly across the parking lot, heels clicking on the pavement. Inside her silver Audi A4 she put the key in the ignition, then leaned forward, resting her forehead on the steering wheel of the car her husband had bought for her just two months ago.

What had she been thinking? She'd almost tried to seduce a perfect stranger. And all because she thought her husband might possibly be cheating.

Was it out of revenge? Or because she was desperate?

She turned the key in the ignition and backed out of the

parking space a little too quickly, just barely avoiding the car behind her.

When had things began spinning so out of control?

My guess is that you need to make some life adjustments.

She drove westward along the sea until she reached the furthest peninsula in the Reykjavík area, the place with a lighthouse on the end, situated on a small spit that became an island during high tide. Parking the car, she got out and stood looking across the tall grass with its sturdy straws, down to the shore where the waves whispered on the black sand, leaving a lacy layer of foam as they hushed back to sea. The water shimmered, and the big sky cupped its palm high above it.

There was a house. On the West Fjords, harboring many of her best childhood memories. Closing her eyes she could hear the whisper of happy voices on the breeze – now, calling. It was a house that her grandparents had owned, that held a part of her within its walls, a place of refuge. It had been there since she was small, not always visible, but permanent nonetheless.

CHAPTER TWO

She drove fast, the Audi hugging a road that advanced audaciously through the landscape like a snake, past black sand beaches littered with driftwood and fjords with grumpy grey clouds overhead. Three days had passed since her meeting with the doctor; three days in which she had come to accept her need to get away to someplace safe, where she could rest, reflect, take walks, take stock, and try to understand.

She craved peace, craved silence. She longed for respite from the endless chatter in her head about unimportant details, such as whether to wear the beige or blue suit to the next diplomatic function, whether she had put on weight, what to serve at the next embassy dinner, or whether they should replace the oil painting above the sofa with something more modern because it clashed ever-so slightly with the décor. Or whether the sofa should go instead. Or whether her lipstick was too red, or too pink, or too this or too that.

Past craggy shores she drove, past green pastures with horses grazing serenely, imposing mountains and rocky hillsides, fat woolly sheep with their perky little lambs brazenly crossing the highway – *Oh Christ!*

Frida slammed on the brakes and the car did a sidespin, coming to a screeching halt like a slash on the road.

She had just missed hitting a ewe trailed by a pair of lambs; one white, one black. They were on the opposite side now, having bolted as she approached, and were staring at the car with astonished expressions. They were lucky. Icelandic sheep made excellent dinner fare, their wild summer roaming giving their meat a game-like flavor, but she didn't care to slaughter them herself, here and now.

Up ahead, some five hundred meters away, another car had stopped by the side of the road with its hazard lights flashing. It was a navy blue Cherokee jeep, a few years old. A man was getting out. Now he headed towards something next to the road that Frida couldn't see. She felt her anxiety rise. Something had happened, she was sure of it. She should stop, see if there was anything she could do, even though the prospect of seeing an injured animal caused her to break out in a cold sweat. She couldn't bear to see animals suffer.

Coming to a stop behind the jeep, she saw the man lean down towards something on the ground. It was a sheep, lying on its back, legs flailing helplessly in the air. She got out of the car. The man was holding a knife. She froze – the sheep was injured, it had probably been hit. No doubt he would now slit its throat, to put it out of its misery. She braced herself. Suddenly he tossed the knife aside, leaned down and yanked at the sheep. A second later it was running away, bleating pathetically, until it was far enough to feel safe, then it stopped and turned, looking accusingly at them both.

The man came towards Frida with a self-assured stride. He was tall and had on a matted brown and white Icelandic wool sweater, grubby jeans and green rubber boots. He was younger than she'd thought at first – probably no older than thirty, if that.

"It just needed some help getting up," he called out by way of explanation.

"I thought it was hurt." Frida called back.

Closer now, the man came to a halt. "It's a major design flaw," he said, gesturing towards the sheep that had now started grazing. "They end up on their backs like that and they can't get up. Especially when they're in between two tussocks. That one got lucky."

"Good thing you came along," she said. He had irregular features, with a hawk-like nose and deep-set eyes. He exuded health and a quiet confidence and his gaze was warm and direct.

She wondered for a moment if she knew him from somewhere – there was an ease in his manner, almost like they had met before.

"If I hadn't, someone else would have. It's just lucky it was that close to the road."

He cast a glance at Frida's license plate and then back at her with a hint of surprise. She recoiled inwardly. Those damn green CD diplomatic plates that were on her car. They were so unbearably conspicuous.

"Well," he said, grinning, "drive safely and mind the sheep."

Frida grinned. "Thanks. Same to you."

He climbed into his jeep, gave a brief wave, and then drove off.

~~

Fagrifjördur had not changed much in the last twenty-odd years. Situated at the bottom of a fjord from which it drew its name, the village consisted of a collection of houses fanning upwards from the harbor. Frida guessed that the freezing plant was still in operation – there were cars parked around it, and those large plastic tubs so ubiquitous in fish processing were stacked here and there. Not all villages had been fortunate when the fisheries management system had been implemented; in many cases the fishing quotas had been sold to the highest bidder, generally large-scale fishing vessel operators who were based elsewhere. With the quotas gone there was not much left in terms of work, and such communities had gradually seen their population drift away, usually to Iceland's capital, Reykjavík. Yet this town, for which she felt such affection, appeared to thrive: the streets were swept, and the homes were well maintained. It was a cheerful town, with no hint of abandoned storefronts and other ghastly signs of neglect. But perhaps this was because in the entire village there was just one store – the one adjacent to the gas station.

It took Frida all of three minutes to drive through and make a mental note of the main amenities: the gas station, the store, a small restaurant, the swimming pool, a gym, a school. And then she had passed through and was heading west, towards the mouth of the fjord.

There it was – about two kilometers from the edge of town. A small, square timber house, clad with corrugated iron that was white on the sides, red on the roof, red around the window frames. It was so much smaller than she remembered and almost obscured by trees – were those really the tiny saplings she had helped plant all those years earlier?

She pulled off the main road and into the small parking enclosure in front of the house. Someone had scattered gravel on the ground, though not very much – if there was a contest between the grass and pebbles, the grass was surely winning.

She sat in the car for a moment, allowing her memories to catch up with the present. The clock on the dashboard read 16.33. It had taken her just over six hours to drive from Reykjavík. She opened the door and got out, walking slowly towards the gate in the picket fence that enclosed the garden. It needed a coat of paint. She pushed open the gate – it creaked, but was firm on the hinges.

Her grandmother had sold the house after her grandfather's death. It had been the passing of an era – she and Egill and his sister Lóa had spent almost every summer there from a time she was first able to remember, until she was nine. Egill and Lóa had been more like her siblings than cousins – all of them more or less raised by their grandparents, for different reasons. Egill and Lóa's parents had been busy getting rich, whereas her father had drowned when she was four, and her mother … well, she just had not handled single parenthood very well. "Married to the bottle," she remembered overhearing one of her grandmother's friends say once in a disparaging tone. She could still remember the deep sense of shame that had engulfed her, and the overpowering need to protect her mother and to hide her secret from the world.

Years later, after Egill had become a successful businessman in his own right, he had bought the house back. The family had used it a lot when his children were young, but after he and Francoise separated and she moved to France with the kids, he'd stopped going there so often. So when Frida got in touch with him and timidly asked if she could borrow the place for a couple of weeks, Egill was more than forthcoming. "Stay as long as you like," he'd said. "I'm relieved to know of some life in the house." His main concern was that there was no Internet connection, which Frida quickly assured him was more of a pro than a con in her mind. She wanted rest – from everything.

As Frida walked through the gate, memories came flooding back. Eating outside in the summer, the sun just warm enough to allow it, the kitchen table with the chrome legs looking curiously displaced on the grass, their spirits high with the novelty of it. Her grandfather chopping gnarly old birch branches for burning in the old wood stove on a large tree stump especially brought over from Norway – since trees that size did not grow in Iceland. She walked around to the back ... and there it was! The little playhouse their grandfather had built for them, just as she remembered it, only it had been painted like a miniature version of the main house – white and red. Tufts of grass pressed outwards from its sides and white-and-red big-checkered curtains, gathered to the sides with a sash, hung at the windows. A little garden elf stood guard in front of the entrance. It was that garden elf she had come to see.

"The key is inside the garden elf, wrapped in a plastic bag."

Frida found this exceedingly foolhardy. Or had she merely become distrustful during her years abroad, where she would never, ever have made herself vulnerable to invaders in this way?

Probably.

It was an old key, long and rounded. Frida deftly unlocked the back door, letting herself into the small storage pantry. Light poured in through a high window, particles of dust dancing slowly in the rays. The built-in shelves, white-varnished and cheerful, were still there. There was also a modern washing machine and an old woman's bicycle, black with a basket in front, the kind she always associated with Amsterdam. Shelves lined the walls, on which were stored all manner of things from paint cans to cardboard boxes to tools.

The pantry led to the kitchen, where Frida turned a full circle, grinning from ear to ear. It was just as she had remembered it – where had Egill found all this stuff? He had painstakingly worked to recreate the old house that clearly held as much value for him as for her. The lace curtain at the window, the decorative dish rack hanging on the wall, the embroidered cloth on it with the date *1945* and *HB* – her grandmother's initials. The only thing she really remembered being different – apart from the modern appliances, of course – was the kitchen table. There was now a small, white-painted wood table, with a checkered tablecloth – the same checkered fabric as had been used for the dollhouse curtains.

She moved to the living room, with its big window set with many small windowpanes that looked out into the garden. When she was small, it used to look out onto the road and the fjord beyond, but now the trees almost obscured the view. Frida cast a glance around the room. There was a dining table with six chairs and a decidedly modern leather corner sofa opposite a small flat-screen TV set atop an old stereo console. The radio still worked, or so Egill had said. The rocking chair was there next to the window, the one that her grandmother had resolutely refused to sit in because she said it made her feel old. On the wall above the sofa there were family portraits … there was that picture of her and Egill the summer after her father drowned. In the center of the room was the same old brass chandelier as she remembered, suspended from the ceiling with three chains, a cone tapering to a point underneath. In the corner was a modern wood-burning stove.

While the downstairs looked much the same as it had when Frida was a child, the same was not true of the upstairs. It looked like it had been gutted and everything put in anew, including skylights on the sloping ceilings. It was modern, airy and very Scandinavian, with white floorboards and wall paneling. It even smelled new. The double bed in the master bedroom was fluffy with duvets and covered with a white bedspread. There was a hush in the room, soothing and gentle, like the feeling when it rained outside and her grandmother sat humming in the sofa with her legs tucked up beneath her, knitting needles clicking in the quiet of the late afternoon.

~~

"Grandpa's died."

Egill, sitting on the side of his bunk still wearing his pajamas, she and Lóa rubbing the sleep from their eyes. He stared at the floor. “When nana woke up this morning he was already dead in the bed beside her.” He pursed his lips to keep from crying. Frida blinked, her eyes dry. At nine, she was already old enough to dismiss her feelings. At eleven, so was Egill. At four, Lóa was too young to really understand.

They all went downstairs very quietly in their bare feet, Egill taking the lead, Lóa after him holding her rabbit with the long floppy ears, Frida coming up behind. Struck by the gravity of the event, they spoke in whispers, making their own breakfasts of cereal and toast, washing and drying the dishes when they were done. Nana was upstairs saying goodbye to grandpa. It was something to be revered.

Just as they were putting the last plate away nana came down, looking pale and tired. She stopped without saying anything and reached out her hands to them. Then she led them upstairs to the room where he lay against the pillows. Frida thought the air in the room looked blue, the bed linen stark white in contrast. Grandpa looked strange, like his soul was already gone, his face pasty and white and not like him at all. Frida was afraid to touch him. Egill touched him and later told Frida that he had been cold – making Frida wish she'd done it, too. Lóa stood against the wall near the door, sucking on her stuffed bunny's ear, looking bewildered.

It was their last summer there. After that, nana spent all her time in the city. And by Christmas, the house had been sold.

~~

For a couple of years after her grandfather's death, Frida saw very little of her grandmother. She did not see Egill or Lóa at all. They had disappeared from her world, like a pair of migrating birds that had flown away for the winter.

She lived with her mother in a basement apartment in downtown Reykjavík, in a neighborhood dubbed “the shadow district”. Their flat was dug deep into the ground so that she could see people's shoes as they passed by on the sidewalk outside. Frida's mother was a nurse and sometimes worked at night. At other times she didn't work, but stayed out during the night anyway. Sometimes she brought company home, and stayed up with them drinking until early in the morning when they all fell asleep. Frida would get up and go into the kitchen, closing the door and cleaning up as much as she could so she could have her breakfast. She was meticulous about breakfast; someone had once told her it was the most important meal of the day, and that if you had a good breakfast your day would always go well. She knew how to make porridge, and that was what she always had – porridge with apples and raisins and milk. Except when her mother had forgotten to buy either apples or raisins or milk. Or rolled oats. On those days, Frida just ate whatever she could find. She then left the apartment and went to the library, because it was a place that was almost always open and she could sit there and read and nobody bothered her, even though it did not escape her attention that the library staff sometimes whispered to each other and cast glances in her direction. Once one of the women who worked there tried to strike up a conversation with her, asking her what kinds of books she liked, and then moving on to more personal questions like where she lived. After that, Frida avoided going into the department where that woman worked.

When Frida was around twelve, her mother said she had to go away for a few days. Frida went to stay with her mother's friend, Jóna, and her two sons. She remembered very little from that time, except that she did not like to leave the room that she had been allocated. The two sons had been moved into one single room, and Frida had been given the room of the younger one. He had a lot of books, and Frida mostly lay on the bed and read. Jóna was kind to her, but she felt like a stranger in their home, and they treated her as such. When her mother came back, about two weeks later, she looked thin and frail, her hands trembled and she smoked twice as much as she had before. But the drinking had stopped.

~~

One Saturday in November, when the afternoon light had been obliterated by the long winter shadows, a knock came at the door. Frida's mother went to answer it. Outside stood Frida's grandmother, tall and elegant, wearing a wool cape with a fur collar. There was a moment of tension. In a flash of recognition, Frida realized that it had always been there.

"Halldóra." Frida's mother's voice was flat.

"Hello, Ásta," said Frida's grandmother. "How are you?"

"Can't complain."

"I've just heard ..." she lowered her voice so that Frida couldn't hear.

Frida's mother stood motionless in the doorway.

Her grandmother said something else that she couldn't make out.

Frida's mother stepped outside and half-closed the door.

A couple of minutes later, she opened the door again and both women stepped inside.

Frida's grandmother's face broke into a smile. "Hello, my darling!" she said, extending her arms to Frida who was already on her feet. She picked her up and pressed her close. "You've grown so big!"

Frida glanced nervously at her mother. There was a strained look on her face, but she was heading for the kettle.

Later, when two cups of coffee sat empty on the table and a few lipstick-stained cigarette butts rested in the ashtray, Frida heard her grandmother ask whether she could take her granddaughter to the theatre tomorrow. There was to be a Sunday matinee performance of the People and Robbers of Cardamom Town at The National Theatre. She was sure Frida would love it.

Frida held her breath.

"Frida? Would you like to go to the theatre with your grandmother?"

She nodded hesitantly.

"All right, then."

She glanced from her mother to her grandmother. She was tentative, uncertain of this new situation and what was to be done about it. Still, it seemed to her like the cramped basement flat with its myriad shadows had just a little more brightness in it now, and the heavy stone that had settled in her heart was just a little bit lighter.

Her grandmother picked her up early that Saturday afternoon. Frida had on her only dress, blue with a white collar and buttons, and together they walked hand-in-hand down the street that led to the theatre. At the box office, Frida's grandmother removed her leather gloves and paid for two tickets. A somber man in a blue and gold uniform tore their ticket stubs at the door. Glancing around, Frida was overwhelmed with the lavishness of the lobby – the ornate chandelier, the thick, brightly-patterned carpet, the paintings on the walls of famous actors now deceased, the smell of chocolate and mints, people dressed in fine clothes, rushing to their seats. Frida and her grandmother removed their coats and handed them to the cloakroom attendant.

Inside, the auditorium buzzed with the laughter and voices of children. Wide-eyed, Frida looked around. The stage was hidden by a sumptuous red velvet curtain with shiny gold stripes. The lights went down, and the curtains were pulled aside as a band started playing. Frida was enthralled. She had never seen anything like the magic that was happening on the stage in front of her. It was like she had been transported to a place where beauty was tangible and everything was good.

In contrast, the outside world seemed flat and dull afterwards. Frida dreaded going home to the bleak contrast of the flat and her mother sitting in the kitchen, reading the newspaper while she drank innumerable cups of coffee and smoked one cigarette after another. She was immensely relieved when her grandmother suggested that they go to a café for a cup of cocoa. Especially since she had lots of questions about the play. "You can't just steal a lion, can you? It would eat you, right? So the play isn't real, the person who writes the play just pretends that it's real. Right?"

After that, trips to the theatre became their special time. The following season, Frida's grandmother bought season tickets for them both and they went regularly, always going to a café afterwards to talk about the production. They saw not just children's plays, but grownup ones, too – A Streetcar Named Desire, The Caucasian Chalk Circle, Hostage, even Who's Afraid of Virginia Woolf. Each time, Frida was transported to that unique place of suspended reality. But the part she loved most was the curtain call, when the actors stepped out of their roles and became real people that let themselves be celebrated.

~

The following year, Frida and her mother moved into a slightly larger flat on the first floor of an apartment building. Ásta had stayed sober, and had shed her previous posse of friends. She had new friends now, friends she had met in AA, and as she cleaned up her life, so things started to improve around her. She took more shifts at work, and was promoted. Things were looking up.

Frida's excruciating shyness had begun to dissipate somewhat, though she still had a painful sense of being different from everyone else. She had few friends, and no close friends. Now in junior high school, she joined the drama club and got roles in the school musicals. One year a small role in Hair, the following year the role of a Kit-Kat girl in Cabaret, and in the third year the role of Anita in West Side Story. She loved being in plays. On the stage, she was no longer shy. She stepped out of herself and into a different character, where she could be free.

She continued going to the theatre with her grandmother, growing more sophisticated in her understanding of plays and performances. Her grandmother delighted in sharing her granddaughter's expanding views and deeper comprehension. Until one day when she was forced to cancel a "play date" because she wasn't well.

A nagging dread began to settle in Frida's mind. Her grandmother had never missed a play date before, and neither had she. Their trips to the theatre were sacred – it had to be something serious for them to be disrupted.

Two days later, the verdict was in: Frida's grandmother had lung cancer, and the prognosis was bad.

~

Frida watched her grandmother wilt before her eyes.

On a Saturday in late March, she was keeping a vigil by her bedside. Her grandmother was at home and the nurse, who came twice a day, would return later that afternoon. Frida was studying for exams – she would complete her matriculation in May.

She glanced up to see her grandmother watching her calmly.

She set down her book. “I didn’t know you were awake.”

“You look so pretty sitting there.”

Frida reached out and touched her grandmother’s arm. “How are you feeling? Can I get you anything?”

Her grandmother shook her head. Her breath came in raspy spurts. She reached up and gently stroked Frida’s long hair. “What are you going to do, Frida, once you’ve graduated?”

“I’m not sure.”

“What do you want to do?”

She furrowed her brow. “I don’t know. I can’t decide. Mom says nursing, but … I don’t know.”

“Theatre studies?”

Frida shrugged. “Maybe.”

“Or acting?”

Frida looked away.

“You should do what you love.”

Frida shook her head. “I don’t think I’m that good.”

“You are that good.”

“You’re biased, nana.”

Her grandmother shook her head, and leaned back against the pillow, closing her eyes. She stayed that way for a while, until Frida thought she must have fallen asleep and picked up her book again. When her grandmother spoke, it was without opening her eyes.

“Don’t let yourself be trapped by your own fear.”

Frida leaned over and gently touched her grandmother’s hand. It was cool, the skin soft and translucent.

After a while, her grandmother fell into a deep sleep. Frida got up quietly to make some tea, and when she came back, her grandmother was gone.

CHAPTER THREE

Frida woke with a start from one of those disturbing dreams she often had, where she was on a stage in front of a large audience and couldn't remember her lines. A whisper of a breeze entered the room through the open window and brushed her bare arm, causing her skin to prickle. She was lying on her side, on top of the white bedspread. The light had dimmed and there were shadows in the corners of the room.

How long have I slept?

She glanced at her watch. It was just a little past four thirty.

She sat up abruptly. Had she been sleeping for most of the night? Throwing her legs over the side of the bed, she stood and went to the window, pulling the gauze curtain aside. The light was hazy and blue, the water on the fjord rippled in a slight wind and the mountain on the other side was swathed in mauve serenity. A small boat was coming in, its engine put-put-putting in the distance.

Which is odd, at four-thirty in the morning.

She looked at her watch again, more closely. The second hand was not moving. It had stopped. She shook her watch and watched the second hand move five times, then stop again.

This meant her watch had stopped at four-thirty that afternoon, just as she arrived.

Turning, she felt a heightened energy in the house. Was she imagining it?

Slipping on her shoes, she left the room and made her way downstairs, taking care on the steep staircase.

Inside the living room, light was still coming in through the big windows at the far end of the room. In front of it, the rocking chair moved ever so slightly.

Frida sat down on the sofa and curled her legs up under her. Leaning her elbow on the back of the sofa, her head on her hand, she gazed outside at the calm trees, the white fence, the slope beyond.

Outside, the cheerful call of a golden plover interrupted the stillness.

~~

The day of Frida's graduation from secondary school, her mother picked up the bottle again. She had insisted on throwing Frida a graduation party, as was common practice in Iceland. Frida felt uneasy about it from the start and tried to talk her mother out of it, but Ásta was adamant: her daughter would get the same treatment as everyone else's children. Frida could sense the slightly manic excitement in her mother, and her own anxiety rose, though she did her best to deny and conceal her feelings. In the end, the party wound up consisting mostly of Ásta's old drinking friends and turned into a boozefest, from which Frida escaped at the earliest possible opportunity. When she came home that evening, having made the rounds of a few parties of her classmates, the party was going stronger than ever.

For the next two years, Ásta struggled with her addiction. Things quickly spiraled out of control, she went into rehab, and came out broke and desolate. Throughout high school Frida had worked evenings at a local café – now she increased her hours to nearly full-time, and also took a job working afternoons at a dry cleaners. Most of her salary went towards helping her mother with the mortgage, though she managed to save a little on the side – a small fund that she hoped to make use of in due course.

She remembered well the last conversation she'd had with her grandmother. The dream to attend theatre school would not leave her alone, yet each time the auditions for the Icelandic National Theatre school rolled around she lost her nerve. Her grandmother had left her a small inheritance, earmarked for her education. Frida kept it stashed safely away in a bank account, securely hidden from her mother. Were Ásta to find out about it, Frida knew she would not leave her alone until she had usurped some or all of it from her. And even though she felt too confused and scared to do anything with it now, the thought of it there was like her lifeline. It was her ticket to freedom, whenever she felt strong enough to make her escape.

Then one cold March day, nearly three years after her grandmother's death, Frida was flipping through the newspaper at the dry cleaner's when an advertisement caught her eye. It was in English, and was from a place called the Actors' Studio in London. They were coming to Reykjavík to hold auditions.

All through the day, the thought of this occupied her mind. She was completely scattered, forgetting to give back change, checking off the wrong items on the tickets, and on her way home she kept walking when she got to the corner where she should have turned to go home. Acting school. London. She would leave Reykjavík, get away from the dreariness here, and do what she wanted. But could she still act? She'd been good in high school, but what about a professional theatre school? In England, of all places? Was she good enough for that?

In the evening, when her mother had gone off to work a night shift, she went down to the storage room in the basement and found the old scripts from the musicals she had been in in high school. She brushed up on her singing, and found two monologues. She rehearsed. She rehearsed some more. And then she went to the audition.

Waiting to be called, she was so nervous she thought she would die. All around her were self-assured young hipsters, walking around singing songs and doing vocal exercises as though they were alone in the world, acting for all intents and purposes like the audition was just a formality – they knew they would be admitted. Finally it came time for Frida to go in. The audition board was made up of three people – two men and one woman, who sat at one end of a large dance studio and regarded her critically. She did her two monologues, sang one song, and was amazed at how strong her voice sounded, considering that her knees felt like putty. One of the men then asked her if she could do a dance routine, and when she said she had nothing rehearsed, they played some music and asked her to dance. Frida did as she was told, feeling like a complete idiot. Afterwards they whispered briefly among themselves, then asked if she could sing another song – anything of her own choosing. She decided on an Icelandic lullaby, one that her grandmother had sung to her when she was little.

A few weeks later, an envelope arrived, and she was informed that she had been admitted to the acting program. Dazed, and almost paralyzed with guilt, Frida informed her mother that she was moving to London.

~~

London opened its arms to receive her. Everything seemed to come together; she even had a flat fall into her lap. Her mother's cousin's daughter, Gréta, who had been in London studying engineering, was moving to Germany to do a Masters and offered Frida her flat. It was a tiny bedsit affair, located above a bathroom fixtures shop in Ealing. It took Frida about forty-five minutes to get to school on the tube, but it was cozy, in a safe area, close to the tube stop, and, most importantly, it was her very own. She couldn't believe her luck.

And now here she was, sitting in the school's rough theatre workshop, surrounded by fellow first-year students. Hans Walker, director of the acting program, sat on a stool in the middle of the stage. He was long and lean with an elongated face and a mouth that drooped at the corners.

"Firstly," he said in a narrow, nasal voice, thrusting his chin upwards, "I'd like to congratulate you all on being here today. I'm sure you're aware of the implications – we have chosen you, thirty-four bright young things, from among more than eight hundred applicants. So you'd better prove your worth. In case you think this means you've made it – think again. This program is going to test everything you have – physically and mentally. You'll find things out about yourself that you never wanted to know. You may think you know who you are, but you don't. You'll question your sanity. You'll question your identity. You'll question your sexuality. And about half of you will give up."

Silence. Frida cast a furtive glance around. *Are we supposed to laugh?*

She caught the eye of a big burly guy who wouldn't have looked out of place on an American football field. He put his fingertips into his mouth like he was pretending to be *really scared*. Frida smiled.

"And that's just for starters," Hans continued, his voice growing more nasal. "Needless to say, we expect you to be punctual – the door to the classroom will be closed when class commences, after which no one, and I mean NO ONE, will be admitted. A missed class will constitute a truancy. Three truancies means you'll be cut from the program. We also expect you to pass three academic subjects: World Literature, History of Art and Theatre History. And you'll have phonetics, too. HEY!" A couple of guys at the front who had been whispering to each other stopped abruptly. "Let me make this perfectly clear! You may think you're the next James Dean, but if you learn anything here it will be this: humility."

Silence.

"You've been given a reading list. Go out and buy those books – and read them. You'll be tested. And last – but not least! You'll notice that you have a double lunch every Wednesday. That is not done out of the kindness of our hearts. Every Wednesday a production will be put on in this very auditorium by the students themselves. THAT MEANS YOU! It's up to YOU to showcase your talent, to prove to us that you're learning something. Otherwise, come Christmas, you'll almost certainly fly from this program, head-first." He paused. "That's all."

Standing up, the guy next to Frida leaned over and murmured, "Is this guy Son of Hitler, or what?"

Frida raised her eyebrows.

"I'm Kevin."

"Frida. Hi."

~

Son of Hitler turned out to be right, though, because by the end of the first month Frida was already losing it. Her mind was like soft pudding, her body stubbornly refusing to provide her with the energy needed to complete all the tasks she was required to do each day. There was exercise on top of endless exercise: to train the singing voice, train the speaking voice, train the body, train posture, train lungs, train diaphragm, train concentration, train train train. Hopping, skipping, humming, stretching, walking with book on head, tongue twisters for enunciation, hanging upside down, emitting loud barking sounds. Frida ceased to be Frida. She became clay.

Clay was not a good substance to be when it came to academic performance. The phonetic alphabet was something Frida was utterly unable to master; and writing essays and exams was impossible with her mental energy at zero by the end of each day. Each evening she went to bed with excellent intentions – book in hand, ready for the Big Read, but then her eyelids would droop and her book would crash to the floor before fifteen minutes were up. She would slip into soul-wrenching dreams of being onstage in a play she didn't recognize. Waking in the dark, she'd be soaked in sweat and unable to get back to sleep. Aha! she'd think, the perfect scenario for getting reading done but no, her mind would buzz like an out-of-tune radio and not a single word would stick in her brain.

At school, getting a positive word or encouragement was like coming across a chunk of gold on a pebble beach – not impossible, but almost. Criticism was the order of the day, week, month, year – the justification being "We're doing it for your own good – just wait until you get out there in the real world". Harsh words, harsher demands – until the spirit withered and the flesh was weak and all she wanted to do was curl up under the covers and weep.

~~

"Is it true that you're a homosexual?"

The question was spoken in a level voice and aimed at Kevin, who occupied a single stool up on the stage – bare, vulnerable and exposed. That stool was The Hot Seat and it was Hans Walker's favorite teaching activity. Everyone in the class would be subjected to The Hot Seat before the semester was out. It was his way of tearing down the students' defenses, he said, of getting to the tender core. "Something you'll have to get used to doing each time you are onstage."

The smile on Kevin's face faded.

"No," he said.

"Have you ever had a homosexual experience?"

His expression was tense, frozen.

"Answer the question, please," Hans's narrow, nasal voice, loud at the back of the theatre.

"No."

Someone snickered.

"He answered the question," said Hans, leaning against the back wall with a smug expression. "He may be lying, but he is entitled to lie if he wants to. Just remember that lying won't get you far in acting. Being a good actor is about telling the truth."

Kevin face was pale and his hands trembled.

Sitting there watching Kevin in his extreme discomfort, Frida suddenly felt like shouting at the top of her lungs. She stood up quickly and left the room, pushing through the door and out into the hallway. She leaned with her back against the wall, head pounding.

She couldn't stand it – they were being skinned alive! It wasn't right.

The door opened. Hans came out. He let the door close behind him and took a stance opposite her. She kept her eyes to the ground for a moment before raising them. In a flash she realized that she was terrified of him – his judgment, his contempt. A vague sneer played on his lips.

"One thing I'm curious about," he said. "Why are you here?"

She couldn't answer. Couldn't look at him. Then he turned and walked away, the click of his heels echoing loudly in the empty corridor.

~~

She was cut from the acting program at the end of the first year. The same panel of judges who had been present at her audition were assembled to deliver the news.

Hans sat on the far right, staring at her with an unflinching expression.

She listened stoically to their verdict, then emerged, stony-faced from the room.

"Hey," said Kevin, putting his arm around her. "Don't blame yourself. They do it on purpose, you know."

She turned, allowing him to embrace her. "What do you mean?"

"They admit double the number of people that are actually allowed to graduate at the end of three years. They're not supposed to send any more people out into the business. But they need the funds to keep the acting program running so they take lots of people – particularly foreigners, who pay higher fees – into the first year, charge them tuition, and then send them packing."

Frida shook her head. "You're just saying that."

"No – it's true. My brother knows someone in administration and that's what they said."

"Oh, great. So they just took me in because I'm a foreigner, not because I have any talent."

Kevin hugged her more tightly. "That's not true," he murmured. "You have talent, Frida. You're a great actress. Believe in yourself. These people are nothing. They don't know how to nurture talent. This place is run by a bunch of failed actors who take their frustrations out on the students. It's fucked up."

"They'll keep you, I hope."

"Nah, they'll probably send me packing, too."

In a flash, Frida reached up, took Kevin's face between her two hands and kissed him on the mouth. Then she turned and walked away.

"Don't be a stranger!" He yelled after her.

She gave a half-turn and a wave. She knew she would be. She already was.

~~

"I'm staying here, mamma."

"And do what? Drift around, all alone in that big city?"

"I …."

Frida was interrupted by a lengthy coughing fit on the other end. Her mother's voice had that raspy tobacco sound that Frida remembered from the days she was drinking. And there was something in her tone. She had a hunch that her mother had fallen off the wagon, yet again. The thought of returning to Reykjavík made her skin crawl. Every nerve in her body resisted. Her demoralizing experiences at the school notwithstanding, she felt a sense of liberation at being in London. At being away. And yet the guilt of leaving her mother alone was overwhelming – especially now that she had no proper excuse for being here. It was almost strong enough to make her cave in.

"I just want to stay here for a while." Frida hated the sound of her own voice – pleading, almost whiny. "At least while I still have the apartment. I got really lucky with the apartment," she added quickly.

"Your grandmother would not have wanted you to stay."

Frida knew that was not true. Her mother was pulling out all the stops.

"I have to go," she said. "I need to get to the store before it closes."

Her mother coughed again. It sounded ugly. "Just ... think it over," she said, in between gasps for breath.

Frida replaced the receiver. She had thought it over. For the first time in her life, she'd begun to feel a strength within her that she had not known before. It was weak, but it was there, like a small seed sprouting. The vestiges of her true self. It would be smothered if she returned. She couldn't do it. She owed herself that much.

~~

For two weeks after being cut from the acting program, Frida was hardly able to drag herself out of bed. She was tired; her self-esteem in the gutter. Christmas came and Kevin called and invited her to come with him to Manchester to spend the holidays with his folks. She politely declined. On Christmas Eve her mother called, drunk and slurring her words; Frida's stomach clenched as she tried to communicate with some semblance of reason, but finally gave up and managed to extricate herself from the conversation. Ten minutes later the phone rang again, and she unplugged it. It was six pm, the time when the festivities were beginning in Iceland, and she hadn't even taken a shower all day, much less planned what she'd have for dinner. Her stomach rumbled. In the end, she threw on some clothes and went out for some pizza. On the way home she bought a small tub of ice cream, and spent the rest of the evening eating it from the tub, staring with disinterest at the small TV with the bad reception that had been left behind in the flat.

After about three weeks of moping, she decided that this was enough – if she actually planned to stay in the city, she needed to find something to do. Armed with a self-assurance that she didn't feel, she headed into town to apply for work. Despite it being low season in the tourist industry, she was hired on the spot at the third place she tried, a small bistro located on a side street, halfway between Leicester Square and Covent Garden. It was an upbeat place with jaunty music and hip food, frequented by tourists and Londoners alike. It was menial work in the eyes of some, she knew, but to Frida it was a new world. Learning how to wait tables, working with other young people, being in a place where no one knew the details of her background … for the first time in years she felt light and carefree. There was an easy camaraderie among her colleagues and herself that she had not felt before. It became a reason to get out of bed in the morning, and after a while she began to look forward to going to work. Her sense of fun returned, and she began to laugh more. She was good at her job, too, and that gave her confidence a boost. In short, the job was just what she needed.

Winter gave way to summer, and the tourists started arriving in London. Most days the place was packed, and Frida was grateful that she had learned the ropes during the winter, when things were a bit more quiet. She worked mostly lunch shifts, and after work, she liked to wander down to St. James's Park. She'd made friends with a few squirrels that lived there, and she would sit on a park bench and feed them peanuts, letting them beg, jump up on the bench next to her, scratch her leg with their little paws. She knew they were filthy and germ-infested, but they were just so irresistibly cute that she couldn't help herself.

She had one favorite – at least she thought it was always the same one. There he was now – next to her sneakered foot, up on his hind legs with his little paws in the air, looking at her, snout twitching. "Oh, hello!" She extended the peanut towards him and he snatched it in his mouth, running off a short distance and parking himself in the middle of a spot of grass to crack it open and devour the inside.

Glancing up, she saw that she was being watched. A man sat on a nearby bench, wearing an impeccable blue tailored suit. He had loosened his tie slightly and was reading *The Times*, though keeping an eye on her over the top. When he saw that she had noticed him he raised the paper and hid his face. She'd seen him before, a number of times. He seemed to frequent the same park benches as she did. Extending another peanut to a furry pal, she wondered what he was always doing there. He must be a businessman of some sort, or maybe a banker. At least his suits were impressive enough. He often sat there just looking out across the pond, or at the people walking by. It struck her as strange – most men of his stature had wives back home, or families, and hurried back to them after work. This one, he seemed to take his time, hanging out in St. James's park, watching her feed the squirrels. It was odd.

~~

It wasn't clear who was more surprised, he or she, when he turned up in her section at the café a few days later. She came out of the kitchen and there he was, at a table with a woman – his wife? No. More likely his mother. But dowdy looking, in a drab brown cardigan and skirt, with mousy hair and a dour expression.

"Hello. May I take your order?"

He glanced up at her and she saw a fleeting hint of surprise. Then his face went blank and he looked down at his menu. "The trout for me, please. And a Perrier."

He spoke with an impeccable BBC pronunciation, voice smooth as molasses.

"I'll take the tagliatelli and an orange juice."

The woman's voice was something else entirely – definitely a class lower than he, her speech was nowhere near his refined parlance.

"Trout and tagliatelli. Coming up. Thank you." She took the menus from him and their eyes met for a fraction of a second.

While they ate, Frida kept glancing over at them. They spoke quietly with their heads inclined towards each other; there was a familiarity, almost an intimacy there. And yet it was clear that they belonged to separate social classes. It was strange.

They ate quickly, then he raised his hand and asked for the check. Something about the pair of them was slightly jarring. There seemed to be little joy there; as though their interaction was merely businesslike, but with curious complications. During their entire transaction he had not made any indication that he recognized Frida from the park, nor did he do so when they left.

And so, she was no less surprised than before to see him at the same table again the very next day. This time alone.

"Hello," he said when she brought the menu over, looking directly at her, unlike the previous day.

"Hello," she said.

He opened the menu. She turned around to leave.

"So not only do you feed the squirrels in the park, you feed the people in Covent Garden too," he said behind her back.

She turned. He was still looking at the menu. "That's right," she said.

He closed the menu and extended it for her to take it. "I know what I want."

"Yes?"

"Same as yesterday."

"Which was?" She remembered, but wasn't about to admit it.

"Trout."

"I'm sorry, we don't have trout on the menu today. Today's fish special is sautéed cod with leeks and potato puree."

"Sold."

She gave him a half-smile and turned to leave.

"And a glass of the house white."

Returning with his wine, she found him absorbed in the back page of his paper.

"Thank you," he said, without glancing up. "Incidentally, where's your accent from?"

"I don't disclose that sort of information," she said.

He leaned back in his chair and grinned. He was a good-looking man, no doubt about it. His bone structure was flawless, and his grooming immaculate. The scent of his cologne reached her – just enough to please. Nothing overpowering.

"I'd put my money on Denmark."

"Hopefully you wouldn't wager too much, because you'd lose." She turned and began clearing a nearby table.

Returning a short while later with his food, he said, "Sweden."

She shook her head.

He ate quickly, then signaled for the check. "All right then, Norway." he said, taking his credit card from his wallet and handing it to her. It was platinum.

She took it, shaking her head.

"Holland?"

"Nope."

She glanced at his card as she headed to the cash register.

Damien Lowe.

"I give up," he said as she returned with the slip. His expression was amused.

"You don't strike me as a quitter."

"Tell me."

"Nope."

"Have dinner with me, then."

Frida was startled. Their little exchange had been fun, but she had not expected this.

"Meet you in the park at six? Near your favorite bench?"

She stood riveted to the spot, suddenly confused, not knowing what to say. It was an intensely uncomfortable feeling.

"I'll have it figured out by then," he added lightly.

She spoke the words, almost involuntarily. "OK. At six."

~~

What had she been thinking? She really didn't want to go out with the man. She knew nothing about him, except that he absolutely was not her type, what with his tailored suits and conservative newspaper reading. Plus, he was a lot older than her. She'd accepted his invitation before she'd even thought about it, and now she was telling herself not to be silly, it was just a dinner date, and if she didn't like him she could always just excuse herself and go home.

Or maybe it was just the fact that she'd had no time to go home and change that was complicating things for her. In any case, here she was, all sweaty from work and smelling like the daily special, which had been unusually popular that day.

"Iceland."

She was wearing a denim skirt, flat shoes and a light jacket, with a colorful Indian tote bag slung across her shoulder. He had on a gray pinstriped suit with light gray shirt and a darker gray tie.

"How'd you guess?"

"I have an Atlas. I've been poring over it, studying the northern hemisphere all afternoon."

She saw him glance at her clothes and instantly she recoiled inwardly. "I … didn't have time to go home and change," she said quickly.

He smiled. Offered her his arm. "Never mind. I hope you like Moroccan. I know a great place in Kensington."

~~

She already knew that his name was Damien Lowe, the rest she discovered over dinner that night. He was forty years old and worked for the Foreign and Commonwealth Office. He'd joined the foreign service fresh out of university and had worked in three different embassies (what he called "posts"): Mexico City, Geneva and the High Commission in Singapore

"What's the difference between an embassy and a High Commission?"

"A High Commission is an embassy in a commonwealth country."

"Ah."

For the past two years he had been back in London at the Foreign and Commonwealth Office: "We alternate stints back in London with postings." He lived in South Kensington and had never been married. No children.

The more Frida talked to him, the more interesting she found him. He had seen a lot of the world, and told entertaining stories. Like the time he was robbed by a cabbie in Mexico City, driven to the outskirts and stripped of his clothes – down to his underwear and socks.

"That should teach you to wear nice suits."

He grinned. His eyes shone with a mixture of admiration and desire.

He liked to play tennis, and tried to fit in a couple of games a week at a private tennis club. He also took a great interest in antique cars, and – as she discovered through a bit of prying – owned both a 1961 Triumph and a new Bentley – he liked to drive the Triumph up to Wimbledon each year, to watch the finals of the championships – that is, provided he was in the UK at all. His face became strained as he said it, almost as though he was embarrassed to tell her about it – as though he feared that it would put her off if she knew that he owned such expensive toys. Indeed, it did take her aback. Surely he had some money if he could afford to indulge his passion for cars in this way. And if he had so much money, he had to belong to a certain class, and if he belonged to that certain class, then what was he doing with a someone like herself, who could boast of nothing more than a failed stint as an acting student and a semi-successful waitressing career?

Happily, he liked to talk about himself, and didn't ask too much about Frida, though of course she gave him the basics. She didn't care to elaborate on her upbringing or her absolute relief to be away from the place where she grew up, which held so many soul-crushing memories. Not for the first time, Frida felt relief wash over her for being far away from all that, in a place where she could reinvent herself and essentially be whatever she wanted to be.

"So what do you want to do, now that you've left acting school?"

Frida shrugged. "Take some time. Figure it out. Enjoy life in the city. I'm still young – I have time."

He smiled. The expression in his eyes was warm, and also a little amused.

It was nearly ten-thirty pm by the time they left. Frida felt light-headed with wine and the warm glow of Damien's appreciation

"Let me get you a cab," he said, lightly touching her waist and waving to one on the opposite end of the street.

"A cab – are you crazy?" Frida laughed. "I live in Ealing. I don't take cabs that far."

"Well, you're not taking the tube at this hour and unfortunately I've had too much to drink, otherwise I'd drive you home."

Frida stopped. "I'm not taking a cab." It was an extravagance she could not afford, though she was reluctant to say so.

"You *are* taking a cab," he said. "I insist on it."

A black cab had stopped in front of them. Damien leaned in through the window and spoke to the driver. Frida shifted her weight and glanced around awkwardly. She averted her eyes when she saw Damien take out a roll of bank notes, peel off a few and hand them to the driver.

He turned to her. "I've had a perfectly lovely evening," he said. Putting his arm around her, he quickly pulled her close, leaned down and kissed her mouth. His lips were soft and warm. The scent of his cologne made her dizzy.

"Good night," she whispered. "And thank you."

"Good night Frida from Iceland," he said. "See you soon."

~~

He called her the next day, and they met the day after that. Soon they were seeing each other daily. They had a gentle sort of chemistry, an ease of being with each other, though in other respects they were absolutely different. He liked antiques. She liked modern design. He liked action flicks with Bruce Willis. She liked art-house films. He loved opera. She loved jazz. He liked Shakespeare, but only at the theatre. She absolutely loved Baz Luhrman's Romeo and Juliet.

And she was taken aback by his house.

He took her home with him on their third date. Approaching the house, her astonishment grew: it was located on a street of stately white townhouses, lined with Jaguar and Mercedes-Benz sports cars, their entranceways flanked by Roman columns. At one of those houses he guided her up a small flight of stairs to the front door and pulled out a key.

"This is where you live?"

"This is it."

She glanced around at the neighborhood. Yup – as she had surmised, he had money.

"On which floor is your flat?"

He pushed the door open before he answered, and quickly entered numbers into an alarm system located next to it. Then he held the door wide for her.

"All of them."

"What – you mean you live in the whole house?"

"That's right."

"And you live here by yourself?"

"No. My housekeeper lives in the basement."

His housekeeper. For his *house*.

He led the way through the vestibule and into the living room, where he flicked on the light.

Standing in the middle of the floor, wearing a jeans jacket, her hair in braids, Frida turned around in astonishment. The word 'stifling' came to mind. She dismissed it. It returned. The room was completely unventilated. There was a beige wall-to-wall carpet so thick that she sank into it with every step. At the windows were heavy drapes bleached by the sun to a lifeless beige, blocking the daylight. Above her was an oversized crystal chandelier that shone with unnerving brightness. The furniture was baroque, all curves and flourishes and ornamentation. It felt intensely cloying.

She turned to Damien. He stood watching her with an anxious expression that made her want to put her arms around him and kiss him. Clearly this house was a relic from a suffocating past. Instantly she knew that he carried his own emotional baggage, just like her. A wave of affection washed over her.

"Wow," she said. She had wanted to sound cheerful, but it came out more downbeat than she intended.

"I know," he said apologetically, "it's been left pretty much as it was since my father died." He paused, then added, "Decorating isn't my forte."

He shifted abruptly. "Let's go into the kitchen. I'll make us some tea."

She went slowly after him, her eyes still lingering on all the *stuff*: a porcelain statue of a milk maid, a gold table clock, an elaborate picture frame with a portrait of a stern older man … even a rococo ashtray.

That night they made love in a canopy bed that had the canopy missing, next to an absurdly modern closet with mirrored doors. Remarkably, Damien's outward confidence did not extend to his lovemaking – he was hesitant and timid in bed. Like a little boy, thought Frida, uncertain of where to touch her, melting into the pleasure she gave him freely. Mortified when at one point his erection faded and he had to stop; grateful when she simply lay next to him, pressing her nakedness against him, until he had recovered and they continued, slowly at first, then with increasing intensity until they both fell back, exhausted and satisfied, to drift into carefree sleep.

The next morning, Frida sat at the kitchen table wearing one of Damien's oversized shirts and flipping through one of his conservative newspapers. He had gone out to pick up some juice and fresh bread at a market around the corner. Suddenly a door that Frida had barely noticed opened. In came a woman. She stopped, a look of shock registering on her face, then retreated without saying a word, closing the door with a clatter. Beyond the door, Frida heard footsteps descending.

A startled Frida had three instantaneous thoughts. One: this must be Damien's housekeeper. Two: it was the woman he had lunch with the other day. Three: she had not expected nor wanted to see her there.

A moment later, Damien came in. He set a plastic bag on the counter, then leaned down and gave Frida a kiss on the lips, lingering just a brief moment longer than he might have.

"I think I've just met your housekeeper," Frida said.

She couldn't be sure, but it almost seemed like Damien froze. Only for a fraction of a second, though – then he straightened up and smiled, almost ironically.

"Oh. Mrs. Kelly came up?"

"And beat a hasty retreat when she saw me. I think she received a big shock."

"She's not used to seeing ladies sitting in the kitchen, wearing my shirts."

"Oh? What do they wear, then, your ladies? Nothing?"

He came over to her, reached for her hands and pulled her up. His hands went under his shirt, took hold of her ass and pressed her close. He was already hard. She grinned and lifted her face to his. He still smelled like sex.

"Let's do it on the kitchen table," he murmured into her ear.

"What if your Mrs. Kelly comes in?"

"We'll lock the door."

~~

It took two months for Frida to give up her own flat and move into his. By that time she was floating in a sea of bliss. Even the god-awful furniture, stifling carpet and light-killing drapes couldn't blight her happiness. His life was pretty unexciting – it revolved around his work. He wasn't someone to go out to the pub or hang with the boys and watch the footie … he seemed to have few friends, in fact. That was one thing they had in common. He just wanted to be with her. To go out for dinner, or to the cinema, strolling slowly back, holding hands, sometimes stopping and looking in shop windows. In the evenings, they went for walks. Damien had a soft spot for cats, and seemed unable to pass one on the street without stopping and scratching its head. They had fallen into the habit of walking through nearby residential neighborhoods specifically for the purpose of "hunting for cats".

"I like to get them to the point where they purr and are like putty in my arms," he told Frida one evening with a grin, cradling a yellow tabby that oozed ecstasy as Damien's deft fingers massaged the sides of its head and beneath its chin.

Frida laughed. "They're only putty in your arms as long as they're getting something out of it. The minute you don't do what they want you to do, they see no use for you any more and are gone. Cats are master manipulators."

"Maybe that's what I admire about them. They're their own masters."

Frida observed him with admiration and affection. He looked so vulnerable and gentle cradling the cat in his arms. "Why don't you get a cat of your own since you like them so much?"

He let the cat fall on the ground. "Too much commitment," he said. "I'd rather just canoodle other people's."

"Couldn't Mrs. Kelly look after it?"

His countenance seemed to darken. "No," he said in a clipped voice. Frida sensed that she'd hit a nerve, though she didn't know why.

Indeed, the presence of old Mrs. Sourpuss Kelly, who apparently came and went as she pleased and barely gave Frida the time of day, was the only thing about this new situation that unnerved her. The day she moved in she had found Mrs. Kelly in the kitchen fixing dinner, wearing the drab brown skirt, long cardigan and beige blouse that appeared to be her permanent uniform. Her skin was pallid and her shoulders sagged slightly, and she moved about the kitchen with a strange defiance coupled with weariness. Her entire being seemed as faded as her clothes, like she'd been put in the washing machine a few dozen times until all the color had run out. She was like a specter. Ghastly.

"Can I give you a hand?" she'd asked cheerfully, though with a hint of trepidation. Mrs. Kelly didn't exactly seem welcoming.

The older woman had looked directly with an expression of thinly veiled hostility.

"That won't be necessary," she'd said haughtily, and turned her back on Frida, who had not known whether to laugh or be angry. The whole thing seemed so absurd. Was Mrs. Kelly jealous of her?

She thought that surely Mrs. Kelly would come to accept her with time, but if anything her evident dislike of Frida got worse. Whenever they were in the same room together, Mrs. Kelly exuded repugnance towards her. She never looked at her. If she was forced to speak to her, she never used her name.

Frida debated whether or not she should say something about it to Damien. She was hesitant, mostly because she wasn't sure if she was perceiving the situation correctly. Maybe Mrs. Kelly was just like that with everyone – well, except Damien. He seemed to have this bond with her, and it felt to her like there was like an invisible circle around their relationship into which she feared to tread. It even crossed her mind that Mrs. Kelly might be in love with Damien, but she quickly dismissed the notion. It wasn't that – it was something else. And whatever it was, it was confusing. Crazy making, even.

Finally she could no longer hold her tongue. Choosing her words carefully, making an effort to be casual, she remarked one day in passing whether old Mrs. Kelly might have something against her. To her relief, Damien merely laughed. "No. Surely not. Don't pay attention to her. She can be a bit cranky."

They were standing in the TV lounge, which was the only room in the house that had any semblance of modernity.

"Has she always had free access to your place?"

"She's my housekeeper."

Again she felt that tension she sometimes felt with him when she commented on something to do with Mrs. Kelly. Like it put him on the defensive. She turned away.

A moment later she felt him put his arms around her.

"Don't worry about her. She's been around a while, that's all. She's sort of part of the family."

"How long has she been your housekeeper?"

"Since I was little. She was my parents' housekeeper, first. After they died, she stayed with me."

"I really think she dislikes me."

"She doesn't dislike you. Don't be daft!"

"She ignores me completely."

"She just needs to get used to you." Damien let go of her and sat down on the sofa, reaching for the remote control and flicking on the TV. It was clear he wanted the conversation to be over.

"What was she like with your other girlfriends?"

Damien shrugged, his eyes fixed on the TV. "I never brought any of them home."

Frida stared at him. "You didn't bring them home?"

"No. I told you that."

Frida took the remote control from him and turned off the TV.

"Isn't that kind of unusual?"

"Maybe. I suppose I knew it wasn't anything long-term."

He looked directly at her face. In his eyes there was a curious mixture of vulnerability and defiance. She stared into his eyes for a moment, then leaned forward and kissed him. A moment later she was straddling him, her blonde hair falling around her face. He was panting, his breath hot. She pulled off her top, and a minute later she was naked.

Afterwards, lying on the sofa, her head on his bare chest, he ran his fingers over her back.

"Frida …" he said.

"What?"

"Marry me."

She reached up and kissed him once on the mouth.

"I'm serious, you know."

She looked up at him again. His eyes were somber. She sat up, pulling a blanket around herself.

"You don't even know me."

"Yes I do. I know you and I know me."

"You *don't* know me. You only know me in this setting. In London. You've never been to my country, you've never met my family …"

"So we'll go." He shifted towards her and took her hand. "As soon as I can arrange a holiday."

Her heart was beating fast. She could hardly look into his face.

"I can't wait to meet them all. I can't wait to see your country."

"It's not ... *all*. It's really just me and my mother."

"Well, then – I can't wait to meet your mother."

Frida's anxiety was rising and she feared she wouldn't be able to keep her composure. Marry him. *Marry him*. The sad little alcoholic's daughter from the shadow district. A little voice inside her whispered that it was a preposterous thought: *as soon as he finds out who you are, he will want nothing more to do with you.*

Damien was speaking. She had to struggle to hear the words.

"Tell her to come for a visit. We'll send her a ticket. Ask her to come soon."

"No," she said quickly. "No, she won't want to."

"Why not?" He was grinning playfully. "You really don't want me to meet her, do you?"

Frida smiled bashfully. "No ... it's not that. It's just that ... well, she'll want to pay her own way." The words tumbled out of her mouth before she knew what she was saying. Ridiculous words, that meant nothing. They weren't even true.

"No," said Damien. "We'll pay. And don't email – call. Go on. Call her now."

She looked at him with surprise. He was still smiling, but his voice was commanding.

"All right," she said carefully. "If that's what you want."

CHAPTER FOUR

There was a sharp knock at the door.

Frida bolted upright in bed, hurled from the land of dreams. Glancing at her phone she saw that it was almost eleven. Did someone just knock? *Who?*

Another knock. Moving swiftly she got out of bed, pulled on her jeans and adjusted the camisole top in which she had been sleeping. Glancing in a mirror she quickly brushed her fingers through her hair, pulled on a cardigan, then swiftly made her way down the stairs. Through a little diamond-shaped window in the door she could see part of a throat and chin, and a shoulder wearing a tweed blazer. It was a man and he was looking up.

She collected her thoughts quickly, then pulled open the door.

"Oh! Hello … I hope I'm not intruding …" He appeared flustered, whoever he was. He was short and spoke English with a strong Icelandic accent.

"It's all right," Frida replied in Icelandic, struggling to compose herself after her rude awakening.

"Oh, you're Icelandic," he said, switching languages. He smiled, an ingratiating smile. "My name is Jón Jónsson. I'm head of the town council."

She smiled and blinked. What did he want?

"I just wanted to stop by to let you know that we'd be happy to show you around the town. We're especially proud of our aquaculture project. We're *thrilled* that you've taken such a keen interest in the place." He smiled again, revealing coffee-stained teeth.

Frida's smile was frozen, her mind working overtime. What on earth was he talking about?

"Anything we can do for you, feel free to ask. It's no trouble at all. We want you to feel at home here. And if you see anything here that might be of interest to the British Embassy, so much the better. We are always looking for new opportunities, in trade, collaboration, or whatever." He reached into his pocket for a business card. "I'm in my office by nine every morning, so if you wish to tour the plant, feel free to call. I'd be happy to show you around personally."

A sneaking suspicion was crawling into her mind. "Thank you … er …" – glancing at the card – "Jón."

" … Call me Nonni."

"Nonni. That's very kind. But how did you know I was…?"

"Oh – oh, goodness, my apologies! The Embassy called to tell us that you were in town. I spoke to your husband personally – we met this past summer in connection with a business delegation from England and had an interesting talk. We met again last week, in fact. My English isn't great, but good enough for your husband and I to understand one another perfectly."

Frida suddenly felt cold. *No. I'm being paranoid.*

"Ah. Well, that's good." Frida heard her own voice as though it was somewhere outside of her. "But to be perfectly honest ... Nonni, I really only came here for a rest. My husband worries needlessly that I'll get bored or lonely, but I never do." She smiled her most dazzling smile.

He looked confused.

"How very kind of you to stop by, though," Frida added, taking half a step backwards and preparing to close the door. "I hope you'll excuse me, but I've only just woken up. I'm already committed to my mission of resting, as you can see." Another flash of a smile.

He looked a little deflated as he ran his palm across his prematurely thinning hair. "Oh, yes. I understand. Again, if there's anything we can do, anything at all, you know where to find me."

"That's so very kind. Goodbye."

Shutting the door, Frida leaned her back against the wall. She clenched her fists.

"*Sonofabitch!*"

Fifteen minutes later she was striding towards the seashore, a pair of oversized rubber boots on her feet, an old jacket flailing around her. If anyone happened to see her they would probably take her for a madwoman, but she didn't care. She was furious. Manipulative bastard! Even up here he couldn't leave her alone. *Scheming, controlling* – already he had a spy in town, and he wanted her to know it.

She crossed the road, splashed through a puddle, then ran down an incline to the shore. Trampling along, pebbles crunched beneath her feet. She leaned down, picked up a rock and hurled it into the sea. "Fuck!!" And another. And another. "Fuck!! Fuck!!" A bigger rock, requiring both arms – "Motherfucker!!"

She stopped. Blood rushed through her veins. There was a ringing in her ears. She started walking again, at a regular pace now. Suddenly she smiled. She'd never done anything like that before. It felt good. Damn! She picked up another rock and hurled it out into the sea with all her might, letting out a Tarzan-like yell: "Aaaaaaarrgghh – !"

Then she froze.

Out of the corner of her eye she sensed, more than saw, someone watching her.

Just a few feet away, up on a grassy slope, stood a man.

She turned around slowly.

It was him. The man from the highway, the one with the knife.

He lifted a hand in salute. She stood perfectly still, wrapping the jacket around herself. Then she nodded her head.

He jumped down from the grassy slope and came walking towards her with that same easy stride she had first noticed out on the road. She was relieved to see that he was grinning.

"Having a bad day?"

She grinned back. Impishly. "I guess. I didn't think there was anyone around."

"Don't mind me. I was just passing."

"Rescuing more sheep?"

"Not this time. Just coming down to check on some flotsam.

We had some stuff come loose off one of our pens."

"Pens?"

"From our aquaculture project."

"Ah."

"Normally there's not much traffic down here. So don't worry, you can hurl rocks all you want, nobody will see you. Normally." He extended his hand. "I'm Baldur."

She took it. He had long fingers and his grip was warm and firm. "Frida." Pause. "We met out on the highway."

"Yes I know. You're the lady with the diplomat plates."

The lady with the diplomat plates. She winced inwardly. Just the thing she did not want as her epitaph.

An awkward moment passed. She searched her mind for something to say, but came up with nothing.

"Well, I'll leave you to it," he said, as though he'd sensed her awkwardness. He grinned. "See you around."

She nodded, watched him take long strides up the slope, and disappear. A moment later she heard a car start, and drive away.

~~

Frida and Damien had their first major fight on the day of her mother's arrival. It was about whether or not Mrs. Kelly should be allowed to prepare dinner that evening.

"She always looks after things when I entertain!" Damien's voice was irritable and slightly whiny. A new side of him that Frida was as yet unfamiliar with and immediately disliked.

"But this isn't entertaining. It's my mother coming. I want it to be just family."

"Mrs. Kelly is family. Practically."

"Next you'll be suggesting that she sit down and have dinner with us."

He stood up abruptly. "Yes – and why not? What's wrong with that? I don't get caught up in all that class nonsense, and I wouldn't have thought that you did, either. Being from such an egalitarian country and everything." She thought she detected a hint of sarcasm in that last remark, but she couldn't be sure.

Frida's heart was pounding. She was completely on edge, she knew. Her mother had been on the wagon now for several months, but there was always this fear that it wouldn't last. She'd put it off as long as possible to contact her and ask her to come, as she'd promised Damien she would. Not that she did not want to see her mother. She was just afraid to upset her equilibrium. All her life she had walked on eggshells around Ásta – first when she was drinking, because her moods could swing so unpredictably, then later when she was not drinking, for fear that any upset would make her fall off the wagon. And she did not want this trip to be the event that would tip the scales. The last thing she needed was for Damien to experience her mother drunk. Also, she knew that her mother hated to fly, and that she self-medicated with alcohol. There was a fifty-fifty chance that she would come off the plane a mess, slurring her words and reeling. But she would not tell Damien that.

And here they were, fighting about old Mrs. Kelly. Frida wondered, not for the first time, whether she was losing her mind. Was it so wrong for her not to want to have Damien's housekeeper, who clearly disliked her, at the dinner table with her and her mother?

In the end Damien grudgingly relented. That grudge hung in the air between them in the car as they drove out to the airport to pick up Ásta.

Waiting in Arrivals, Frida tried her best to act normal, but was failing miserably. The tension inside her was unbearable. Would her mother emerge drunk, or would she not? She shifted her weight and tried not to chew her fingernails. Damien cast the occasional glance at her. He probably thought it was all due to their fight, Frida thought, and that was OK. Better that he think that than know the truth.

There she was. Ásta looked wan and emaciated, her skin sallow and her face drawn. She stopped to orient herself.

"Mamma!"

Ásta looked confused for a moment, then broke into a smile. She walked with small, rapid steps towards her daughter. Frida put her arms around her mother, trying to catch a whiff of her breath without her noticing. The strong smell of stale tobacco filled her nostrils, but at least there was no alcohol. She breathed a sigh of relief and felt some semblance of normality return.

"Damien, this is my mother, Ásta."

"Such a pleasure." Taking Ásta's hand, he touched it lightly to his lips. Frida cringed with embarrassment. What was he thinking? Her mother appeared bewildered.

"My mother's not used to such gallantry, Damien – the women of Iceland are known for their independence."

"Even so, I find it hard to believe that they don't appreciate a little gentlemanly attention."

God.

Outside, it had started raining. Damien pulled out a small umbrella and opened it, holding it for Ásta. Frida stood to one side, unable to avoid the thought that her mother was closer to Damien in age than she, herself, was.

"No – it's all right ..." Ásta appeared bemused.

Despite Damien's efforts at gallantry – or perhaps because of them – the drive back to Kensington was fraught with tension. Ásta's English was limited, yet she anxiously tried to respond to Damien's rapid-fire questions, which seemed to be less about genuine interest and more about avoiding any moments of silence, however brief. It also occurred to Frida that it might be his way of keeping her and Ásta from speaking to each other in Icelandic, something which would, of course, automatically exclude Damien and thereby his efforts to control the situation. She was extremely relieved when they reached the house and Damien took Ásta's suitcase upstairs.

Her mother was looking around much in the same way as Frida had the first time she entered Damien's house.

"What do you think?" Frida asked quietly in Icelandic.

"About ... this? Or about him?"

"Both."

"The house is a bit dated, of course ... and as far as he goes, I can't really say yet." She paused. "But ... how *old* is he, Frida?"

For one brief second, Frida considered lying to her mother about Damien's age. Then she swallowed. "He's forty."

Damien came down the stairs before Ásta could answer.

While her mother went to settle in to the guest room, Frida got dinner ready. Damien lent a hand, though their earlier fight hung in the air between them like a cold mist.

Dinner itself was tense. Damien brought in some wine and offered some to Frida but not to Ásta, which gave rise to heavy friction. Frida was furious: she had mentioned Ásta's drinking problem to Damien – could he not have skipped the wine for one evening? All through the meal, Ásta seemed distracted and Frida knew she was battling the longing to drink. This, combined with the language barrier, made conversation at the table virtually impossible. Frida was incredibly relieved when it was over, even as she shuddered at the thought of what the next ten days would be like.

After dinner, Damien excused himself and retired to his study. Ásta helped her daughter carry the plates into the kitchen.

"He's not much for equality, is he?" she said, clearly striving to keep her voice light.

Frida tensed up at the negative tone in her mother's voice. It was like she could never see anything but the worst in people.

"He's not normally like this," she said defensively. "He's nervous about meeting you, I think. Also, we had a bit of a fight earlier." The moment she said it, she wished she hadn't.

"Oh. What about?"

"Nothing. Nothing important, anyway."

"Just a general fight about nothing?"

"Yep."

Ásta scraped leftovers from the plate into a garbage can. "So, you're going to marry him?"

There was something about Ásta's voice that made Frida instantly defiant. The truth was that she hadn't given Damien a definitive answer yet – she had wanted for him to meet her mother.

"Yep."

"Do you love him?"

"Of course I love him. I wouldn't marry him if I didn't love him."

"People marry for all sorts of reasons, not just for love."

"Well, I love him."

Both of them stopped, facing each other.

"Well in that case, I wish you all happiness."

The antagonism between them evaporated, and both were left feeling slightly awkward.

Ásta turned to the sink. "But I still say that he is a bit old for you. And anyway, what are your plans for your life, Frida? I know it may be enough for him to have you as his wife, but you have to think of your own future. What about school?"

"I'll figure it out. Don't worry."

"I just wonder what you'll have to fall back on if it doesn't work out."

Frida flushed with anger. "What do you mean, if it doesn't work out? Why wouldn't it work out? Can't you just be happy for me?"

Again they stared at each other, as if across a chasm. In a flash of recognition, Frida saw the heaviness in her mother's face, the weariness in her eyes. All of her life, she had been battling demons, and it had nothing to do with her, Frida. She saw that now. Her mother's demons were her own demons, and if she could not be happy for her, then it was simply a result of her own unhappiness. Nothing to do with her.

"I *am* happy for you," Ásta said, squeezing forth a smile. "If you're happy, I'm happy." But her eyes were dim, and the shadows in her face seemed deeper than before. She put down the tea towel. "I'm just so tired. I got up early this morning and the flight took a toll. I hope you don't mind if I just go to bed. I'll be better in the morning, and maybe we can go out and do something tomorrow. It's been so long since I was here, I'm sure London has changed a great deal."

Frida wanted to tell her mother that she was proud of her for not drinking, for having resisted, for staying sober when she clearly wanted so very much to have a drink, but she said nothing. It was one of those things they didn't discuss. The big taboo. Also, she could not be sure that the tiredness was not a ruse, that her mother would not go upstairs and find a way to sneak a drink – maybe she had one of those little bottles of liquor they served on the planes, or maybe she'd come down and take the rest of Damien's bottle upstairs when they'd gone to bed. And Frida knew well enough that once she had one drink in her, that was it. The trip would be ruined, and she might even have to take her mother back to Iceland herself, holding her hand and making sure she didn't scandalize on the way.

But of course she said none of that, only put her arms around her mother and gave her a gentle squeeze. "Yes, mamma. We'll go out for lunch tomorrow, and then maybe do some shopping.

And we'll have to take in a show while you're here."

Alone in the kitchen after her mother had gone upstairs, Frida's resentment at Damien returned. He had behaved like an idiot, and then escaped to his study. He had a habit of doing that, especially if something bothered him. Frida often felt shut out. She wished he'd talk to her about whatever it was, but he always said he didn't want to trouble her with it, which was considerate enough, she supposed. And once he was in there, she didn't feel like she could bother him. One time she'd knocked at the door, then tried the handle, only to find that the door was locked. When he'd opened the door, he'd stood there in the doorway like he didn't want her to come in. He was working, he said, and it disturbed him when his concentration was broken. He hoped she didn't mind.

She said she didn't, but when she walked away she'd felt an overwhelming sense of loneliness.

And now she, too, felt tired. It had been a tough, emotionally draining day. It was still early – only around nine-thirty – but perhaps she should just go to bed. Read a bit, then allow herself to drift off. Tomorrow she and her mother would spend some quality time together, just the two of them. She'd let Ásta decide where she wanted to go.

When she went upstairs, she saw through the crack in the doorframe that the light in her mother's room was still on. Frida knocked gently, then opened it.

Ásta was in her nightgown, sitting on the edge of the bed and brushing her hair. Seeing her in the half-light, looking so frail and brittle, Frida felt an overwhelming surge of love for her mother. She hadn't chosen to be the way she was. She hadn't done it on purpose. And she had loved and cared for her, Frida, as much as her disease would allow her to.

In that instant, Frida decided that it was time to release all anger and resentment from the past. She wanted things to be good between the two of them. After all, her mother was all the family she had in the world. She needed to remember that, and cherish it. Blood was thick – thicker than water.

"I just wanted to say goodnight again," said Frida, stepping inside the room.

"Goodnight, darling. It really is good to be here. I've missed you."

Frida hesitated for one moment, then walked rapidly over to her mother and awkwardly put her arms around her. "It's good to have you here. It's really, really good, mamma."

Ásta stroked her daughter's cheek. "You've got everything going for you, Frida, and your whole life is ahead of you. I just want you to use it well. Time passes so quickly – it's hard to believe at your age, but it does. Nothing lasts forever."

Frida kissed her mother's cheek. "Goodnight, mamma. Sleep tight."

"Goodnight, darling. See you tomorrow."

~

A loud wail cut through the dull greyness of the morning. Frida bolted up in bed.

There was the sound of running on the stairs. Frida was already on her feet, reaching for her robe. Damien was behind her. Someone banged loudly and urgently on the bedroom door.

She threw it open and in an instant registered the panic in Mrs. Kelly's eyes. Pushing past her, she took three steps down the stairs. There, at the bottom, lay the crumpled form of her mother in her nightgown. A shattered glass lay next to her head. Death was evident in the way her limbs were splayed, in the peculiar stillness of her body.

~

The succeeding days were a blur of activity. Frida moved through them as if she were in a trance, and allowed Damien to take charge. People from the Icelandic Embassy came, there were papers to sign, and arrangements made to have the body transported back to Iceland.

Frida was a mess. Feelings of guilt and grief would tear at her one minute, then the next she would turn numb and disoriented, almost forgetting what had happened. Then the horror would return, the searing coldness of death, penetrating right through skin and bone, shuddering through every cell.

Her mother was gone. She had been there, in the guest room,

giving Frida a weak smile from the edge of the bed as she left the room. And then suddenly, without warning, she was no longer there – her spirit flown, just her crumpled body left at the foot of the stairs, like a discarded shell. *At least she is free now*, Frida told herself, *free from the spiritual malaise that dogged her throughout her days and always made her fall prey to her disease again, sooner or later.*

She did not want to think the thoughts that nevertheless accosted her mind: whether her mother had gone down to get a drink or, worse, whether she was already drunk and was heading down for more. She had not had the courage to go near the body for she dreaded the smell of alcohol. It was ridiculous, but true: she hated her mother's drinking, and she didn't want to know. And now she hated herself for it – if only she had gone to her one last time, kissed her one last kiss, touched her. Then, at least, she would feel as if she had said goodbye.

Instead, two weeks later, Frida and Damien were in Iceland, standing hand-in-hand with a small group of mourners in a barren cemetery, shivering as they watched Ásta's coffin being lowered into the ground. The minister released a handful of earth onto it and made the sign of the cross. People started filing past the grave, paying their respects one by one. There weren't many people – a few relatives who still kept in touch, a few of her mother's colleagues, her mother's old drinking buddies, and some people who Frida had never seen before but whose faces told many stories. They had paid their respects to Frida at the church, and one woman said she had known her mother from Vogur – the alcohol treatment hospital.

It was Frida's turn. With everyone's eyes on her, she stood at the edge of her mother's grave, looking down. The coffin was white, and there was a bouquet of blood-red roses on the lid. She raised her hand and made the sign of the cross.

Goodnight mamma. Sleep tight.

~~

There were millions of things to take care of, stuff to sort through, old letters, clothes and trinkets to take to recycling depot, some of which would get passed on to the Red Cross.

Damien was there, then he was not, he had to go to London for his work, but would return soon. Frida felt intensely alone – now, more than ever, she felt how small their family had been, basically just her and her mother, no one else. The feeling of being an orphan, of being abandoned in all the world, cut her like a knife.

And so it was, when Damien returned, that she found herself standing in the District Commissioner's office with him slipping a ring on her finger, and she a ring on his. It was just the two of them, plus the witnesses supplied by the DC's office. Just the two of them, because they were both orphans now.

~~

Back in London, things returned to normal, only nothing was normal. Damien went to work, and Frida … she floated through the days in slow motion, not fully awake. Numb. When she looked at the place where her mother's body had been at the bottom of the stairs, she felt nothing. No horror, not like she had felt that very first day – just, nothing.

And there was this ring on her finger. She had always said that she would only get married in Iceland, so Damien had insisted that they do it now, because who knew when they might be there again, what with the demands of his job? His logic was so flawless that she couldn't argue, and so she'd sleepwalked through that, too, wearing an old dress she'd dug out of a box because she couldn't bear the thought of going out to buy a new one in her twisted, dark state. They'd gone out for dinner at a restaurant, but even that felt hazy and strange, and their wedding night had been spent in her old bed with a million old ghosts. Damien said they'd do the honeymoon later, and she said she didn't care about that, and it was true – she didn't.

The days all flowed into each other. Most mornings she didn't get up until she heard Mrs. Kelly puttering around downstairs, doing the hoovering and dusting and wiping and laundry and dishes and whatever else it was she had been doing for decades in Damien's house. She hated the sight of Mrs. Kelly. She despised her mousy hair, her colorless face, her vapid presence – it was like she was a ghost moving around in the house. And so, she usually got dressed and slipped out of the house before Mrs. Kelly came up to the second floor. She'd get a coffee and something to eat at the local Starbucks, sitting there looking at the paper, pretending to read and not registering a word. Afterwards she would go out and wander the streets, occasionally stopping to look in shop windows at nothing in particular, just trying to act normal, because she was sure everyone was looking at her and if she just acted normal they wouldn't see that she was falling apart. Sometimes she'd go to the cinema, particularly if the weather was bad; she'd see films and look for meaning in them, sometimes she would find it and sometimes not, and either way, by the time she got outside she knew it didn't matter.

Most of all she was terrified that Damien would find out what was really going on with her, so by the time he got home in the evenings she made a point of having showered and dressed for dinner, which Mrs. Kelly would have already made. She'd stopped battling Mrs. Kelly in the kitchen. She didn't want to cook any more. Mrs. Kelly could do it for all she cared. In fact, she cared about very little, except staying out of Mrs. Kelly's way.

And so, she would greet her husband, having already set the table and heated up dinner – depending on how late he came home, of course. He always asked her how her day had been and she always responded "fine", and that sufficed him – he didn't need to know the details, or how she had filled the hours. Indeed, it seemed to suit him fine that she didn't elaborate too much – it gave him a chance to talk about his day, his work, his colleagues, some of whom were exceedingly funny, but most of whom were idiots, according to Damien. Frida had the performance down to an art. She laughed in all the right places, probed in all the right places, showed compassion, shock, admiration, sympathy in all the right places. Anything to hide the fact that she was crumbling inside.

This went on for four months. Then, one day, Mrs. Kelly had to go away. Damien knew but did not say where, and Frida strongly suspected there might be a medical reason, although of course it could also be a family emergency, for all she knew. She didn't really care – but she did care that Mrs. Kelly was out of the house. It felt less oppressive, and for the first time in months, Frida felt like she could breathe freely indoors.

For the first three days, she lay in bed and slept until mid-afternoon. On the fourth day, she slept until noon, then got out of bed and threw open the window, as she had just noticed that the room felt terribly stuffy. In fact, the whole house felt stuffy, so she opened all the windows and aired out all the rooms.

On the fifth day, she surprised herself by digging out an old pair of trainers and some of her dance clothes from theatre school. She then put everything in a bag and headed to the local gym – the one that Damien occasionally went to after work. After running three kilometers on the treadmill she felt not tired, as she had expected, but completely energized. The following day she went back and hired a personal trainer. Gradually the gym became her anchor, and working out on the treadmill became her lifeline. Slowly but surely, Frida began to return to life. She was beginning to see a future again, and even to believe that she had a place in it. Her problem was that she needed something to do, some purpose in life. Power-walking on the treadmill or doing laps on the elliptical machine was all good and fine, but it was hardly something that would infuse her life with a sense of purpose, at least not in the long run. Still, it helped her think about how she could potentially fill her time, and after three days and about twenty kilometers of thinking she settled on four things: a) she could get a job. b) she could go to school. c) she could do charity work. d) she could renovate Damien's house.

A few more kilometers were spent considering these options. The problem with a) and b) was that she didn't know what she wanted to do. Sure, she could go out and be a barista at Starbucks, but that would hardly give her life meaning. Similarly she could sign up for, say, a literature course at the university with all the other bored housewives, or a course in underwater basket weaving at the local community college, but the prospect was about as thrilling as the beige drapes in Damien's front room. c), of course, would ostensibly give her life some purpose, but maybe, just maybe, she needed to put the oxygen mask on herself before she went out and tried to help someone else.

Therefore, after much deliberation, she decided that d) made the most sense.

She was waiting with bated breath to sell him on the idea over dinner that evening. However, the moment he entered the house, she could tell that he had something else on his mind. He looked elated – almost impish.

"What?" she asked, seeing his expression.

"Don't ask what. Ask where."

"All right: where?"

"Berlin."

"Berlin!?"

"Head of trade and investment."

He was pumped with excitement.

"Oh Damien, congratulations! That's great!"

He put his arms around her and gave her a big kiss on the lips. Releasing her, he walked past her into the main hall.

"So, when?"

"March."

"Okay."

That was five months away. She could still get started on the house.

He rubbed his hands together. "Boy, it's cold out there. What's for dinner?"

"Shepherd's pie."

"Mmm! Mrs. Kelly make it?"

Resentment stirred in Frida's belly. "Yes."

"I can't wait to tell her the news. She'll be so pleased."

The ensuing silence was like a dead weight between them.

"Why will she be pleased?"

"Well … because, of course …"

"Because … what?"

"She'll like it over there."

"She's *not* moving with us?"

Damien glanced at her sideways. "Of course she is."

Frida stared at him in disbelief. "How can you just decide that without talking to me?"

"Decide? There was nothing to decide. She always comes with me."

"You never told me that."

"I'm sure I did. I told you about her being in Mexico with me. You just don't remember."

"You didn't!" God, she hated the sound of her own voice. She sounded like a petulant child.

"Oh, for God's sake Frida, I'm not going to stand here and argue about it. I know I did."

His voice was dismissive. For a moment he hesitated, then he turned and left the room. She heard him go into his study and lock the door.

Slowly she walked to the kitchen and turned off the oven, removing the Shepherd's Pie that Mrs. Kelly had made. Leaving it on the counter, she walked slowly upstairs. She felt that same thick black fog as before begin to engulf her and pressure begin to build at her temples. The temptation was intense to undress and lie down under the covers, fall into a state of oblivion for the next twelve hours, wake up and feel directionless, like someone whose life was a mistake.

No. She would not go there. She drew herself up to her full height and looked at herself in the mirror. She needed to get out of here. Go for a walk. Get some fresh air. Leave this toxic place.

She put on some warm clothes and crept back downstairs. The house was perfectly still. She wondered what Damien was doing in his study that required so much secrecy. Maybe nothing special, maybe he just needed a symbolic barrier to put up between him and her. Which he seemed to need more and more, all the time.

She went out, closing the door quietly behind her, then started walking at a brisk pace. Walking was good, it cleared her head and helped her to think.

Things were not good between her and Damien, that much was obvious. But these fights they kept having were always about the same thing – or, rather, the same person. Mrs. Kelly. If she wasn't in their lives, the problem wouldn't exist, and hence not the fights.

And now he wanted to take her to Berlin with them.

Frida clenched her fists. *Over my dead body.*

When she returned just over an hour later, the light was still on in Damien's study. Walking up the front steps, Frida cast a furtive glance down into the flat below. The windows were covered by bars to keep out intruders, and inside she could see Mrs. Kelly in her slippers, watching television and munching on a biscuit.

She let herself into the house. All was quiet, still. She padded into the kitchen – everything had been put neatly away. The shepherd's pie was on the counter, covered with foil. She lifted it slightly and saw that the pie was half-eaten. Frida's stomach clenched. Silently and feeling like a criminal, she opened the dishwasher a crack and looked inside. There were two plates there. Mrs. Kelly had joined Damien for dinner.

With quick steps, Frida walked to the door to Damien's study. She listened briefly, but heard nothing. She raised her hand to knock, but held it suspended in mid air. Suddenly she felt overwhelmed with fatigue. Weak. She let her arm drop.

She'd deal with this tomorrow.

~~

"We need to talk."

She stood in the doorway to their bedroom, her arms folded across her chest. He was hanging up some of his clothes.

"About what?"

"Mrs. Kelly."

There was a moment's hesitation, almost imperceptible. Then he said, "What about her?"

"I don't think she should come with us to Berlin."

"Why?"

"Three's a crowd."

He stood facing her now, his lips pressed tightly together. "I don't understand what your problem is with her. You're making a big deal out of nothing."

"I'm your wife, right? Shouldn't I be the mistress of this house?"

"Are you suggesting Mrs. Kelly is the mistress?"

"No …. "

"She's my *housekeeper*. She's been the housekeeper here for over forty years."

"Then let her stay here."

"She comes with me."

"And I have no say in the matter?"

"You're being irrational."

"It's me or her."

They faced each other, defiance etched on each of their faces. Then Damien went back to hanging his clothes, his every jarring movement a reflection of his anger.

"Have you thought this through?" Frida continued. "Have you pictured us all living together in Berlin, one big happy family? You going to work, and me staying home with a woman I barely know and really don't care for – and who can't stand me?"

"You're being overdramatic. Mrs. Kelly has nothing against you."

"Are you kidding? She barely speaks to me. She sends me evil looks."

"That's ridiculous."

This conversation was going nowhere.

"I don't want this interference in our lives." He was turned away from her. She walked over and put her arms around his waist. "I want us to be happy."

He stiffened. Then he gently disengaged her arms.

"I would have thought it would suit you to have someone take care of the home," he said, his back still turned. "It would leave you more time to do whatever you wanted to do during the day."

"Like what? What do I have to do during the day? I *want* to take care of house. I don't want to feel like an intruder in my own home."

He turned to her. His anger was dissipating, she could tell.

"Having household help is part of being a diplomat's wife. It comes with the territory."

"Having household help doesn't necessarily involve someone living with you."

"I can't just *leave* her here!"

Frida was startled by his outburst.

"Why? She'll find other work. With good references, all the experience she has – she'll find work in no time."

He shook his head. "Not at her age."

Frida felt her heart soften. Her husband was a good man. The woman had been in his life for all those years – it was probably natural for him to regard her as family. But she would be damned if she agreed to take her with them.

“Let her live here, rent-free. Pay her a little something to look after the house.”

He put his head in his hands, rubbed his eyes. Finally he raised his head and stared straight ahead, his expression blank.

“All right,” he said in a flat voice. “We’ll do it your way.”

CHAPTER FIVE

On the wall, between the living room and the kitchen, hung an old black telephone. When she was little, Frida had called her mother every Saturday, right after Egill and Lóa had spoken to their mother and father. The phone was still up there, even though it no longer served any practical purpose. When her cell phone rang, Frida automatically got up and headed for the phone on the wall. Stopping, she shook her head, remembering that it was 2008 now. She scooped up her cellphone from the table where it lay. It was Damien.

"Hello, my dear."

My dear. Frida seized up inside at the sound of his words. They were not an endearment but an address used in marriages devoid of passion.

"Damien."

"I just thought I'd check in. Since you've decided not to." There was a pause. "How are you?"

"I'm fine. You?"

"Are you enjoying the solitude?"

"Not as fully as I would have liked, thanks to you."

"Oh?"

"Thank you for informing the town council of my presence."

"I thought you might want something to do."

She said nothing.

"Right. Well, things are fine here, too, thanks for asking. I had the mayor over for dinner last night. Also the CEO of Kaupthing bank and the head of the Financial Supervisory

Authority. And their spouses, of course. They asked about you. I made excuses. Said you were abroad."

All those little lies all the time – to save face, to avoid discomfort, to hide the truth.

"So being in Iceland but unavailable was not acceptable?"

"Well, it would have demanded more elaborate explanations, which I wished to avoid. How are you feeling, by the way?"

"Just fine at the moment, thank you. Being away does me good."

"I understand. Being a diplomat's wife is such a burden."

Their exchanges had become filled with this sort of caustic bickering. She despised it.

"Listen, I'm a bit busy at the moment."

"Fine, I'll get to the point: When do you plan to return?"

"I don't know."

"You're part of my job here. Coming here to Iceland was as much for you as it was for me. In a sense this is your career as much as mine."

"Consider me on sick leave."

"I need to know how long."

She did a quick mental calculation of how long it would take her to paint the side of the house, plus the fence. Probably three or four days.

"Four weeks."

There was a hesitation on the other end.

Then he hung up.

She stood still for a moment, flicked off the phone. Stared out of the window.

It was strange, she thought, how unaffected she felt by his manipulation. How strong she felt, now that she was here.

A run on a treadmill would do her good. And afterwards, a soak in a hot tub.

~~

The fitness center was attached to the local swimming pool. The girl in the reception was young and doe-eyed; she handed her a key and told her to go change in the swimming pool change rooms. The pool was busy, the change rooms full of German tourists. The good thing about the Germans, Frida thought, was that they weren't afraid to strip down and shower naked. Icelandic pools required all bathers to wash themselves thoroughly without a swimsuit, but few tourists did, much to the disgruntlement of the Icelanders, who liked their pools to be clean – and hygienic.

The fitness center was small and basic – one treadmill, one stationary bike, one elliptical machine, and an assortment of nautical equipment. Frida ran five kilometers at a steady pace, blasting Radiohead on her iPod and working up a good sweat. She'd neglected her fitness regimen this summer – no doubt that had been part of the problem. She needed to keep active and fit, for her mental condition if nothing else.

After a good stretch, followed by a soak in the hot tub, Frida felt rejuvenated. On leaving, a poster on the bulletin board by the front entrance caught her eye. It showed Látrabjarg, "the westernmost tip of Europe" – a sheer sea cliff reaching almost half a kilometer up in the air. The picture was inlaid with a close-up photo of a puffin, and another of a wide beach with reddish sand. It was written in somewhat faulty English.

Látrabjarg and Raudasandur

Saturdays, 10 am.

Látrabjarg is Iceland's highest cliff at the sea with one of largest bird colonies in the world. Home to puffins, kittiwakes, fulmars and other sea birds, an experience not to be missed. Raudasandur is the red sands, a beautiful beach. Guided tour leaves from the campsite Saturdays at 10 am in summer.

"Have you ever been?"

Frida registered the voice before she turned around: Jón Jónsson, the town council man.

She turned, smiled graciously. "Oh, hello."

"It's a wonderful tour. Are you likely to go?"

Amazing how this man got on her nerves. He was so ingratiating. Or was it just the feeling she couldn't shake: that he was spying on her, and would report back to Damien on everything she did?

"I'm afraid Saturday isn't good for me."

"Oh, it's not just this Saturday. It's every Saturday through the summer."

"Yes, I know. Just as it says." She smiled to soften the sting of sarcasm.

"Of course." Self-depreciating smile. "Of course. We have other tours as well, though. Trying to boost the local economy with tourism, you understand. Using every possible angle."

"Naturally."

How long is he going to stand here?

"Well, it was good to see you again," Frida said, making a mental note to read the rest of the bulletin board notices at a later time.

"And you. Remember, if you want a tour of our aquaculture project ..."

"I'll keep that in mind!" Frida called over her shoulder.

Getting in her car, Frida felt a pang of hunger and had a mental image of the inside of the refrigerator back at the house, which was wretchedly devoid of contents, save for the few items she'd brought with her from Reykjavík.

Time to check out the local shop.

It carried a surprising number of items for such a small place, though on reflection that was probably not so strange, given that it was the only market in town. Frida collected a few things in her cart, staples like milk, eggs, bread, butter. Over at the cash register, someone was asking the clerk if they had any smoked salmon, and she overheard the clerk refer them to another place, down by the harbor, that sold salmon, and also "the best fish pate in the country." Frida felt her mouth start to water.

"What's that other shop you mentioned to the gentleman who was in here a moment ago?" Frida asked the clerk when she got to the register.

"There's a small processing shop down by the harbor – they smoke their own salmon and also make fish pate, fish balls, that kind of thing. They're really great." She lowered her voice slightly. "It's run by my cousin, but that's not why I'm saying it. They really are good. And they're local."

"Are they open now?"

"They're open from one to five every day."

Frida could see it from the road: a simple sign, red letters on a white background: SHOP. As far as she could see it was just a single door in an industrial-style building, flanked by piles of fishing nets and plastic tubs. The door was open.

She parked the car and went inside. The space was immaculate with a wet floor and white-tiled walls, smelling of fresh fish. There was a stainless steel counter and another door on the far end of the room that stood open. Through it Frida glimpsed the door of an industrial refrigerator. A few products were arranged on the counter, clearly for sale. It was obvious this was a processing plant with a little sales outfit on the side. From the other room she could hear the voices of people talking, echoing off the bare walls.

"Yeah, well, she doesn't want to go." A woman.

A man said something that Frida couldn't make out.

"There's almost always someone with her. And she's eating more now."

"What about last week?"

"What do you expect us to do? It's not like people can just walk into the psych ward and demand admission. It's not a freaking hotel. Don't you listen to the news? They're turning people away as it is."

"It's worth a try. At least we could talk to her old doctor. She's not getting any better, believe me. You're not with her all the time. She's getting worse if any …."

"I'm not discussing it. She stays here!"

There was a silence. Then suddenly a man appeared and walked quickly past her to the exit. Astonished, Frida saw who it was. There was a flicker of recognition in his eyes, then he strode past her and was gone.

A woman came out of the back room behind him. She was stout and wore white rubber boots, a white plastic apron and a hair net over her hair. She looked tired, her face red and puffy.

"Afternoon," she said.

"I was told you had smoked salmon for sale."

"That's right." The woman went behind the steel counter with slow, heavy movements. "We have smoked salmon, cured salmon and seafood pate. And fish balls."

"I'll take a package of each."

The woman got her purchases together and put them in a bag.

Frida paid, thanked her, and left. Pulling out of the parking lot onto the main road, she waited for a car to pass. It was the blue Cherokee jeep. Sitting next to the man whom Frida had just encountered in the shop was a pretty young woman with a thin face and large eyes. She stared at Frida as the car drove past, looking pale and drawn, her countenance vapid through the car window.

Driving back to the house, Frida couldn't keep from wondering if this was the person she had overheard the Cherokee man and the matronly woman discussing in the shop. Was it his wife, she wondered, or his girlfriend? Or even his sister? Whoever or whatever she was to him, it was clear that he was concerned for her well-being, and was not in agreement with whoever else was involved.

~~

Over the next two days the weather was fabulous: sunny, with just a scattering of clouds, temperatures in the double-digits, and – most importantly – no wind. Still, there was no denying that autumn was just around the corner. Frida could feel it in the air ... the hint of a chill, making its presence felt, like a slight warning on the breeze. 'Be forewarned,' it seemed to say, 'don't be lulled into thinking it will stay this way forever.'

That's just what Frida was thinking as she stood on the ladder that leaned against the side of the house, wearing paint-splattered coveralls and wielding a paintbrush. Egill had mentioned to her that he'd started the job but been unable to finish; she'd said she'd be happy to do it for him; he'd said only if she felt like it and the weather was decent. She was happy to assist him in this way – a small token of appreciation for what he had done for her by lending her his property. She had the radio on and could hear it through the window – there was a debate happening, with some man expressing doubts about the merits of Iceland's astonishing economic growth, while two others babbled overtime to convince him of the misguidedness of his views: Iceland was, quite simply, an economic miracle, a "bumble bee economy – no one knows exactly how it manages to fly, technically it should be unable to, but nevertheless it does". All the leading economists agreed, was the argument, especially those who worked in the research departments at the three largest banks – they were experts in their fields and they had the data to back up their assertions. The banks had experienced astronomical growth, it was true, but that was all down to the Icelanders' intrepid behavior in all things business, their quick responses, absence of bureaucracy and willingness to take risks. The Viking spirit. The "outvasion" as it was called in Iceland – being done in reverse now, the opposite of "invasion". And anyway, they claimed, the nay-sayers were just jealous, especially the Danes, who could not stand to see their former colony come in and buy up their own treasured assets, like the Hotel Anglaterre and Magasin du Nord, the famous department store that had graced the Kongens Nytorv square in Copenhagen for over a century. Or the British, who were losing most of their treasured high street shops to foreign interests – and Icelandic interests, at that.

No one listening could be in any doubt that Iceland was on its way to conquering the world. The first man protested weakly – these takeovers were mostly leveraged, he said, done on borrowed capital, and eventually the time would come when the "outvasion Vikings" would have to pay. He was quickly silenced by the host, who announced it was time for some music. A moment later, a jaunty tune emanated from the speakers.

Frida climbed down from the ladder and surveyed her work. She'd have to put on one more coat before she left. Hopefully she'd have enough paint – the nearest paint store was bound to be in Ísafjörður, which was at least a two-hour drive away, if not more.

Perching on the old tree stump that her grandfather had used to cut firewood, she looked up at the mountain slope that rose above the house. She closed her eyes and inhaled. There was so much peace here. She wished she could stay like this forever. Yet deep inside there was a disquiet, and she knew that sooner or later she would have to leave, to go back to her life. At the thought, she felt a powerful resistance deep in her belly. The thought of going back to her life with Damien was somehow inconceivable; she could not picture it.

She had changed. She was unsure of just when and how, but the change had come. Perhaps it was when she had made the move back to Iceland. It had been a hard thing to do, to come back and face down the ghosts of the past – the feelings of unworthiness, shame and alienation, born of her mother's alcoholism. Those feelings had driven her to leave in the first place and had kept her from returning to this beautiful country that, now that she was back, had reclaimed so much of her heart.

And yet, the thought of abandoning her life with Damien was equally hard. After all, he had come here for her. She had begun to grow wistful, longing to return and yet being afraid to. She had shared some of her thoughts with Damien, and one day he had come home and announced that Iceland would be his next posting, and not only that: it would be his first ambassadorial post. She'd had no idea that he had even put Iceland down as a request – he had done it without her knowledge, wanting to surprise her, he said. At first she was equal parts shocked and anxious, and even angry with him for forcing this upon her ... but as she began to grow more familiar with the idea, she started to warm to it. And then, before she knew it, there they were, moving into the residence on Laufásvegur – that on top of everything was not far from the shadow district. She still encountered her former self occasionally, especially on certain streets or in certain situations, but on the whole she felt strong.

~~

Frida and Damien came to Berlin in 2001 minus two things – Mrs. Kelly and Damien's baroque furniture. Both had been left behind in London. Frida would have preferred to have both discarded permanently but she wasn't about to argue. She was happy to be starting afresh, in a new country, with just the two of them. Life was a blank canvas now, infused with promise, theirs to fill.

Their new German flat was beautiful – Frida fell in love with it the minute she stepped inside. It was situated on the first floor of an elegant house in the Prenzlauer Berg district, which had largely escaped destruction during the war and thus had an abundance of beautiful old buildings that were slowly being gentrified. The flat itself was serene and airy with spacious rooms, high ceilings and tall windows that looked out onto a small park with a playground in the middle. The floors were of natural polished wood and in the living room there were two Roman columns. The bathroom had a corner tub with a Jacuzzi. There were three bedrooms and a large kitchen with sliding doors, outside of which was a patio. From there a set of steps led down to a small garden.

"Ven does your container arrive?" asked the woman from the rental agency, making that strange German guttural sound with her throat: *'agrrraiv'*.

"In a few days' time, I expect," Damien replied jovially, "although we're not bringing much furniture over. My wife disliked the furniture we had and insisted we leave it behind."

The woman glanced at Frida, who looked sharply at Damien. What a bizarre comment to make to a stranger. He, on the other hand, appeared unaware of what he just said or how inappropriate it was.

Which is strange for a man who is always conscious of what he says or does.

"I've given her permission to 'go wild'," he continued, "just so long as she keeps away from my study."

The woman laughed affectedly.

Frida's stomach clenched and she turned away. Oh, so she'd been given permission to go wild? Great, then that's what she'd do.

~

"Mein Name ist Stefan. Wie ist Ihre Name?"

"Mein Name ist Frida. Wie ist Ihre Name?

"Mein Name ist Stefan. Ihre Name ist Frida. Wie ist Ihre Name?"

"Mein Name ist Frida."

~

Learning German came easier than she'd expected. It bore a distinct similarity to Icelandic and by the end of three months she could utter basic sentences in shops and manage reasonably well when it came to comprehension. Her German was far better than Damien's, something that, oddly enough, he liked to boast about at cocktail parties.

"My wife's command of German is much better than mine. I've only managed to learn how to ask for a loaf of bread in the bakery, whereas she can order five different types of rolls."

This particular cocktail party was being thrown by the head of the British Council for the head of the Goethe Institute in London, who happened to be in town.

The head of the Goethe Institute in London nudged Frida. "You know Gerhard Schröder, he does not speak good English. So he goes to London and asks his advisor, *Wie sagt man 'Apfelkuchen' auf Englisch?* The advisor says to him, *Applecake.* So Gerhard goes to the bakery and says *Applecake*, and gets applecake. He's very pleased! So the next day he does the same thing and again he gets applecake. The third day he's in the mood for bread so he says to his advisor, *Wie sagt man Brot auf Englisch?* The advisor says, *Bread.* So Gerhard Schröder goes to the bakery and says *Bread.* And the lady says, *White bread or brown bread?* and Gerhard Schröder hesitates and then says, *Applecake*."

He roared with laughter, his double chin shaking with the effort, and held up his glass to be filled by a passing caterer. Frida smiled, and looked around for an exit.

Excusing herself, she went out into the corridor, intending to search for a toilet – the old cocktail party escape. There it was – and someone was going in ahead of her. She took her place outside the door, leaned against a railing, and gazed through a window straight ahead. In the next house someone was watching television. The news was on. A bluish hue flickered on the windowpane.

"Is this the queue?"

She turned. A friendly face matching a pleasant voice. A tall and burly man with a beard and wavy hair, wearing a tweed jacket over jeans.

"I'm afraid so."

He leaned next to her against the banister. "Oh, I've seen worse. Been here long?"

Frida grinned. "No. Not too long."

He stuck out his hand. "I'm Simon French – I teach in the

English department at Humboldt."

"Frida Lowe. My husband is with the embassy."

"Ah. You must be new. Haven't seen you at any of these before."

"We are."

Silence. They stared in opposite directions. Beyond the door, the toilet flushed.

"So …"

"How long …"

They both grinned. He gestured for her to speak.

"How long have you been in Berlin?"

"Oh – far too long! Isn't that the standard answer? – Let's see – six, seven … nine years."

"You must like it here."

He shrugged. "It's all right. Could be worse." Pause. "Where's your accent from?"

"It's Icelandic."

"You're from Iceland! What's that expression they have up there … 'All the dead lice now fall from my head!'"

She laughed. "How do you know that expression?"

"I had a girlfriend from Iceland once. Hrefna. Do you know her?"

"Hrefna! Yes, of course I know Hrefna."

He laughed. "I suppose it isn't *that* small…"

"No. It's not *that* small."

The door opened and a thin, stern-looking woman in a suit came out. She smoothed her skirt and nodded at them before hurrying past.

"There you go – vacant," said Simon.

Frida shook her head. "It was only an excuse to leave the party for a moment."

"Ah! Crafty!"

"So you go ahead if you …"

"No, no. I'm out here for pretty much the same reason as you."

There was an awkward pause.

"Your accent isn't very obvious, though. You must have spent some time in the UK, or somewhere else."

"I went to the UK to go to school…" she thought for a

moment, "two years ago. Almost exactly. See, I have to count, too."

"Wow. And you graduated in two years?"

"I didn't finish. I ... stopped."

"What were you studying?"

"Acting."

"Oh, you're an actress? Fantastic! We're looking for people to join our theatre group. It's English-speaking.

"We ...?"

"I run an English-language theatre group out of the University. We do two plays a year. Are you interested?"

Frida was at a loss. This was unexpected. "Um ...."

"Come on. We actually have a Nordic theme this year. Yes, seriously. We're putting on Miss Julie. You can audition for the lead if you want. It would be great to have someone with a slightly Nordic accent."

Frida laughed. She felt giddy. All of a sudden the idea of staying in this city for the next four years had become a whole lot more appealing.

He touched her arm casually. "Will you think about it? You could come by and do a reading."

"I'll think about it."

"Here's my card." He pulled one from a worn, brown wallet.

"Thanks."

"Call me soon."

~~

Sitting in the back of a taxi after the party, Frida rested her head on Damien's shoulder.

"God, I'm knackered," he said. "Third cocktail this week. The things you do for Queen and country."

"Do you plan to work tonight?"

"I'll have to do a little."

Damien worked almost every night. Frida had begun to wonder whether he was a workaholic. It wasn't normal the way he went into his study every evening after dinner and locked the door. He hated being disturbed, he said – he always managed to concentrate so well at that time of day. It was his optimal time as far as his biorhythm was concerned. What he really should do was sleep all morning and report to work at noon: "They'd get the best out of me that way. But unfortunately normal work hours do not seem to revolve around my biorhythms."

Frida moved closer to her husband, until they were touching. She shifted and placed her hand on his thigh, nuzzling into the crook of his neck, kissing it. His body was tense and he did not move.

"Can't it wait until tomorrow?" she whispered.

He gave a slight nudge with his arm, a signal for her to move away. "We're not alone," he whispered under his breath.

She looked up and saw the taxi driver glancing at them in the rearview mirror, then look furtively away. She straightened up, and smoothed her hair. She felt stupid, and slightly ashamed, even though she knew she had no cause to be. What did it matter if some taxi driver they'd probably never see again saw them kissing? No – the real concern was what was happening to their marriage. Lately, it was as though Damien did not desire her any more. She didn't know if it was her, or him, or if there was something else. And worse, she knew there was no way to get him to talk about it.

~~

"OK. Can you give me the monologue one more time?"

"Sure." Frida cleared her throat and stood in the middle of the stage.

> We must go away, but we must talk first. That is, I must speak, for until now you have done all the talking. You have told me about your life – now I will tell you about mine, then we will know each other through and through before we start on our journey together. …

She went on, continuing through to the end. When she had finished, she stood perfectly still. She felt centered, like there was a strong energy running through her, from the floor and up through the top of her head, flowing upwards. She felt stronger than she had in a very, very long time, yet at the same time utterly vulnerable. Strange, she thought, how those two feelings could be present, both at the same time, and complement each other so perfectly. Surely this was what actors were supposed to feel when performing – but she had not felt this way before, and certainly not at acting school, when she had only felt weak and afraid.

Simon was watching her intently from a chair. “That’s good, Frida. And your teeny Icelandic accent complements the role perfectly.” He rose from his chair. “I’ve got a couple of others that I need to listen to, but …” he grinned and took hold of her shoulders. “I’ll let you know. OK?”

She nodded.

“You’d be up for it?”

“Definitely. Mind you, I haven’t discussed it with Damien.”

“Would he object?”

“No. I mean – I don’t know.”

~~

“I’m going out this evening,” said Frida, deliberately casual, avoiding Damien’s gaze. They were sitting in the dining room eating dinner – she’d made shepherd’s pie, Damien’s favorite.

“Oh? Where to?”

“There’s a script reading at Humboldt. You know Simon French? He’s invited me. He’s considering me for the lead in Miss Julie.”

She sensed as much as she saw Damien’s astonishment. He put down his knife and fork.

“When did you meet Simon French?”

“At the British Council cocktail party.”

“Oh?” His intonation was laden with meaning.

Frida felt herself tense up. “What’s the matter?”

“You didn’t mention it.”

“I must have forgotten.”

“Ah.”

Silence. Frida’s mind began to quiver, then vibrate with anxiety.

“What play?” he asked, deliberately casual, returning to his food.

"Miss Julie. Like I just said." She wished she didn't have to sound so defensive. But Damien's disapproval terrified her – that was the miserable truth.

He opened his palms and looked at her quizzically as if to say, *And...?*

"Strindberg?"

He shook his head.

"Miss Julie is a famous play by August Strindberg, who was a Swedish playwright. He's considering me for the lead. Miss Julie." As an afterthought, she added: "They're focusing on Nordic plays this semester."

"Oh, are they."

"Yes."

"Did you tell him you got dropped from the acting program at the Actors Studio?" Damien said nonchalantly.

Frida stared at her husband. His eyes met hers. They were cold. Something inside her froze. Her mind struggled to comprehend Damien's meaning. Was he being deliberately cruel? Or was it she who misunderstood? She frowned, her mind suddenly filled with confusion.

"I'm just worried that it would interfere with your duties here," he said, his voice thick as molasses.

"What duties?"

"I'm just wondering if rehearsals and things … you know, presumably a lot of them would be in the evenings. I need you to accompany me to events, and to help with the entertaining." His voice was gentle, yet his eyes were hard.

"We haven't done any entertaining."

"Because you haven't got the place decorated yet." He smiled sweetly, then picked up his plate and took it into the kitchen. A moment later she heard him go down the hall, and the door to his study open and close. She strained her ears to listen: yes, there it was, the sound of the lock turning quietly.

Frida sat still for a few moments, staring down at the table, trembling. *You haven't got the place decorated yet.* He was right. Guilt slowly coiled around her, sapping all of her energy. She'd persuaded him to leave all his stuff behind and he'd given her free rein to start decorating, but she hadn't done a damn thing. The place was bare. They had a dining room table and an old

IKEA sofa that one of Damien's colleagues had been planning to throw away but had given to them instead, to tide them over until they got some proper furniture. Paintings, borrowed from the British government, were not yet hung on walls – they were leaned up against them, patiently awaiting the time when someone would hang them properly. She glanced at the window – it was bare, no curtains or blinds, nothing. It hadn't bothered her, seeing as how there was just a park across the street and no one to look in at them. But it made the room seem bare and uninviting – she saw that now.

She'd made a commitment to Damien to stand by him, to be his wife, to support him in his work. She'd taken it on as her own job. She'd promised.

She'd made him leave all his furniture behind. And Mrs. Kelly.

Mrs. Kelly would have had the place up and running by now.

She stood up swiftly and gathered the plates, quietly so as not to disturb Damien, then carried them into the kitchen. There she looked around, shame engulfing her once more. A large hole gaped at her where the not-yet-bought dishwasher should be. There were boxes on the floor, containing their good glasses and tableware and various other things that she knew were important to Damien. They should be in a cabinet, she knew, or at least periodically in use. Indeed, they should have entertained by now – they'd been here four months already. Instead they were living in the midst of a mess.

Damien was right. She needed to make this her priority now. She owed him that much. He had never said anything about it, but of course he would have been annoyed. Angry, even. She'd been so caught up in her own stuff that she'd barely given a thought to what he thought and felt. How could she have been so selfish? Was that why he spent all that time in his study? No doubt! He didn't know how to deal with her lifestyle, her laid-backness. What he must think of her! She'd been behaving like a schoolgirl – a lazy teenager. A child who occasionally got dressed up in woman's clothes and went out with him to some function or another.

It was no wonder those nightmares had returned, the ones in which she was in a play but couldn't remember her lines. The ones where she stood on a stage in front of a full house of people, mute, and realized with soul-crushing panic that she had not memorized any of the dialogue. Now she understood. It was a message. She was being made aware that she had completely misread the script. She was playing the adolescent in a play that required her to be a woman.

That's why he was avoiding her, putting in all those hours in his study.

He uses work as an escape.

Because he couldn't deal with her.

Her insides churned with a rancid cocktail of pity, shame and self-disgust.

She would change. Now. As of today.

~~

It took Frida a mere six months to reinvent herself. She went from being a vaguely bohemian girl with long hair who favored jeans and sneakers, to an elegant woman who left perfume in her wake and rarely left the house without putting on high heels. Her makeup was always carefully applied and appropriate to the occasion, her hair was smooth. She made sure Damien hardly ever saw her unkempt or disheveled. In bed, she surprised him with new lingerie, which she had chosen especially with him in mind. He seemed to like it, and even started surprising her with impromptu gifts of the same. For a time their earlier passion was rekindled, though she noted that it was only if she was wearing the sexy underwear she'd bought. Impromptu sex without props seemed to be a thing of the past. He simply seemed disinterested in sex. She chalked it up to his age ... after all, Damien was forty-three now and she'd heard that men's libido started to wane markedly after the age of forty.

She attended Wives' Club meetings with other diplomatic spouses, went on their little outings to museums and charity events, did lunch, joined the literary club, entertained. She became adept at giving orders to caterers and other help – the former for dinner parties, the latter for helping around the house on a twice-weekly basis, or more, if needed.

Their home became unrecognizable from what it had been before. Frida enlisted the services of an interior decorator who drew up plans and color schemes and with whom she went out and selected fabrics and textures. The first time the interior decorator – Ines – had come, Frida had been deadly nervous, feeling like a country hick masquerading as an urbane sophisticate who would soon out herself as the bumbling clod that she was. But on sitting down with Ines she surprised herself, discovering that she actually had a pretty clear idea of what she liked and what she didn't, and what sort of look she ultimately wanted for their home. She had wanted a smooth, sensual, sandy kind of feeling, something to remind them of a beach at dusk: soft lighting, minimalistic furniture, lots of light-colored oak, throw rugs, and the occasional avant-garde art piece. The whole undertaking had cost a fortune, and at first she had dreaded Damien's wrath, but he did not seem to mind. On the contrary. He seemed to love everything she did with the place.

Frida was pleased. This new role was less foreign to her than she had anticipated. In her mind's eye she saw her grandmother, who had always been elegant and gracious without a trace of affectation or haughtiness.

The image of her grandmother appeared in Frida's mind as she stood in front of the mirror in her and Damien's bedroom, putting on her earrings. The light was subdued, and she could almost feel her there in the room with her, watching her with approval. This was not unusual. She often felt her grandmother's presence of late, and it gave her comfort and strength. She had never been particularly interested in the paranormal, but sometimes that feeling of having her grandmother with her was so powerful that Frida was convinced she was actually there.

Her serene reverie was broken by Damien coming into the room. In contrast to her, he seemed frazzled. He was wearing a white shirt and putting on his tie as he walked. They were expecting his boss, the British Ambassador and a German CEO of a large corporation with British interests, plus their spouses. "Have you seen my jacket?" he asked tensely, opening the closet and rummaging through it.

"Over there, on the chair."

He put on the jacket and stood just behind her at the mirror, straightening his tie. They made a stunning couple. He with his smooth, taut skin and handsome features; she with her fine bone structure, long hair and flowing movements. Looking at her dashing husband, she recalled what she had overheard one of the wives say during a cultural outing the other day: "We're going to see a lot more of Damien Lowe."

"You look very handsome," she said, turning around and standing very close to him. She was wearing a low-cut dress with delicate gold lace. In the soft light, her skin glowed like honey.

He glanced at her briefly, then looked back into the mirror. "Damn! I can't get this button fastened. The buttonholes are too small. It's a new ..."

"Here, let me try."

She stepped closer, he relaxed and let his arms fall to his sides. She felt his warmth. "There." Button fastened, she stepped closer to him, feeling her body touch his, lightly, their two scents mingling.

But he was distracted, his energy somewhere else. He gave her a light kiss on the cheek and then put his hands on her waist, gently moving her to one side.

"Why don't you ever kiss me on the mouth any more?"

She hadn't meant to say it. The words just escaped her lips.

He gaped at her. "What?"

She dropped her gaze. "Nothing."

"Because I don't want to mess up your lipstick," he said defensively, after a moment.

She walked past him and sat down on the side of the bed, pulling on a pair of sling-backs.

The doorbell rang.

"They're here," said Damien, glancing once more in the mirror, then quickly putting on his jacket and leaving the room.

She sat on the bed for a moment. Outside the window, a falling leaf drifted through the air on its way to the ground. Frida stood up. At the door, just before she headed out, she shut her eyes briefly. Then she breathed deeply, lifted her chin, and went out to greet her guests.

~~

Frida stood on the edge of a pond in the Tiergarten park, throwing bread to the ducks. Only a handful of the feathered critters was interested – the majority sat on the banks of the pond dozing or smoothing their feathers, having clearly eaten their fill. Good thing at least some of them were hungry, Frida thought – coming down here with bread was the sole focus of her day. Some days she simply had to invent a purpose, something that would provide the momentum for her to get out of bed. Now, just past noon, there were few people wandering around, mostly mothers with strollers, but also a few office types on a late lunch break.

She shook out the last of the breadcrumbs, then sat down on a bench. It was a beautiful September day, and the sun warmed her skin. Last night there had been a thunderstorm, which had cleared the air. Today, it was like the world had awakened anew, fresh and ready to take on … itself.

On the other side of the pond there was a mother with a toddler. The small cluster of ducks that had been on the receiving end of Frida's generosity had now moved over there. The toddler, a boy, was throwing bread their way: he'd take a morsel, run forward three steps, hurl it clumsily into the water, watch enraptured as a duck gobbled it up, then turn to his mother and laugh, clapping his little hands. His mother stood nearby, on the alert, ready to spring forward if he got too close to the edge, laughing and clapping with him. Frida could hear her cooing, hear their laughter and delight.

The mother glanced up and saw Frida looking at them. Frida looked away quickly, embarrassed. She shouldn't stare like that. The mother would think she was strange.

Why?

She wasn't strange. She wanted a child, that was all.

The realization hit her like a bolt of lightning. She was stunned, not by the realization itself but by the fact that she had not recognized it before. The signs had all been there. She would stand wistfully at the window, looking out at the children playing in the playground. She saw children everywhere – not difficult in Prenzlauer Berg, which had the highest birth rate of all the neighborhoods in Berlin, or so the estate agent had told them. Whenever she looked out over the front garden, at the back of her mind there was always the thought that it would be perfect for a child. She stopped at windows that displayed baby clothes, thinking of how cute they were and what she would choose, *if*. And just the other day when she had been out buying towels, she had been thinking of how perfect they would be for wrapping a child in after a bath.

She realized in a flash that she was, quite simply, obsessed, and also that she hadn't wanted to acknowledge it.

She got up slowly and started walking back home. All of a sudden she was overwhelmed with sadness. She and Damien hadn't made love in weeks, and it was screamingly obvious that he did not desire her any more. She felt lonely and unfulfilled in so many ways. Yes, she wanted him sexually, but she also wanted to make love and conceive a child. She longed to enter another dimension with a lover, in which they met in a sacred place beyond space and time, and made something new. Made a new life.

Maybe if they had a child, they could recapture some of the magic in their relationship. Maybe if they met in that space together, everything would change. If they had something to care for, a little person that they both loved equally well.

She would have to speak to Damien about it. And yet, strangely, the thought terrified her. The topic of children had never really come up, and – in another flash of insight – she knew why. It was because they avoided it. It was a pink elephant in the midst of their chic living room, a subject that could and should not be broached, for whatever reason. The reason lay with him. Damien. And somehow she picked up on it subconsciously and made a firm decision, also subconsciously, to avoid it. And now, the thought of breaking that barrier that had been created between them at that subconscious level terrified her so much that it set her heart palpitating and made her knees weak.

What enormous control he has over me!

Coming out of the park, the streets seemed strangely empty. Fewer people were about than usual. There was a kind of hush that Frida found unsettling. She went down into the subway; things down there seemed normal. All the same, she had a strange feeling, like something was not quite right.

Coming out of the subway on Ebenswalder Strasse, Frida's

phone beeped. She'd received a text message – no, a voice mail. Just as she was about to check it, the phone rang. It was Damien. His voice was level and measured, but Frida discerned a hint of panic beneath the controlled surface.

"Where are you?"

"I've just come out of the U-Bahn. Why?"

Just then, she heard screaming. Not a single cry from a single person, but more of a collective shout, coming from all directions. A stone's throw away a crowd thronged around the window of an electronics shop.

"Oh my God! Another plane just flew into the World Trade Centre."

"*What?*"

The phone cut out, the call was disconnected. Glancing down the street again, Frida debated whether to head towards the electronics shop and try to ask someone what was going on. She feared her German wouldn't be good enough, so instead she turned and walked quickly in the direction of home. About halfway, she started running.

Opening the door to their apartment, her hand was shaking. Inside, she threw off her jacket and went directly to the TV, impatiently flicking the channels until she found CNN. Every news station had more or less the same footage – a plane flying in slow motion into one of the World Trade Centre towers, crashing into glass and metal in a great explosion of fire and smoke … and then another, into the second tower.

The phone rang. It was Damien.

"The phone went dead …"

"Must be the provider. So many calls being made now."

"What happened?"

"A passenger jet flew into the World Trade Centre about half an hour ago. We thought it must have been an accident, until the second one hit just when I was talking to you. There's total chaos everywhere in New York and here, too. It's obvious that it's a terrorist attack."

"Oh my God."

"We're waiting for word from the Foreign Office – we don't know if there will be other attacks in other cities."

Frida had her eyes glued to the screen. People were hanging

out of the windows of the burning buildings, some of them waving clothing. Others were throwing themselves out, falling to the ground like debris. "Oh my God, Damien, they're jumping. They're jumping from the windows."

"Look. Stay where you are, all right? Don't go anywhere. Don't go outside."

"No."

"I need to get to a meeting. I'll call you later."

Frida put the phone down and perched, stunned, on the sofa in front of the television. She watched in abject horror as the events unfolded in front of her eyes, a third plane hitting the Pentagon, a fourth going down in a field. She cried out when the first tower collapsed, screamed when the second one went down. She held her head, could not believe what was happening. It was like their entire civilization, everything they had taken for granted and considered safe and secure, was crumbling with those two massive towers.

She was still sitting there when Damien got home, the apartment dusky, the only light the flickering images from the television. She'd curled up and put a blanket around herself, and was flicking the channels, trying to get more coverage, better coverage, to discover something else, some answer that eluded her as to why this was happening.

Damien came and sat down next to her. He put his arm around her shoulders, and she put both of hers around his waist. They sat like that for a long while.

"How were things at the office?" she finally said.

"Chaotic. Some of the local staff went home. Everyone's scared, thinking they might target other places. Like British missions. But we got word to sit tight."

"What's it all mean?"

"Terrorist group, they think. Islamic extremists, probably."

"What's it going to mean for the world?"

He shook his head. "I don't know. But nothing will be the same."

"All those poor people," she said. "All those passengers on those planes. Can you imagine? And those people who jumped ..." she shuddered.

He kissed the top of her head.

Later that night, when they were in bed, she clung to him, taking comfort in the feeling of his naked body next to hers, his warmth, his solid, tangible presence. She had been shaken to the core that day. The horror still resided deep within her. She wanted him to wipe it away, to make it better.

"Let's make a baby."

She felt his body stiffen. He was lying on his back; she lay in the crook of his arm. He was silent so long that she thought he must be asleep. Gently she raised her head to look at his face. His eyes were open, staring at the ceiling. His expression was strained.

"I can't believe you want to bring a baby into this crazy world," he finally said, not looking at her.

"We have to have hope," she said with urgency. "If we give up we are letting the evil win."

"Bringing a baby into this won't help a damn bit."

"Why not?"

He released her and sat up in bed. His expression was unlike any she had ever seen him wear before – like a strange, twisted combination of pain, rage and disgust.

"Excuse me, but haven't you been watching the news today? This world is filled with crazy, sick people, who will stop at nothing to get across their fanatical viewpoints. And it's not just that. There's climate change, and all the misery associated with that. Pretty soon they're going to be fighting wars over fresh water supplies. Food is starting to go up in price already, due to the shortage that will inevitably arise." He shook his head. "No. I don't want to bring a child into this."

"I want a baby."

She hated the sound of her voice, like a spoiled, petulant child.

"Well, I do not."

It was steel on steel. The tension inside her was unbearable now, and she had to get away from him. She got up and put on a robe, then left the room. In the living room, she curled up on the sofa, pulling a blanket over herself. She felt cold. Damien's bleak sense of futility had reached into her very core, and she felt hopeless. Hopeless and without a purpose.

Surely this was not what life was about. Surely there was

more than this.

She heard movement in the bedroom. Hugging her knees closer to her chest, she waited for the sound of Damien retiring to his study and locking the door. It didn't come.

She didn't know how long had passed before she saw his silhouette in the doorway. She might even have fallen asleep.

"Frida?"

"Hm?"

There was a starkness in his voice. "I would not be a good father."

"That's such a lame excuse."

"I don't want children. I've never wanted children."

"Why didn't you tell me that before we got married?" Her voice sounded faint.

"I did."

"No you didn't."

"I'm positive I did. You just don't remember."

Her mind was becoming filled with that strange anxiety, that sense of confusion, that she often felt with him. The kind that made her doubt her own judgment and conviction, and which ushered in an insidious crumbling of her self-esteem. She fought to retain a clear head.

"I would have remembered something that important…"

"What about you? You never told me you wanted children."

"I thought it was a given."

"You've never talked about it before."

He was right. She had not talked about it before. She'd been terrified to talk about it. Why, she didn't know. It was all due to that heavy taboo that she sensed all around it, whether that feeling was right or wrong.

"I don't know," she said.

"So why now? Because you're lonely, you need something to do?"

Again, this confusion, creeping up on her, sapping her energy. She had a sudden image in her mind of a huge spider digging its teeth into her, drawing the very lifeblood out of her.

"No," she said weakly, shaking her head. "No."

He had come closer and now stood over her in the dark. His voice was soothing, almost hypnotic. "Believe me, this is no life for a child. This gypsy life. It's not good for a child to have to pick up and relocate every three or four years, move to a new place, get used to a new culture, go to a new school where they may have to speak a completely new language, always starting over."

"Maybe it makes people stronger ..."

"I think stability makes people strong."

"There are boarding schools."

He laughed: one loud, clipped "HA!"

She waited.

"Boarding schools have their own darkness," he said.

"What do you mean?" She still lay under the blanket, turned away from him, hugging her knees. It occurred to her that she seemed to be cowering. She sat up straight.

"Boarding schools can be horrible places," he said, and there was something strangely disconnected in his voice, something alien, something that made her skin crawl. Here in the dark, she couldn't see his face, only the outline of his body with the light in the hallway behind it. "I wouldn't want to inflict that sort of torture upon anyone."

With those words, he turned and left. This time she heard him go down the hall to his study and lock the door.

Frida sat behind in the dark. Something had happened in his childhood. Something that he did not want to tell her about. He was deeply wounded, that much was clear. Thoughts swirled in her head. She felt drained. She hoped that they would one day be able to talk about it. If only he could tell someone, talk to someone, perhaps the ice in his heart would melt and he would be able to welcome a baby into their lives. As it was, he did not want his child to have to experience the same things that he had – and that, in itself, was an act of kindness. Yes, there was something deep inside his heart that he was unable to release, but she felt sure it would happen with time. In the meantime, she needed to stand by him, to demonstrate that she would be there for him, no matter what. That's probably what he needed, if he was to heal the wounds of his past. He needed to feel safe.

She would be there for him.

CHAPTER SIX

Látrabjarg and Raudasandur. The last tour of the season.

That was the thought that Frida woke up to on Saturday morning.

She had never been to Látrabjarg, and she should probably grab the chance while she was here. Everyone said it was an amazing place. She didn't know how good the road was – likely not good enough for her car to make it. So going with a planned tour in a properly outfitted bus was probably the thing to do, if she was going to do this.

She got out of bed, pulled the window curtain aside and looked out. It was sunny, with a bit of wind. White-capped waves raced towards the shore, and in the distance there was a bank of white, puffy clouds. It was a good day for it, seeing as how it was already September. There might not be another day like this before she left.

She got dressed quickly, then went downstairs and assembled a few things while her coffee was brewing. In one of the cupboards she found a small thermos – perfect. She also found a collection of Tupperware boxes. One of those would do nicely for a packed lunch.

She was running late, and people were already boarding the mini-bus when she drove into the parking lot in front of the pool. She parked and jumped out of the car. Turning, she saw who stood at the mini-van door, waiting for people to board. It was the man in the blue Cherokee, the one who kept crossing her path. What had he said his name was, again? Baldur, was it?

Yes, Baldur.

She felt nervous as she walked toward the bus. It was awkward, after all. These compromising situations in which they had each witnessed the other.

"Hi," she said, striving to appear casual, "Is this the tour to Látrabjarg?"

He turned and nodded. She thought she saw that same flicker of familiarity in his eyes as had been there the last time she saw him, in the makeshift shop, but she couldn't be sure. In any case he gave no particular sign that he recognized her. "Yep," he said, "hop on – there are still a couple of free seats."

"Do I need a ticket?"

"You can buy one from me. Once we're on our way."

"I only have a card ..."

"That's OK. We take cards."

He flashed her a smile. There was something so likeable about him. She felt instantly that he was a good person. It seemed to her suddenly that it was rare to find someone like that, someone genuine, who seemed to have no hidden agenda, no need to twist circumstances to suit their own needs.

Then she recalled the conversation she'd overheard in the shop the other day.

Everyone has an agenda I guess.

The mini-bus was almost full. She took a seat at the very back, next to an elderly couple who were speaking quietly in German. Baldur got in the front, next to the driver, and as they set off he said a brief welcome through a small intercom. A moment later they were on their way.

Frida gazed out of the window at the passing landscape and was suddenly gripped by nationalistic fervor. She loved this country with all her heart. Its spectacular beauty, the down-to-earth people, the traditions, the stories and legends, the raw landscapes, the magnetism. Now that she was back ... she never wanted to leave again. Never.

The implications of this for her marriage flashed into her mind, stark and insistent. But before she could consider them, the man in the seat next to her addressed her.

"Do you go here the first time?"

He was a kindly gentleman and spoke English with a thick accent.

"Ja," she replied, switching to German, "my first time."

"Ah! Sie sprechen Deutsch."

"Ja."

"Are you with the diplomatic corps?"

The question caught her off guard. Then she realized. *Those damn plates.*

"No – I'm not." For a fleeting moment she thought about volunteering more information but thought better of it. "No."

"You are Icelandic?"

"Yes."

He was looking at her inquisitively. "Your German is very good."

"Thank you." Change the subject. "Is this your first time here?"

Just as the man was about to answer, Baldur's voice came over the call system, speaking in English. "Hello everyone. As you know, we are headed to Látrabjarg, the westernmost point of Iceland, and therefore also the westernmost part of Europe. Látrabjarg literally means 'the cliff at Látrar' – Látrar being the name of the area. Látrabjarg is actually three cliffs, but they are generally referred to by that one name, in the singular. At its highest point it rises four hundred and forty-one meters above sea level – almost half a kilometer."

He continued speaking, offering various bits of trivia about the cliff and its bird life and entreating people not to get too close to the edge. "The wind is not all that strong where we are now, but on top of the cliff it is *always* strong, and one misstep can have serious consequences. Also, please keep in mind that puffins nest along the top, digging holes into the ground along the cliff's edge. By which I mean to say, the ground is hollow next to the edge, though it may look solid. In other words: *keep your distance*."

As they drew closer to their destination, the bus left the main highway and took a gravel road leading towards the sea. It rocked from side to side as it traversed the more difficult spots, and the German couple hung on to the handles attached to the seats in front of them, clearly alarmed. Occasionally the man glanced at Frida and gave her a polite nod and a smile, but he did not make further attempts at conversation. She was relieved.

They were there in less than an hour – sooner than she had expected. The group climbed out of the van. Ahead of them the open sea stretched out infinitely to the perfect horizon, deep blue, with lacy whitecaps dancing on the waves. Oh, and the wind! It literally took Frida's breath away as she got out of the bus, blowing her hair in all directions. She struggled to get it under control with an elastic she'd had the good sense to wrap around her wrist, turning her back on the rest of the group to better be able to manage. When she turned around, she saw that Baldur had hung back and was waiting for her.

"Hi," he said, as though he was only now able to place her.

"You didn't recognize me back there, did you?" she said, smiling as the wind tore at her clothes.

"Oh, I recognized you."

"You did not."

He cocked an eyebrow.

"Well I guess you could say we're even now," he said.

"You mean about the embarrassing situations we've both unwittingly witnessed?"

"Yes."

"Your secrets are safe with me."

He grinned.

"This your first time here?" he asked as they came closer to the ledge.

"Yep. Not yours, I take it."

He shook his head. His hair was blowing around as much as hers was, and he now lifted his hood to cover it.

Just then they both saw the elderly German man stepping precariously close to the edge. He was wielding his camera, trying to get a shot of the puffins perched on a ledge just below the top edge.

"Oh, jeez." Baldur rushed off.

It sure was cold. Frida rummaged in her pockets for her gloves, thanking God that the sun was out – at least it helped to offset the chill slightly. Off to her left was an Icelandic family – a couple with two boys – who had laid down on their stomachs and were inching close to the edge in order to take photographs. Frida did the same, laying down flat and crawling slowly towards the edge, holding her camera in one hand. It was a Canon EOS digital device – a Christmas gift from Damien the year before last.

When she got to the edge, she looked down with trepidation and felt a fluttering in her stomach. It was sheer, all right. There was no surviving a fall down there. Then, suddenly, directly beneath her, a whimsical little head appeared – a puffin, with his colorful beak and adorable little face. "Oh, hello," Frida said under her breath, maneuvering her camera to be able to get the shot. "Hello there cutie …" *click.* And again, *click.*

She lay there, completely absorbed and delighted by the experience of being so close to the bird. Suddenly it jumped off the ledge and hung suspended in mid-air, floating on an air current, its legs comically splayed behind it. It looked so funny that she laughed out loud. Just then, she felt someone next to her. It was Baldur, grinning from ear to ear.

"Look at this little guy! I just love how they float in the air like that," Frida enthused.

"I know. It's great."

"They're so funny-looking."

"I know. They always remind me of professors."

"Totally!"

Across from where they lay, the cliff jutted out so the sheer face was visible to them. It was like a tenement building, with hundreds of screeching birds – gulls of some kind – perched on every available ledge.

"What are those birds over there?" Frida called out. The wind made it very difficult to hear.

"They're fulmars. And some kittiwakes."

Frida reached inside her waist bag for her zoom lens – she desperately wanted a picture of them. She got it out and unscrewed the lens on her camera. Baldur reached out his hand to hold it for her while she attached the zoom lens. That done, she began snapping photos, zooming in on the different birds – some perched solo on their ledges, others with their mates, still others with their young.

"Do you ever get tired of this?" she called out to him.

He inched closer to her, to better be able to speak to her above the roar of the wind. "Never. It never gets old."

"Do you come here every week?"

"No. But I come here often."

"How does tourism fit in with the aquaculture project?"

"Anything to help the region. We don't want any more people to leave. But it's not just that, it's also fun."

She nodded, and snapped a couple more pictures.

"How long are you staying here?" he asked.

"What? Here?"

"No, I mean how long will you stay in town."

She put her camera down. "Not exactly sure," she said. "I really like it there."

"It's a nice place."

"It is."

"Relaxing."

"Yes."

"I have some wonderful childhood memories from there."

"Oh?"

His gaze flickered from her and to a point behind her. He was clearly keeping an eye on the group for which he was responsible. Just then, something caught his eye, he nodded at someone behind her, and inched his way back from the edge. "Sorry – looks like I'm needed."

Frida took a few more shots, then looked around for her puffin friend, but it was gone. She inched her way back from the edge and stood up, brushing the grass from her clothes. The group was scattered; a few people had strolled further along the cliff, up a small slope. Frida wandered, read a sign telling of an intrepid rescue of the crew of a British trawler, and snapped a few more photos until she saw the group gathering by the mini-bus.

Next stop was Raudasandur. On the way her German seatmate was a bit more talkative than he had been on the way to Látrabjarg. Clearly fired up by the proximity of certain death at the edge of the cliff, he began chattering excitedly about Iceland's many charms. He and his wife had been there four times already, he said: "… and this is our fifth. Our friends, they travel to Spain, Portugal, the Greek islands … they think we are crazy, always going to Iceland." His wife looked on, smiled and nodded. "But we love it here. Still, we have noticed a change here in the last few years. An unfortunate change." The expression on his face darkened. "People are so caught up in materialism. And the people are more stressed out, much more."

"Oh, Icelanders have always been suckers for material things," Frida said absently. Baldur was coming up the aisle holding a credit card reader, and she reached into her bag for her wallet.

"That may be so, but it has never been so bad as now," the German continued. "I am afraid for Iceland. I am retired now, but before I worked as a financial analyst. There is a storm brewing, and I worry that your bankers and all those businessmen – especially the ones who have been buying all those shops in England – have been a little bit reckless."

Frida was growing exasperated, and wished he would shut it. She was so tired of foreigners who thought they knew everything about Iceland, even better than the Icelanders themselves. The Germans were especially bad.

Baldur had stood above them while the German was talking. Frida noted that he did not interrupt by barging in, like most Icelanders did, but waited politely for the man to finish. He nodded to him, then smiled at Frida. "It's just you I need to collect from."

"Because I'm the typical Icelander who always shows up at the last minute," she said wryly, handing him her card.

"You said it, not me."

She saw him look at her card for a beat longer than needed. He was reading her name. The card had her married name on it, and for a reason she didn't quite understand, she cringed. Elsewhere she quite liked people knowing that she was part of the diplomatic corps, or that her husband was a man of a certain rank. Here, for some reason, she wished she could conceal it.

"Thanks," he said, handing back her card and a receipt. He looked at her again, and their eyes met. Something passed between them; a kinship, or connection. Frida quickly dropped her gaze.

The mini-bus bumped and rolled its way along a road considerably worse than the last one. Baldur was speaking over the intercom now, about the area. Not long ago, Raudisandur had been a thriving community, but today it was made up only of summer homes. The name Raudisandur meant 'red sand' and drew its name from the wide stretch of sand colored red by crushed scallop shells. Nearby were the ruins of a farm, he continued, at which one of the most famous murders in Icelandic history had been committed, when a man and his mistress, who lived on adjacent farms, murdered their respective spouses and were sentenced to death.

"This I love about Iceland," the German seatmate said to Frida, leaning close to her, "the many stories. Every place, almost every stone and hill, has a story."

And there, she had to agree. Iceland was not rich in monuments or architecture or historical works of art, but it was enormously rich in stories.

A moment later, they turned a bend on the treacherous mountain road that was now leading them downward, and a stunning vista opened up: the spectacular red sands, flat and wide and rippled, with bands of shimmering water snaking inland from a glittering turquoise sea. Directly below them was a grassy lowland with scattered houses, quaint and lovely, grouped together in a small community. Children played in between them; laundry hung on lines outside some of the homes, blowing in the wind. There was a collective gasp within the bus, and a moment later almost everyone was grappling for a camera.

At the bottom of the slope, the bus drove on a short distance, then stopped. Baldur announced that they would stop there for about thirty minutes, and the passengers filed out, Frida last. Baldur stood waiting for her. She felt a fluttering inside her belly, but quickly checked herself: of course he would wait for all the passengers to get off the bus. He was the guide, after all.

"What do you think?" he said, moving to stand by her side.

"It sure makes me proud of my country."

"I noticed you were speaking German."

"Yes."

"Are you fluent?"

"More or less. I lived there for four years."

"Where?"

"Berlin."

"Nice. Were you studying?"

"No." Frida hesitated. "My husband was posted there," she added, looking away from him, out over the sands.

Several members of the group had started walking out onto the beach. Without saying anything, both Baldur and Frida headed after them.

"I never get tired of this place either," Baldur said, "no matter how often I come here."

"I can see why."

"If you ever have a chance, there's an amazing hiking route that leads up past Sjöundá, the farm where the murders were committed, and out to Skor, which was a fishing station and one of the most remote farms in Iceland. Mind you, don't try it if you're afraid of heights. You have to take a very narrow path where there's almost a straight drop down. That's part of the kick, though." He glanced at her. "Do you do any hiking?"

They were walking slowly, and the gap between them and the others widened. Frida felt a warmth inside of her. Something about the way he spoke to her, like he was giving her his full attention, and the interest he took in her, made something in her respond. "I haven't done much," she answered. "I would love to do more. I'm just discovering this country all over again. I was away for quite a few years."

"Hiking is the best way to see Iceland. That, and horseback riding. The places you can go to, that you can't reach in any other way. There are so many hidden gems."

They walked on a distance without saying anything. Frida breathed deeply, taking in the salty air. It was invigorating.

"Have you always lived in Fagrifjördur?" she asked.

"No," he said, "I moved there when I was eight, and left at sixteen to go to menntaskóli in Reykjavík."

"Because there's no menntaskóli here," she observed. Menntaskóli was the type of upper secondary school that Icelandic adolescents attended from age sixteen to twenty. They were scarce in rural areas, so most youngsters had to attend somewhere else.

"There's one in Ísafjördur," he answered, "but I wanted to go to Reykjavík. The big city," he added with an ironic chuckle.

"And why did you come back?"

He glanced away, into the distance. "My wife's family lives here. And I wanted to help with the development of the area."

Wife. Frida glanced down at his hand. He wore no ring.

So his wife must be the pale woman she had seen with him. The mention of her unnerved Frida. She raised her camera to hide her disconcertment, angry with herself for being so silly. Baldur waited.

"You mentioned that you spent some time in the village as a child," he said when she was finished. "Did we ever meet back then?"

She looked at him. The tousled waves of his hair were tinged gold from the sun, and there were light freckles on his skin. His eyes were a deep blue. It seemed to her such a natural question: had they ever met before, because it felt to her that they must have. She felt like she knew him. Perhaps they had played together as children, somewhere in the village or maybe down on the seashore – though she had no specific recollection of it.

"I was there almost every summer until I was ten. How old are you?"

"I was born in 1980. I'm twenty-eight."

So he was that much younger than she was. Six years.

She smiled, squinting against the sun. "In that case, no. During my last summer there, you would have been four. And you wouldn't have lived there yet."

"Why did you stop coming to the village?" he asked.

"My grandparents owned the house, and my grandfather died. After that, the house was sold."

"Wait a minute. It's that white house with the red roof, right? The one just outside of the village?"

"Yes."

"Egill. The man who owns the house now. I thought *his* grandparents had owned it."

"Egill is my cousin."

"Ah!"

"He bought the house back a few years ago from the people it had been sold to."

"He must have had good memories from there too, then."

"I think he did. Just like me. The best memories are from there."

He smiled at her, and something lovely passed between them. Frida blinked twice, rapidly, and looked away. There was an awkward pause.

"It's such a great day," Baldur said.

"It is," said Frida.

Again they grinned at each other, like they shared a secret, or at least the understanding that remarks about the weather were always good for getting back on neutral ground. Like a conversational reset button.

Suddenly Baldur stopped, and touched her arm. "Look," he said, pointing, "over there."

"Where?"

"A couple of seals. Right there."

Oh, yes. Two rotund gray seals with pitch-black eyes, basking on a piece of rocky coastline about a hundred meters away. She raised her camera to capture the moment. Slowly she moved closer. The seals did not seem bothered; they raised their heads and looked at her, eyeing her with interest.

"They're so curious. They always have to check everything out," Baldur said in a low voice at her side.

"They're adorable, aren't they? The Germans call them *Seehunde* – sea dogs."

The German couple had sidled up behind them and heard her German remark. The woman repeated the word, and laughed. The group was moving closer to the seals now. Suddenly both of them maneuvered their heavy bodies to the edge of the rock on which they lay and then slid smoothly into the water.

Heading back to the bus, Baldur was occupied with the German couple and a couple of Frenchmen, who wanted to know all about the history of the region. Frida hung behind, relishing the beauty of the place and the sun on her bare face, offsetting the coolness of the breeze. She felt serene.

But not for long. Just as she was about to step onto the bus, her phone rang in her pocket. She took it out and looked at the display. It was Damien. Instantly and without thinking she glanced up and at Baldur. He was looking at her. Involuntarily, almost like a spasm, her thumb pressed down on the reject call button.

It rang again, just as she had settled in her seat and they were setting off. This time she turned her phone off. Looking up, she saw that Baldur had turned around. He smiled at her. She smiled back. One of the French tourists sitting near the front caught his smile and turned around to see what he was smiling at. Frida looked down quickly, feeling her face flush red.

On the drive back, she felt strangely conflicted. On the one hand elation, so that she had to work not to have a permanent smile on her face, on the other hand an insistent feeling of dread. Almost like a part of her was dying, while another part was being reborn. Both at the same time. All of a sudden she had developed a hyper-awareness of Baldur sitting in the front, like he exerted some sort of magnetic pull over her consciousness and his smallest move registered on her radar and sent miniature shock waves through her. She tried to force her mind to focus on other things, but with limited success. She felt enormously self-conscious, and to protect herself she immersed herself in the photos she had taken on her camera. She wished she'd taken one of him – but that would have been inappropriate, and would have given her away completely.

Given what away?

By the time they arrived back in the village, Frida was desperate to get away, to be alone, to sort through her feelings. She climbed off the bus, glanced furtively at Baldur, gave him a quick wave when she saw him looking at her, then made her escape. Her car left skid marks in the gravel as she sped toward home.

~~

Back at the house, Frida found it hard to focus. Her mind was scattered; her equilibrium upset. Thoughts and feelings swirled insistently around inside her, all vying for her attention. She loaded photos into her laptop and started processing them, but found that she was too restless to sit still. Finally she gave up, put on a sweater, a windbreaker and some boots, and headed down to the sea.

Walking along the shore calmed her. She breathed in the fresh, cool air and let the sound of the waves wash over her, so gentle yet so powerful, capable of lulling you to sleep and also of tearing you apart, limb for limb. Gradually, her mind began to settle and she could think more clearly about what was making her feel so unsettled.

It was Baldur, and the effect he had on her. She did not like it, she reproached herself for it, and yet she had to face it. He had stirred something in her. Still, it was just as likely that her feelings were an illusion, a falsehood born out of yearning for something that wasn't available in her own marriage. It was a story as old as the hills: lonely housewife develops crush on younger man. And a married younger man, at that.

The real issue, of course, was what she should do about her own marriage. She couldn't cower here forever. The time to grow up and take responsibility for her own life had arrived, only she had run from it, high-tailed it to the relative shelter of the West Fjords where, boxed in by tall mountains and a shimmering sea, she could almost pretend that her real life was a mirage and this was real.

But was her life with Damien all that bad? They had grown apart, certainly, and he was probably … or, to give him the benefit of the doubt, *possibly*, having an affair. She had not found the right moment to ask Kristín about the earring, but she thought it unlikely that it belonged to her or any of the other girls who worked in the house. Very unlikely. And yet Damien had been adamant and, well, she'd had no cause to doubt his fidelity in the past.

And anyway, this wasn't just about Damien or his earring. It was about her feelings towards *him*.

She stopped and stood with her eyes closed in the middle of the black sand beach. She tried to listen. To her feelings. She drew a blank. As she stood there tears welled up in her eyes, not from sadness or grief but from the sheer frustration of not feeling anything in particular for the man who was her husband. Yes, she cared for him, she cared about his well-being and safety, but on the whole she felt alarmingly indifferent towards him. Even the point about the earring was more about the principle of the thing, rather than anger about his possible infidelity.

And, if she was brutally honest, she had to acknowledge the fact that … and here she almost faltered … she had to acknowledge that she loved her *life* with him more than she loved him. She loved having money and status, she loved her silver Audi A4, she loved travelling, and she even loved having servants – even if she felt hopelessly embarrassed when they opened car doors for her.

Perhaps they would be able to rekindle their passion. Maybe they could see a marriage counselor – although deep down she suspected that Damien would never agree to that. He was too concerned about his image. Or maybe she could just settle for the charade, as she knew many wives did; buy herself a little sanctuary, spend most of her time there, and re-appear every now and again in the play that was Damien's life. She had set out to be an actress and perhaps her plans were finally coming to fruition, though in a slightly different form than she had originally envisioned.

CHAPTER SEVEN

The first thought that came to Frida as she looked out of the window the following morning was that this looked like a good day to paint the fence. The weather was much the same as the day before, the sun out in all its cool, semi-autumnal glory, but judging by the white caps on the fjord it appeared to be less windy. For a second she marveled at the beauty of the sky, so clear and penetratingly blue. There was nothing quite like the light here in the north, with clarity and visibility that seemed to go on forever.

And so, just before noon she was out in the painters' garb that she had found stuffed in the far corner of the pantry – an old sweatshirt and oversized coveralls that hung sack-like from her shoulders. She had the radio on for company, blasting the volume almost as high as it would go. They were playing songs by an Icelandic singer-songwriter who had recently sold his entire song portfolio to one of the banks. However, that programming ended a moment after she had positioned herself, opened the paint tin and taken the first brush stroke. The news came on. Frida groaned inwardly – there seemed to be nothing on these days except endless dull reports about the financial markets, particularly in the States: some bank going bust, mortgage lending companies with silly people's names who were in trouble for reasons that she couldn't comprehend, the status of share prices, fluctuations in the exchange rate. There must be a serious drought in other, proper, news, she thought, if they had to incessantly wallow in this yawn-inducing stuff.

The sound of a car approaching jolted her out of her thoughts. Quickly she straightened up, shielding her eyes from the sun. She registered a flash of blue. Instantly her heart leapt into her throat. The Cherokee slowed, then pulled off the road and up in front of the house.

Baldur stepped out, a big grin on his face. “Hello!” he called. There was something so refreshing about his bright, infectious energy. Instantly her nervousness and anxiety fell away.

She put the paintbrush down and stepped forward to greet him.

“Hi,” she called. “How are you?”

“Good!” He was outside the gate, but didn’t open it. The grin was still there, affixed to his face, and suddenly she realized that he was nervous.

“You’re painting!” he said, stating the obvious.

“Yeah,” she said, slightly bashful, almost like he’d caught her in an uncompromising situation – not for the first time.

He held something up. “Miss these?”

It took her a moment to register. “Oh! My gloves. Actually, no, but I would have soon enough. Where did you find them?”

“In the bus, under the seat you were in. I remembered you wearing them.” He seemed slightly embarrassed to reveal this fact.

“Oh wow. Well it’s so nice of you to bring them here. Really.”

“No problem at all. It’s not far.”

There was an awkward moment: mission completed, now grapple for an excuse to stay.

“So,” he said, “painting?”

“Yeah.” Frida laughed and gestured, unnecessarily, with her hand. “I wanted to do something to help my cousin before I leave. Just to show him a small token of my appreciation.”

“Oh, you’re leaving?” His voice sounded unnaturally casual.

“Well, yeah. I have to leave eventually,” she said.

“Oh, so you’re not leaving, like, tomorrow or the next day.”

She shrugged. “Not tomorrow, anyway. I’ll probably put on another coat of paint before I go.”

He smiled at her. She couldn't help it: his smile was blinding. It obliterated everything else.

"Do you want some help?"

She stood there, at a loss, wondering what to do, what to feel, what was right and what was wrong, wanting so much to say yes, yet fearful of what it might mean – for her, her emotions, her life.

"… not that I want you to finish any faster," he added quickly.

There it was. It was out there now.

Or was she reading him all wrong?

"You don't have any clothes. For painting, I mean," she added quickly.

"I've got some old clothes in the car. And I'll be careful not to make a mess."

"It's amazing how much can get on you, though, even with the best intentions."

"That's a pretty cool outfit you have on." He grinned.

"Oh, this old thing?"

"I'm guessing you didn't bring it with you."

"What gave it away?"

He beamed a smile at her. There was such ease in their rapport. She felt that same warmth begin to spread, just like yesterday.

He went back to the car to get his clothes, returning a moment later.

"Is there someplace I can change?"

"Sure. Just go inside the house. Change anywhere in there."

A few minutes later, after Frida had fetched another paintbrush, they were positioned on either side of the fence, Baldur outside the yard, Frida inside it. He had changed into a worn pair of jeans and a faded black sweatshirt, both of which had grease stains on them, like he had worn them to fix his car.

"So this is how you spend your Sundays, huh?"

"Not usually." She grinned. "Is this the way you spend yours? Doing good deeds for your neighbors?"

"Absolutely."

The news had finished on the radio, and now music came back on – too loud, now that there was suddenly a prospect for conversation.

"I'll just go in and turn that down."

He was painting with strong, fluid movements when Frida came back, handling the brush like a pro.

"You look like you know what you're doing," Frida said, observing him.

"Sure. I'm an old hand at this. I worked as a house painter when I was in school, every summer."

"In Reykjavík."

"Yes."

"Which school did you go to?"

"You mean secondary school? MR. You?"

"MH."

"And then university?"

"I worked for a couple of years after I graduated. Then I moved to London to go to acting school."

"Acting school!" He stopped, straightened up and looked at her. "What was that like?"

"It sucked."

He laughed. "Why?"

Frida shook her head. "Never mind. It just wasn't a very good experience." She paused. "How about you? Any university?"

"Yep. Five years."

She found that she was surprised, and instantly reproached herself for her prejudice. Somehow she hadn't pictured him as being academically inclined.

"What did you study?"

"Economics. BSc and then a Masters."

It was her turn to straighten up and look at him. "Really."

"What?"

"Economics?"

"What's wrong with that?"

"You don't strike me as the type."

"What type?"

"The economics type."

"What are economics types like?"

"They wear suits."

He laughed. "Yeah, well. Been there done that."

"You wore suits?"

"Yeah."

There was a brief silence. She wanted to probe further, but she sensed a reticence in him, like some door had been shut, if only halfway. She decided to take a different track.

"So as an economist, maybe you can tell me why I can't get any decent news around here these days because the news hours are filled with senseless blather about the global financial markets."

His brow furrowed and it was like a cloud crossed his face. "Yeah. That's a bad situation. One I try not to think about too much, frankly. I cling to this illusion that by living up here, removed from the craziness of it all, I'll be able to avoid what's coming, but that's a fallacy. It's going to hit us all."

She stared at him. "What are you talking about?"

"The global financial situation. Isn't that what you're talking about?"

"Sure, but I was joking. I've been listening to this day after day on the news, wondering what the hell it matters to me here in Iceland that some bank in the USA teeters on the verge of bankruptcy."

"It matters because we're all interconnected. No country is an island any more."

"Not even Iceland?"

"Not even Iceland."

"So what do you know that I don't know?"

"Well I know that the Icelandic banks will most likely go bankrupt."

She stared at him, wide-eyed. Then she laughed.

"Come on." she said. "Banks don't go bankrupt."

He looked at her and smiled, with a mixture of something that unnerved her. She realized that he was serious.

"Unfortunately they do."

He said it so matter-of-factly that she instantly felt a twinge of fear. And yet, it was an outrageous proposition. Banks were solid. They were like vaults.

"You're saying the Icelandic banks are going to go bankrupt."

"I'm pretty sure at least two of them will."

"Which ones?"

"Glitnir and Landsbanki. Kaupthing may survive."

"And when is all this supposed to happen?"

"I can't tell you that. And obviously I hope I'm wrong. But I'm pretty sure I'm not."

"But we'll get lots of warning, right? I mean, we're talking years, not months."

He shook his head and pressed his lips together. "I don't know. I'll just tell you this: I had shares in Kaupthing. I used to work for them. I've sold all my shares and put my money in a safe account. I also had some shares in other companies, and in Straumur-Burdarás, the investment bank. I've sold those, too. I've also spread my money around so that there's no more than three million krónur in one account. That's the amount the deposit insurance scheme will cover. I thought of moving my money abroad, but since I don't live abroad it's kind of tricky to open an account somewhere else. I figure these precautions are sufficient for someone at my level of solvency." Again, there was humor in his eyes, but the previous frivolity of their interaction was gone.

She had stopped painting. "You're serious."

"Very serious."

"How do you know all this?"

"It's obvious to anyone who wants to see it. You just have to look at their financial statements to see how much equity they have, and combined with the news of the impending financial crisis, it's not hard to put two and two together. It's going to be a lot harder to get credit in the coming weeks and months. Years, even. Credit has been cheap for the last while, everyone has been prepared to lend money. That's the problem with those sub-prime mortgages in the United States, they were lent to people who had no way of paying them back, and now they're defaulting en masse and there's a lot of bad credit. And the Icelandic banks, well, they're not that different. They've been making loans to people without good collateral. Besides, they've been relying heavily on credit from other banks to refinance loans and stuff. They're going to run into serious problems."

"But why isn't anyone saying anything? Why do they all just go on like there's nothing wrong? Shouldn't someone be ringing warning bells?"

"Where are they going to ring them? The same people who

own the banks, own the media. Iceland has turned into an oligarchy. Anyone who tries to say anything is silenced, or made to seem ridiculous. People outside of Iceland have been saying this kind of thing for a few years now, warning about the rapid growth of the economy and the fact that the banks can't possibly sustain this growth. But what happens? They get ostracized for it in the Icelandic media. The 'research departments' at the banks – that are really their marketing and image departments, make no mistake – pull out all kinds of spreadsheets and figures and PowerPoint presentations to prove that they're wrong. Documents that really mean nothing. Then these respected journalists and analysts who try to give warnings get told by the people who run this country that they need to go back to school. The arrogance is unbelievable. And to top it all off the politicians put on a road show, go with the bankers to hold these presentations overseas to convince anyone who cares to listen that everything is fine and the Nordic Tiger can still roar." He dipped his brush into the paint tin. "Believe me, even though everything is hearts and kittens on the surface, there is a lot of panic within the Icelandic banks right now. A lot. But banking is a delicate business. If there is one thing the banks avoid at all possible costs it's ringing the alarm bells. The last thing they want is a run on the banks. So they'll keep their poker faces as long as they can."

"But … they keep talking about these enormous profits they're making, and everyone is all gung-ho."

"Sure. Yep. I know. This country is caught up in a collective madness and few people seem to realize, or even care."

"Why don't you say something?"

He shook his head. "I tried. It didn't work out too well for me."

"What do you mean?"

He shook his head. "Never mind. Let's just say that it's not all what it seems on the surface. There's a lot of stuff that *is* available for scrutiny … but there's also other stuff that isn't."

"Like what?"

She sensed that he was becoming increasingly reticent.

"I don't know exactly. I just have this suspicion that there are books being cooked in the back rooms. But I have no proof. I may be wrong."

From the tone of his voice, though, Frida could tell that he did not really think so.

"Anyway," he continued, "I'm so glad to be away from that world. I'm so glad to be back here, helping out with something that is real and tangible, like this aquaculture project. And the tourism, trying to attract people to this region. The West Fjords are such a fantastic place. But it's getting harder to live here all the time. The more people leave, the less money gets spent on maintaining the infrastructure. The health professionals leave, the roads fall into disrepair, which in turn causes more people to leave. If we don't do something to reverse the trend, this place could become depopulated in a few years, just like Hornstrandir, the northernmost region of this area."

"Oh, has Hornstrandir become depopulated?" Frida said, embarrassed about her own ignorance.

He smiled, the first smile he'd shown since they began talking about the economic situation. "Years ago. It used to be a thriving fishing region. But now there's nothing there. Just birds and foxes, and lots of hikers in the summertime."

Baldur's face lit up as he talked about the West Fjords. He was passionate about the area, she could tell, and eager to do his part to help build it up. But it was an arduous task, "like pushing a large boulder up a hill."

"Have you seen much of the region?" he said as they were finishing, packing the brushes into plastic bags so they could be reused later for a second coat.

"I can't say I have. I mean, apart from some picnics with my grandparents when I was a child, and the trip to Látrabjarg and Raudasandur yesterday – which was amazing, by the way – I've seen very little of this area. It's a scandal, really. I haven't even been to Ísafjördur. But … " and now a memory came to her, "I remember years ago going to a place where there were a lot of strange sculptures. Lions and things."

"Selárdalur."

"The man who made them was distantly related to us, I remember. But he was dead by then."

"Samúel Jónsson."

"Yes, that's him. It was a strange place. Those sculptures

were bizarre and not very good, but I remember that there was something about them that … got to me. Or maybe it was the story of the man. If I remember it right he never travelled abroad, but made all kinds of replicas of things. Is that right?"

"That's right. He was called the artist with the child's heart." Baldur was engaged now, his eyes bright and lively. "They've restored those now, you know. It's a museum."

"Really? Is it far?"

"No. Not far. I can take you if you want."

It seemed like he blurted it out without thinking. Their eyes met. The words hung suspended in the air, strong yet fragile, suggestive yet innocuous. He looked timid and a little scared, and smiled an unsteady smile. "That is if you want," he added.

Thoughts raced through Frida's mind. Warnings, fears. She shouldn't go. She couldn't.

"That would be great," she said.

~~

That Tuesday, the day Baldur said he would pick her up, she was filled with anxiety and apprehension. She had a sense that she was doing something wrong, something shameful but exciting, that she was crossing an invisible boundary into forbidden territory. She reasoned with herself that Baldur taking her on this trip was only a friendly gesture by someone whose company she enjoyed, and who clearly enjoyed hers. They had great rapport and she loved talking to him – she found him interesting and funny and … *nice*, that insipid word she normally hated, but which she now found herself associating more and more with the polite, energetic, intelligent man for whom she had begun to feel such fondness.

Still, when she spoke to Damien on the phone, she neglected to mention their upcoming excursion. When she hung up, she acknowledged it to herself, and also the reasons for it. She was going there with a man, alone, a man whose company she had to admit she enjoyed a lot more than her husband's. A man who moreover was also married, and who she suspected would also not be informing his wife of their excursion.

And yet, apart from these, well, *technicalities*, it did not feel wrong. Their interaction, their relationship, did not feel wrong. It felt right. It felt good, wholesome and safe. Deep in her heart, she recognized Baldur as a friend. For some reason, she trusted him. She knew that he would not intentionally harm her.

She had also been very preoccupied with the subject of their last conversation – that of the banks. It seemed so improbable, so apocalyptic, that the banks would go bankrupt as Baldur said, and yet he seemed so certain – to the point where he had taken very specific actions to prepare for it. She debated whether she should tell Damien about it, but if she did, how would she explain from whom she'd heard? She could tell an outright lie, say she'd heard it on some talk show or other, but that lie could easily snowball into something unmanageable. And if she told him the truth, that she'd heard it from a friend, he would probably cross-examine her on the identity of that friend and the circumstances of their encounter.

In the end, she decided to say nothing. Even if she did, what difference would it make? Their money was safe; they had it stored in a British bank account. Thankfully it was not the account that Landsbanki had rolled out in the UK a couple of years before and that she'd planned to sign up for, just because it was Icelandic. Damien had talked her out of it. For a bank to offer those kinds of interest rates, he said, there was something wrong. It was too great a risk. Best to be moderate and safe. And anyway, they had enough money. What did a few bob in interest matter to them either way?

~~

Baldur had said he'd pick her up at two, and he was there at ten minutes past. She was sitting outside on the step waiting for him, enjoying the late summer sunshine that had been permanent for days now, though a chill lingered in the air.

"Sorry I'm late," he said as he jumped out of the car with that trademark grin on his face. "There was a line at the gas station."

She cocked an eyebrow. "A line? Really?"

"Honest! There were three cars in front of me at the pumps. I swear. Very unusual."

As she climbed into the blue Cherokee she again felt a slight twinge of apprehension. What if someone saw them?

"Won't people wonder what we're doing together?" she asked as they approached the outskirts of the village.

Baldur shrugged. "We're friends. I'm showing you Selárdalur. That's all that matters to me."

She glanced at him. His gaze was directed firmly ahead, but his hands were gripping the steering wheel tightly. Despite his easygoing demeanor, she could see that he was tense.

As soon as they were out of the village and turned onto the main highway, she could feel them both relax. She put down her window and breathed in the fresh air. The road wound up along a mountain pass and then back down, passing along the coastline of a fjord. A tall mountain slope stretched on to their left, and straight ahead was the vast Atlantic, glittering in the sunshine.

"We could have hiked across," he said. "A route that people used in the old days is still there. It is lined with cairns – and the odd marker."

"Oh I would have loved that!"

"It would have taken around nine hours, though."

"Are there berries on the way?" September was berry season in Iceland.

He glanced at her with a smile. "No doubt. Lots."

"I would have had to add another five hours, then, with stops factored in." She leaned back in the seat and looked out. "I'd love to try it sometime. Is it a difficult hike?"

"Not for you, or anyone who is in good shape." He said it matter-of-factly. "Just don't get any ideas of going there on your own. You never should – unless you let someone know when you're going and when you'll be back. Icelandic nature is so unpredictable. Even dangerous."

"You're giving me the Icelandic Tourist Board spiel."

"Oh, sorry. I forget that I'm not showing a foreigner around. Well. You are *kind* of a foreigner." He glanced at her and smiled. She felt something brighten within her. How lovely he was!

They drove on, and before long, three gray buildings came into view. As they drew closer she could see sculptures, randomly placed, yet in some sort of order. Baldur stopped the jeep in front of the buildings and they got out. Frida stood, letting nostalgia flood through her. Yes, this was the place they had gone with their grandfather – she and Egill and Lóa.

There was a low, two-story, concrete building that had once been a home but was now slowly decaying. The corrugated iron roof was corroded into a uniform rust color and the gaping holes that once were windows were like hollow, lifeless eyes. Another two-story building nearby was slightly more stately and whole, had a curious, high curved roof over the entryway, held up by two concrete pillars. There was a freestanding archway in front, as though it was part of an absent fence and gate. The archway was attached to the pillars by two rounded concrete arms. There was scaffolding around the building, like someone had been in the process of making repairs but had had to abscond.

In between the two buildings were the sculptures, completely naïve pieces of ... art, that looked like something a nine-year-old might have made, had that nine-year-old been skilled at making things out of poured concrete. There was a man, standing and shading his eyes from the sun, looking at six lions that were arranged around something that looked like a low pillar with a basin on top. Another man stood in front of a seal, the seal's head and mouth placed at an angle that was rather unfortunate in its pornographic suggestions. She snuck a glance at Baldur, wondering if she should say something, but decided against it. Another pert seal lay nearby, and there was also a sea horse and a swan.

The sculptures were very crude. The paws of the lions were like flat hands with thick fingers, their heads were clunky, there was no definition in their bodies. The same was true of the rest of them. They were not something you'd find in a respectable art museum. In fact, they were not very good at all. And yet, there was something about them, something about the conviction with which they were made, that made them special.

Frida got out her camera and started taking pictures. "Who is doing the restoring?" she asked, circling the sculptures.

"A German man who came here and was fascinated by them. He's working with a volunteer association, a bunch of young people from different countries – you've probably heard of them. They lay paths and things."

"They're so ... I don't know. I don't really like them. They're not exactly pretty. But there's something about them that is so sincere. Like this man who created them was completely free from the constraints of society and just … went for it."

"Which is exactly how it was. Only I'm not sure how free he was from social constraints. He painted an altarpiece for the church in the area, but the congregation rejected it. He responded by building his own church and putting the altarpiece inside it. This one."

He pointed to the third building – a church that was the most whole of the three structures. Like the other buildings, it was made of concrete, and it had three windows along each side, as well as a smaller window set high into a gable near the entryway. The steeple was made of two rectangular pieces set atop each other and a circular section with windows, on top of which was the inverted turnip-shape that Frida associated with the Red Square in Moscow. The little windows were painted red; the top of the steeple white and red.

"You mean he made all this out of anger and spite?"

Baldur shrugged. "I don't know much about his psychology, but it seems kind of strange that he'd go out and build his own church after his neighbors turn down his kind offer for an altarpiece. Kind of like: 'Fuck you, I don't need you, I'll build my own fucking church'."

Frida laughed. "I guess you have to admire his audacity, though."

"Most definitely. I just wonder how happy he was, being pissed off at all his neighbors and beavering away over here in his little corner, building churches and making sculptures that no one really saw but him."

"A misunderstood genius, no doubt."

"Something like that."

She walked around, taking pictures. Baldur followed close behind, saying nothing.

"Thanks for bringing me here," she said.

Their eyes met. Her heart beat faster, and she could see that he, too, was moved – she could see it in his face, which had suddenly gone serious.

"Do you want to see the altarpiece that started it all?" he said.

"Can we go in the church?"

"I have a key."

"Well. Aren't you well connected."

Somehow her flippant remark sounded out of place now – the mood between them had grown solemn, like they both recognized a new dimension in their relationship.

"This is one of the tourist attractions in the area. I have keys to all of those."

The church was less like a church and more like an exhibition space. There were no pews, and naïve paintings lined the walls. Against the far wall there was a makeshift wooden altar with the altarpiece hanging above it. The middle panel showed a picture of Christ, holding out his hands to bless the world, and the two side panels showed angels. The painting was in the same childish style as the sculptures outside.

"So that's the fateful altarpiece?" asked Frida.

Baldur stood just behind her. "That's it."

"So this wasn't good enough for the country folk around here," she said, stepping closer to the altar and examining the painting.

"Evidently not. But to be perfectly fair, they'd just had one made for their own church."

They wandered through the space, looking at the different paintings and models on display. Baldur stayed close to Frida, and despite the lack of proper sanctity in the church there was a quiet hush over the space, a marked sort of reverence.

"Can you imagine living out here all alone, so remote, and just spending your days making art for no one but yourself?" Frida said when she had almost made the full circle of the exhibition.

"I can."

She was slightly taken aback by his answer. She had expected that he would say no.

"Really?"

He was looking at her intently, the look in his eyes both faraway and completely present. "Maybe not making art, but certainly being a recluse."

"You don't strike me as the type."

"You have a lot of preconceived ideas about me."

"I do. I'm sorry. You're right."

"Haven't you ever wanted to just escape from the world?"

They were speaking quietly, facing each other.

"What do you think I'm doing up here?" she replied.

He leaned over and kissed her lips, lightly at first, then more intently as he felt her respond. She moved closer and he pressed her against his hips. The tips of their tongues touched. Momentary bliss; then she pulled away.

"What are we doing?" she whispered.

He kissed her again.

She pushed him away gently. "Baldur."

He was looking at her, clearly struggling with his feelings.

"There are other people involved."

He nodded. "I know."

"Should we maybe talk about that?"

Again, that quiet hush in the air between them.

"Let's go outside."

Frida led the way. They sat down on the low stoop in front of the church door. Here they were sheltered from the ever-present wind, and the slanted rays of the sun warmed them.

She spoke first. "When I came into the factory shop that day and overheard you talking … was that about your wife?"

He had his forearms on his knees and was looking down at the ground. The arms of his sweater were rolled up and she could see the outlines of his muscles and the dusting of light brown hair.

"Yep."

"And a few minutes later you drove by with her?"

"Yep. I saw you there."

A raven glided past them, landed on a rock, and crowed.

"So you got married, and now you're here with me. What happened in between?"

He flexed his jaw. He looked miserable. "I'm sorry. I shouldn't have kissed you. I know it was wrong."

There was a silence. Then she said, "Why was it wrong?"

He turned to look at her. His eyes were somber, but held a flicker of surprise.

"I don't do this, you know. I'm not the type to cheat."

"I believe you."

"I just feel something when I'm with you. I can't really explain it."

"It's OK."

"My wife is a good person. We've known each other since we were kids. I care about her a lot. I love her ... as a sister. But that's not the way love should be. It's taken me a long time to admit that."

Frida sat perfectly still. She could feel his fragility, and her own, the brittleness of the truth, and the risk of speaking it.

"She's ill. She's got anorexia and she's once tried to kill herself. Actively, I mean. Of course she's constantly trying to kill herself. The anorexia is like a slow kind of death."

His words were laced with resentment and hurt. He was like a different person now from the vigorous, dynamic man she had encountered at first, with his easy smile and casual stride.

"It's killing me, too. I need to leave, but I don't know how."

They sat for a moment, letting the words settle around them.

"I'm not going to give you the excuse you need, you know," Frida said gently.

He looked at her, astonished. "No. No, that's not what this is. That's not what I meant."

"Are you sure?"

He shook his head. "I know I'm confused. Confused and unhappy. But this is a breath of fresh air for me. I feel like I understand you, and you understand me. It's hard to explain. I'm not really that good with words."

"It's OK. I know."

"I'm sorry if I'm putting you in an awkward situation, and I'm sorry I kissed you. I know you're married. I just ..." he picked up a pebble and tossed it in front of them. "I'm sorry," he said again.

She took his hand and pressed it. It felt good to feel his fingers, to close hers around them. "Don't be."

He looked at her hand on his and hesitated, then pressed it back.

"What about you?" he said. "Why did you come up here, really?"

She felt her heartbeat accelerate. Not because she was there with him – that felt gentle and good and right – but because she had never admitted out loud that her marriage to Damien might be over.

"A couple of weeks before I came up here I found a woman's earring on the floor of my husband's study."

He waited. His fingers moved, and caressed hers gently.

"The thing that scares me most about that is, not that he might be having an affair, but the fact that I really don't care if he is."

"So you're not in a picture perfect marriage either, then."

"I was young when I married him. It was right after I'd received a big shock in my life and I wasn't really present."

"And now?"

"And now I feel like I'm just part of his work. I'm there to smile and host parties and greet people and look like I'm happy. But we don't communicate. We don't talk. I don't feel like I know him at all, and I don't feel like he knows me." She paused before continuing: "Early last month I was at a party and I passed out. I went for some tests, and there was nothing wrong with me. But one of the doctors said that it could be a wake-up call. That there was something in my life that was causing so much pressure that I collapsed inwardly."

He furrowed his brow. "That is not good."

"I need to leave him. I'm scared, though."

"Of what?"

She shrugged. "I'm not sure. Not being Damien's wife, I guess. It's all I know. And there's security in it."

"There's always security in what we know. It doesn't mean it's the best thing for us, though."

"Why are you afraid of leaving your wife? Is it because you're afraid she'd harm herself?"

"There's that. And the fact that I'm here with her family, helping them, and have invested almost all of my savings into their project. Shallow, I know. And maybe just an excuse not to have to make a decision."

"Couldn't you go back to what you were doing before?"

He hesitated a moment. "I was working for Kaupthing."

"And?"

Again she sensed that same resistance she'd felt in him before when they were discussing the banks.

"I could never go back there," he said decisively.

"Why not?" she asked gently.

"It was the worst time of my life. A nightmare. I started

working there as a bond trader, right after graduation. At first it was great, lots of action, lots of money, this really upbeat, jocular environment. I was doing well, too. Making good money. We'd go out a lot after work, and there was all this pressure to be part of the team. Everybody was so hip and cool. It was like being on a coke-fuelled high all the time."

"*Like* being?"

"OK. *Was* being. Though not all of the time, I hasten to add."

"So it's true what they say … about the coke? Is it a big part of that world?"

"Totally. Getting high in general is a big part of that world, and coke is the drug of choice. It's slick, it's cool and it costs a shitload of money. Basic requirements for bankers." He paused. "Anyway, things took a bad turn with Hafdís. I was out all the time, and she was getting more and more sick, she had cut down on her course load at school so she was way behind me in terms of graduating, and then without telling anybody she just stopped going. She stayed at home all day, or went to the gym and worked out for hours. She was getting more and more thin. I didn't want to face the fact that there was something wrong with her."

"Were you married by that time?"

"Yeah. We got married so we could apply for family housing at the university."

"So what happened?"

"Her mom was the first to realize that something was seriously wrong. Soon after that, she tried to kill herself. I think it may have been to try to get my attention, I'm not sure. I was never around. I was completely caught up in the crazy banking scene, all the excitement and tension. It was completely addictive. Besides, if you wanted to be part of the group, you had to play the game. You had to go out on Thursday and Friday and party all night. You had to meet up at the bar on other nights too sometimes, and more often than not, those nights ended up in some weird macho universe – I say 'macho' with quotation marks, because to me it's not macho – like strip clubs and shit. I always felt totally uncomfortable with that, but felt like I had to go along with it, otherwise I would be ostracized."

"Strip clubs and shit … you mean, like prostitutes."

His voice was tight. "Yeah, that was one part of it. I always managed to wangle out of that, though. That's not my scene. At all."

"So what finally happened?"

"One night, one of the guys on the team took me out and, well, made me a proposition. We'd become pretty close, and in hindsight I can see that he planned it that way, he planned to earn my trust and also to test my character."

"A proposition …?"

"No no, nothing like that. He didn't come on to me or anything. But he basically asked me to do something I knew was illegal. To take part in a pretty dangerous game. And I refused."

"That something you alluded to the other day when we were talking."

He nodded. "After that the attitude towards me changed completely. The clique I was in stopped including me, no one talked to me … the ostracism I'd feared so much, that had been this underlying current for such a long time, that had completely controlled me … it happened. I felt worthless. I started trying to change it by doing more coke, but thankfully I realized what I was doing. Thankfully, too, I don't have an addictive personality. I also realized, surprisingly fast, that the place in which I was working was a cesspool. I couldn't believe how blind I'd been. Soon after, Hafdís's family suggested we move up here so she could be closer to them and I could invest all the money I'd made into their venture."

There was a hint of sarcasm in the last remark.

"When was this?"

"March of this year."

"And now?"

"I find myself caught up in family dynamics that are almost as bad as the place I was working before. They hold me responsible for Hafdís's condition, they say – directly and indirectly – that she got sick because I was never around, and suggest that I can't leave because that will push her over the edge."

"Have you told them you want to leave?"

"Not in so many words. But it's pretty clear that we don't have a regular marriage. I mean, how can you have a regular marriage with someone who is so sick? I love her, but she has the emotional maturity of a child. Her world revolves around obsessively controlling her weight and other people, playing on her condition to make people do what she wants. Her family does the same. It is manipulative and narcissistic, and they don't see it. They probably never will."

"And that argument I witnessed in the shop that day?"

"I want her to be committed. She's been getting really bad. She's a hazard to herself, and it's not fair to the rest of us. But her mother won't hear of it. She doesn't trust the psychiatrists down south. Instead she wants us to watch over her. Which most of the time means me."

"But you're here with me now."

"Because her mother has taken her to Ísafjördur to buy some new curtains for the apartment."

"Oh, she's well enough for that."

"Yep."

Frida shivered. The sun had gone behind a cloud and it was getting pretty cold to be sitting outside. Winter was just around the corner, and it now made its presence felt.

"Are you cold?" Baldur said, putting his arm around her shoulders.

She nodded, her teeth chattering.

"Come." He stood up and pulled her to her feet. Then he put his arms around her and rubbed her back and arms vigorously.

"I don't know if that's going to help," she said.

Then she tilted her head upwards and kissed him.

She felt herself fill with peace, harmony and deep desire. *So this is how it is supposed to feel*, she found herself thinking. *This is it.* She wanted him, wanted to feel his naked skin, wanted him to touch her, wanted to feel him in her. Her whole being wanted him.

They broke apart. She was still shivering. "Let's get in the car," she whispered.

She was glad when he turned on the engine and the heater. While he went to lock the church door, she waited, watching and thinking how strange it would be to know of him in the same village now, and not be able to talk to him or to touch him.

He came back in the car, reached over and buried his face in her hair. She kissed his lips, feeling a mild jolt, like an electric current that travelled straight down into her belly. How easy it would be to give in. How tempting it was.

They drove back in relative silence. About halfway to the village Baldur glanced at her, reached over and took her hand. He pressed it lightly. They held hands for the rest of the way: caressing, entwining, relaxing, releasing. So much communication in the tiny movements of two hands and ten fingers. Frida felt nuances and shades dancing in her soul, sensations flowing through her. The silence between them was soft and good. If she could only live inside that silence, she thought, she would be perfectly content forever.

The sun hung low in the afternoon sky as they turned off the main road and drove toward the town. Frida blinked rapidly and put down her visor. The light was blinding. Risky conditions for driving, she thought, just as Baldur slammed on the brakes. Someone had stepped out into the road in front of them. She sensed, more than she saw, Baldur tense. He let go of her hand. For a brief moment, the man on the road stared at them. First at Baldur, then at her, then back at Baldur. She recognized him – it was that Jón fellow who had come to the house at Damien's bidding. She glanced at Baldur. He was staring back. Then Jón Jónsson retraced his steps back to the curb, and gestured for Baldur to continue. As they passed, Frida looked at him. His face was cold and impassive. She shuddered.

"Who is that Jón character?" asked Frida.

"My father-in-law."

She suddenly felt ill.

"Do you remember when you saw me down on the beach, throwing rocks into the water?" she said after a long pause.

"Sure do."

"It was because Damien – my husband – had sent that man to spy on me."

"To *spy* on you?"

"Well, to keep track of me. I think. He called especially to tell the head of the town council – which is Jón – that I was here, and to pay me a visit."

"He couldn't have picked a better man," said Baldur sardonically as he brought the car to a halt in front of the house.

He killed the engine and turned to her.

"What's going to happen now?" she said softly.

He look at her for a moment, then leaned over and kissed her. It was gentle, light – different from earlier, more guarded.

"We both have things that we need to think about, I guess."

"Are we going to see each other?" she said.

He took out his phone. "What's your number?"

She told him. He entered it into his phone's memory. She went to reach for her phone, but remembered that she'd left it in the house. On purpose.

"I haven't got my phone, so you'll have to get in touch with me."

"OK."

She looked at him for a moment longer. She wanted to demand that he tell her when they would see each other again, what he was going to do now, how everything was going to work out, but she also knew that it was unfair – he had to have space to work out his complications, just as she did. She wanted to open her mouth and say something, but there was just far too much to be said, and when there was far too much to be said, the best thing was to say nothing.

She opened the door quickly and got out. Just as she reached the door, she heard him turn on the engine and back away, his tires skidding on the gravel as he drove off.

~~

Oh, the mockery life makes.

She'd come up here to regroup, to reflect, to step out of the chaos that her life had become – and now here she was, in a complete state of disorder and confusion, far worse than before, her emotions a whirlwind of doubts, fears, yearnings and uncertainties.

Lovesick.

The hours ticked by horribly slowly, each one longer than the last. How in God's name had she got herself into this situation of waiting, hoping, pining … like an obsessed teenager. She had her phone within sight all the time and glanced at it every few minutes, in the unlikely event that he had called and she hadn't been able to hear it, five feet away.

Wednesday passed. Then Thursday.

Friday passed. She finished painting the fence, even though it had grown so cold that her fingers turned numb. All the time she kept hoping to hear the sound of a car on the road. His car. Later she drove into town for some groceries, feeling horribly conspicuous, like everyone – the cashier at the store, the people buying gas, the family exiting the pool – were looking at her and whispering amongst themselves. She felt like a Jezebel, with the wrath of God – or at least the tiny rural community – upon her, and she could not wait to get back in her car and drive back to the house. Nonetheless she kept her eyes peeled for the blue Cherokee, but caught no glimpse of it.

Saturday passed. The weather was stormy with rain, and by the afternoon the rain had turned to sleet. Inside, Frida paced, feeling like a caged animal. Her thoughts circled round and round and round inside her head, like a frantic dog chasing its tail, not for fun, but out of sheer misery and desperation. Finally she dug out a piece of paper from a drawer in the living room, sat down and started to write, emptying the contents of her head onto the blank page. Afterwards, she felt slightly better. Next, she took out a piece of paper and drew a big grid on it, on which she listed the pros and cons of leaving her husband. A few minutes later she tore up the paper in frustration when she realized that the number of pros or cons didn't matter, but rather the weight of each.

Damien had called on Wednesday. She'd waited anxiously for him to say something, like that Jón Jónsson had called and informed him that his wife was very likely having a hot, illicit affair with his son-in-law, but he had said nothing of that sort. Damien's voice had been strained – he was under a lot of pressure at work, he said, and much to Frida's surprise he had not once asked her when she planned to return.

On Sunday morning, the ground was covered in hoarfrost, and Frida decided it was time to go home. Anything could happen now as far as the weather was concerned; if it snowed and road conditions were bad, she might become trapped in the village for an indefinite length of time, and that was something she wished to avoid at all costs.

She spent the morning and most of the afternoon cleaning and setting things in order. By the time she was finished, it was too late to start the journey home – she'd have to drive much of the way in the dark, and she preferred not to do that. Instead, she decided to head into town for a workout on the treadmill. Yes, people might talk; yes they might whisper and send her hostile glances, but she didn't care now. She'd be out of here tomorrow.

In front of the pool building she took a deep breath, then got out of the car. Inside, the girl in the reception barely gave her a second glance. Frida felt comforted: perhaps no one was judging her, perhaps it was all her imagination. She went through to the women's change rooms to put on her running gear. Two women were in there, getting dressed, speaking to each other in loud voices. Just as Frida was putting on her shoes, a third woman entered from the showers. Frida saw her out of the corner of one eye, a vapid presence with long, stringy blonde hair, almost like an apparition. She registered Hafdís's presence with her instinct rather than her eyes, and instantly averted her gaze. After a moment she dared to look up, and even though she had known about her condition, the sight of her naked body was shocking. She was so emaciated that her ribs and hipbones protruded from her sides, and her stomach was almost concave. Her face was gaunt and her skin pallid, and her legs so thin and frail that they looked like they might snap at any moment.

Frida looked away. The other two women had gone silent, and were also averting their gazes. Frida finished lacing up her shoes, pushed out of the change room and down the hall, where the gym was. She got on the treadmill, almost immediately setting off on a run. The sight of Hafdís had filled her with sadness and revulsion, and also a deep sense of pity. She was so obviously ill, and she felt for her. Still, she had to admit, most of all she felt sadness and compassion for Baldur, for having to live trapped inside that sickness. Yes, she knew he chose to do so, but it was not for her to judge him – if she were in the same situation, she had no idea how she would react. Extricating oneself from circumstances like that was more than just saying the words – there was bound to be all manner of complex feelings involved, just as he had said.

As she ran, she no longer felt self-conscious or guilty for her involvement with the man who had become so dear to her. Surely anyone who looked at Hafdís and who knew the two of them, anyone who had any sense of compassion and decency, would understand his predicament. Others might even wonder how he managed to stay in the relationship.

In the midst of these musings, she suddenly saw through the window in front of her as Hafdís exited the building. She stood for a moment with her back turned, then she spun around. Someone had just come out. It was Baldur.

Frida felt like she had been hit in the stomach. She grabbed on to the sides of the treadmill to steady herself. She immediately felt foolish – why did his presence there come as such a shock to her? He was Hafdís's husband, after all. Wasn't it normal for them to be together?

From her vantage point, she watched them. He was a good deal taller than his wife, and was bending down now to see something she had in her hand – a brochure of some sort. They stood there for a minute, almost close enough for Frida to touch them had the glass window not been there. Frida got her bearings back, lifted herself up and started running again, her gaze fixed on them. She saw Baldur reach out and touch Hafdís's waist, as if to guide her in a specific direction. She saw his profile. He looked incredibly tired, his face devoid of the energy and brightness that she had come to associate with him.

At that moment it was almost as though he sensed something, or saw something. She watched him hesitate, then he turned and looked directly at her through the window. Their eyes met. His look was inscrutable. Then Hafdís spoke and he looked at her, removing his hand from her waist. He turned, and Frida watched them walk off in the direction of the grocery store. They moved slowly; evidently Hafdís set the pace, which was in marked opposition to Baldur's energetic stride. After what seemed to Frida like an eternity they turned up a side street and disappeared from view.

Frida slowed the treadmill to a walk, then stopped. She was alone in the gym. She sat down on the edge of the treadmill and leaned forward, hugging her knees. She felt like she'd been cut on the inside with a knife. She wanted most of all to cry, but she knew she wouldn't. Worse, she chided herself, *hated* herself, for these feelings, that she was even hard-pressed to believe were real. It wasn't as though she was in love with the guy. She barely knew him. No. It had to be something else. It had to be because she wanted out of her marriage, and saw Baldur as some sort of ticket to freedom.

Silly girl.

Slowly she got up and went into the dressing room. She took her clothes and left the building as fast as she could. Back at the house, she took a long shower, feeling the water wash over her, cleansing and healing. She would leave early in the morning. This short chapter in her life was finished. She had been sent here to learn something, and she was grateful for it. It was now time for her to go back and face her own life.

It was already getting dark. Frida put on some clean clothes, then stood barefoot in front of the bathroom mirror, combing the tangles out of her hair. Just as she was finishing, there came a sound. It drew nearer. Wheels on gravel.

She stood perfectly still, afraid to move. The car stopped in front of the house, then there came a knock at the door.

Still she stood, riveted to the spot, wondering what to do.

The knock came again.

She made her way down the steep staircase and slowly opened the door.

Neither of them said a word. He hesitated a moment, then stepped inside. She shut the door. An instant later they were clinging together, kissing: passionately, desperately, deeply. Their bodies trembled. They broke apart, he took her face in his hands. So much to say, and yet nothing that could be said. They went upstairs without speaking and got undressed, a little shy, yet unable to keep their hands away from each other. Timidly she enclosed her fingers around his hard penis and felt him quicken towards her; she stroked him and he moaned, his breath hot against her face. Under the covers, their naked bodies pressing together, she sighed with exquisite pleasure and release. Worlds opened beneath the skin, hands feeling, touching, pressing; soft moans, murmurs, unfolding and entering a world beyond this world, where only the two of them existed in perfect unity. She gasped when he entered her and clung to him tightly, closing her eyes and allowing feelings to wash over and through her, like water, like waves. He was in her and all around her; they glided through liquid in exquisite beauty. Slowly, slowly, then quicker, faster, whispering now, words meant only for each other, then finally tensing, contracting, pleasure swelling, then dying away, slowly, slowly.

Afterwards they lay spent, not speaking, holding each other. Frida forced out the distressing thoughts that pressed against her awareness. *Let me stay in this moment. Savor this moment.*

She moved closer to him, feeling his strong, naked body against hers, that body she had so often admired from afar for its graceful movements, its energetic stride. She inhaled the smell of him, a smell that was so familiar and so *right*. She pressed him close.

He tightened his embrace and buried his face in her neck.

"I'm sorry about today," he murmured. "I'm sorry you had to see us."

Frida tensed at the thought.

"Won't she be wondering where you are?" she finally said.

He lay still and said nothing.

She drifted into a slumber, stirring only when she felt him move. In the room there was a sliver of light, the moon rising behind the blind.

"What time is it?" she murmured.

He turned to her. His body was so warm.

"Almost nine." He paused. "I have to go."

She nodded. Acquiescent.

"This is not … meaningless to me, if that's what you think," he said.

She pulled his head down and kissed him.

He lay for a moment next to her, then turned and got out of bed. He dressed quickly. She lay watching him. When he had finished, he crouched down beside her. His face looked strained, like he was struggling to find words. He tucked a lock of hair behind her ear.

"I want to say so many things, but I don't know how to say them," he whispered.

"It's OK," she said.

"I don't want to make promises I'm not sure I can keep."

"Neither do I."

He looked at her once more, a troubled expression in his eyes. Then he left the room. She heard him put on his shoes downstairs, and the front door open and close. Only when she heard the sound of his car on the gravel fading into the distance did she allow the sadness to wash over her.

~~

Frida woke up with an aching emptiness inside.

She'd planned to leave early. Now she didn't want to leave at all. And yet the thought of staying, with all its tension and inherent uncertainty, was also unbearable.

Her mind circled back to the previous night. It had been wonderful. Amazing. An awakening of something that she'd deep down longed for but at the same time believed unattainable. A secret space she had inhabited with another person that was luminous, and good, and right, even if society condemned it. It was adultery, after all.

And now in the stark morning light she felt wretched. She was also all-too aware that they had made love without protection. Her prescription for birth control pills had run out just before she left Reykjavík, and she hadn't bothered to fill it. After all, she and Damien hadn't made love in months, and she didn't understand the point of pumping hormones into her body, artificially controlling her cycle – for what? Yes, the thought of asking Baldur if he had a condom had flickered into her mind the night before, but she'd resolutely dismissed it. She had wanted him naked inside of her. She had wanted to feel the sensation of his seed flowing into her body. She knew there were risks, and that pregnancy was only one of them. But she didn't care.

She dressed quickly and went downstairs. The house was cold. She shivered slightly as she padded across the chilly wooden floorboards. Passing to the kitchen, something strange caught her eye. A flash. She stopped, confused. Now it was gone. No – there it was again. It was her phone, flashing through the side pocket of her gym bag, which she had left on the floor near the door.

She fished it out quickly. It was still on silent from the day before, but she obviously had a message. Hope swelled up in her

– perhaps it was from Baldur. Her disappointment was equally acute when she saw that, no, it was not from Baldur, but from Damien.

There were six missed calls from him. *Six*. And two messages informing her that she had voice mail.

Her fingers trembled slightly as she pressed the keys to listen to her voice mail. With six missed calls, something had to be wrong. Both voice mail messages were from Damien. The first, from last night, asked her to call him – it was urgent. The second sounded irate: where the *devil* was she, and would she kindly return his call – it was urgent, or had he not mentioned that the first time?

She leaned against the wall, her thoughts spinning. Yes, she would have to call him, but she couldn't face it until she'd had some breakfast and, more importantly, coffee.

She went into the kitchen, her nerves already on edge.

As she was assembling her breakfast, the phone rang again. She jumped, and lunged for the phone. It was Damien, again. Her fleeting sense of hope was replaced by apprehension. Something was definitely wrong.

She boiled an egg, ate some toast, then sat down with her coffee and dialed his number. He answered on the first ring.

"Damien. Hi."

"Where the hell have you been?"

She resisted the impulse to throw the phone against the wall.

"I just got up. The phone was on silent. What is it?"

"I don't suppose you've heard the news?"

"What news?"

"The news that Glitnir has collapsed."

It took her a moment to absorb what he had just said.

So it had happened. Already. Just as Baldur had said it would.

"When?"

"They announced it at a press conference this morning." His voice changed. "You don't seem surprised."

She did not answer. "OK," she said slowly, struggling to process the information. "So it's collapsed … what does that mean exactly?"

"It means the state is taking it over."

"And … do people lose their savings?"

“No. They’re saying people won’t lose their savings. But it’s mayhem down here. Frankly the concern is that this is just the beginning, but of course no one says that, at least not publicly.”

“Not publicly?”

His voice was urgent. “Listen. Frida. I need to go to London and I need you to come with me.”

She felt her stomach constrict. “When?”

“I’m leaving this afternoon.”

“I can’t get to Reykjavík by then.”

“Very well, you can come tomorrow.”

“Why do I need to go?”

She hated the sound of her own voice, like that of a petulant child.

He lowered his voice, as though someone could be listening. “Look. We have a serious situation on our hands. A crisis. It involves London, and has people at high levels very worried. I need to get there and brief them on the situation. I’ll need you there with me to monitor the situation, to translate, to keep up with what’s going on.”

He needed her with him, not as his wife, but as his translator. His dogsbody.

She drew a deep breath.

“No,” she said.

“Frida.”

“No.”

“You’re acting like a bloody child.”

“No Damien. You’re wrong. I’m acting like a woman. And I do not want to go to London with you right now.”

She was amazed to hear the composure in her voice – it was a calm she certainly did not feel.

He hesitated. “All right,” he said, clearly straining to control the anger in his voice. “You don’t want to go *now*. Will you come later? On Wednesday, perhaps?”

“No,” she repeated. “I am not prepared go to London with you to be your translator.”

His voice turned icy. “You do know what this means, don’t you?”

“Not exactly. But I suppose it means I may be fired from my job.”

There was a beat, then he hung up.

For a long time afterward, Frida sat perfectly still and stared out at the faded leaves on the trees outside. Something was imminent, over which she had no control, over which none of them had any control.

CHAPTER EIGHT

As soon as Frida drove into Reykjavík, she became filled with a sense of apprehension and foreboding. The city felt different. The speeding, impatient drivers that normally dominated the streets all appeared to be elsewhere now, and instead the traffic proceeded in an orderly fashion. At traffic lights, people sat perfectly still in their cars, as though they were holding their breath, anxiously waiting for something to occur.

Perhaps, like Frida, they were listening to the radio. She had listened on the drive all the way back to town, moving from one station to another, trying to absorb everything that was being speculated and said. Frida comprehended only about half of what she heard, but she did understand the sense of impending doom that permeated the voices of almost everyone who spoke about the collapse of Glitnir. There was much instability on the financial markets. The krona, apparently, was in free-fall, having depreciated by about twenty-five percent against the dollar in September alone, and it showed no signs of stabilizing. People kept referring to the "tempest" on the financial markets, and the question on everyone's lips seemed to be whether the Icelandic banks were sturdy enough to withstand it.

She took the road along the sea. A freighter was coming in, stacked high with containers. All the consumer goods that the Icelanders imported – from food to clothes to building materials to machinery. All those goods needed to be purchased in foreign currencies, and with the vast depreciation of the króna, everything had just become at least twenty-five percent more expensive. Where would it end?

She had a sudden flashback to the past: her mother, coming out of her bedroom in the middle of the day, wearing a stained robe, looking like she'd just been hit by a truck. Turning her back to Frida, ashamed to let her daughter see her that way, scribbling something on a piece of paper and handing it to her – a list of things that Frida was supposed to get at the corner store, where her mother had credit. At the top of the list was inevitably a pack of Winston cigarettes. Frida would go, her eyes to the ground, feeling the stigma dripping from her like slime, knowing deep down that her mother had sent her because the shop owner would not try to collect from her, because she was just a child and they felt sorry for her. Frida would slink along the aisles, collecting the items, then take them to the cash register, keeping her head down, avoiding their eyes, taking care not to see the glances they gave one another.

And now, here she was. Back in the place she had left five weeks ago. It was only a short time, yet she had changed irrevocably at some profound level. How would she fit back into the mold that awaited her here?

There were lights on in the ambassadorial residence. Instantly her stomach clenched – could it be that Damien had not gone to London, after all?

Parking the car in the embassy garage next door to the residence, she dragged her suitcase out onto the sidewalk and then up the pathway to the house, cringing at the noise it made. She felt strangely conspicuous and that made her intensely uncomfortable. Her hand trembled slightly as she put the key in the lock and pushed open the door.

Inside the house, all was quiet.

"Hello!" she called, but there was no answer.

She took off her shoes and padded silently through the downstairs in her stocking feet. Everything was in perfect order, clean and tidy. *Like a museum.*

He appeared from the kitchen, stepping out in front of her in the hallway, silently and without a word. She shrieked.

"Jesus, Damien! You scared the hell out of me." His face was white and expressionless. Something about him made her shudder.

"What are you doing here? I thought you were leaving for London this afternoon."

"My flight was postponed. I had some things to take care of." He stood there, macabre in his controlled stillness, making no move to welcome her home; indeed, showing no expression whatsoever.

"Oh," she said, her shock turning to irritation. "Why didn't you say anything when I came in?"

"What would you have liked me to say?"

"Hello, maybe?"

"Hello, Frida. How was your drive?"

She shook her head, turned around and took her bags upstairs. The appearance of Damien had stunned her – she had not expected to see him there, and indeed, would have preferred it if he hadn't been there. She needed to reorient herself and sift through her feelings about what had happened the night before. Alone.

There was a light on in their bedroom. The bed was made. A pair of Damien's shoes were lined up next to the door; his dressing gown hung in the bathroom. She realized that she felt like an impostor, like someone who did not belong there. This was not a place where she felt free to shed her defenses, to raise her voice, to speak her mind, to laugh loudly and raucously. It never had been. She had just become so accustomed to her self-censorship that she hadn't noticed. But now, with the contrast of the past five weeks fresh in her mind and soul, it was suddenly brought into stark focus. She did not belong here. This was not her home.

Carefully she opened the closet, almost expecting to see someone else's clothes. But no, those were her dresses and things – *my uniforms* – all hung in neat rows.

She couldn't bring herself to go back downstairs. There had been something about Damien, something about how he had looked at her, that set her nerves on edge. It bothered her. Did he know that she and Baldur had been seen together? Had that Jón character contacted him? Was he really Damien's spy – or was she just paranoid?

She went to the bathroom to draw a bath. There, too, everything was immaculate – the marble tiles gleaming, the chrome shining, the plush clean towels neatly folded on the towel rack. Perfect and soulless, like a hotel bathroom.

Just after she'd got in the bath, the door opened, and Damien stood there.

She raised herself up in the tub and crossed her arms over her breasts.

For a moment, neither of them spoke.

"It's good to see you back," he said, but there was no warmth in his voice. It sounded like something rehearsed, something he'd realized he should have said, but had forgotten to say.

She nodded.

"I'll have to pop over to the embassy for an hour or two," he continued. "Will I see you when I return?"

"Not sure. I'm pretty tired."

"I'm sure you are." There was something in his tone – a snide sarcasm, just barely noticeable. Or was she imagining it?

"I wanted to ask if you'd changed your mind about coming to London with me."

Frida shook her head. "No. I haven't changed my mind."

"Very well," he said. He gave a perfunctory smile, then left.

Frida slid down into the tub and immersed herself in the water. She couldn't stop her mind from turning, over and over, thinking of the man she'd left behind in that beautiful fjord out west. Neither could she stop thinking about making love with him. Involuntarily her hand went between her legs and she pressed her mound, a momentary sensation of the bliss they had shared spreading through her body. What sharp contrast to the soul-crushing deadness she experienced with the man that had just stood over her with his contemptuous sneer, all because she refused to do his bidding.

She quickly surfaced and inhaled deeply, filling her lungs with air.

Downstairs in the kitchen she flicked on the light and winced at the bright glare of the fluorescent bulb. Frida hated that light. Why anyone would choose to have a fluorescent light in their home was beyond her capacity for understanding. No doubt she could request to have it removed and something more genial put in, but she couldn't be bothered. For some reason she felt an overwhelming sense of apathy about this house.

In the fridge she found some leftover casserole that she popped into the microwave. While she waited for it to heat up she turned on the TV that hung on the wall by the kitchen table. Kastljós – the current affairs program that followed the evening news – was on. The Chairman of the Board of Glitnir bank was being interviewed about the collapse of the bank and at times appeared almost on the verge of tears, at other times like he was having trouble controlling his rage. Frida couldn't get her head around half of what they were saying ... something about sinister motives and political incompetence and some huge power struggle between different camps that seemed incredibly harsh and, to her ears, hopelessly inane.

She flicked off the TV and leaned against the counter, covering her face with her hands and rubbing her temples. It seemed like everything was coming undone – not only her own life, but the society all around her.

Later that night, when Frida was in bed, she heard Damien come in. She lay still, straining to hear his movements.

A few moments later the door opened and he stood in the doorway to their bedroom, a perfect silhouette. He stepped inside, quietly, and got undressed, then slipped into bed beside her. She turned over on her back. Moving closer, he pulled her to him and molded his body against hers. She felt herself tense. He found her lips and kissed her. His hand slipped up under her lace-trimmed slip, caressing her thigh, her buttocks. "I've missed you," he murmured, pulling off his shorts and pressing against her thigh. She closed her eyes and allowed herself to surrender to the sensation of his hands on her skin. Hesitating for a moment, she lifted the slip and deftly pulled it off over her head, then took off her panties. His body was warm and the touch of his naked skin sent a thrill through her. Her body responded instinctively and she pressed closer to him. Then she felt his erection wilt.

He kissed her, hard, fervently, moving his body against hers, as though hoping to re-evoke the desire. But it was gone.

She lay still, saying nothing, a million unspoken words between them.

Moments passed. Then he turned over quickly, angrily, and

got out of bed. An instant later he had put on his dressing gown and left the room.

Frida lay under the covers, her nerves taut, perfectly still as though she did not dare to move. She didn't know what had just happened. She didn't understand him, and she didn't understand herself. Why had she surrendered to a man towards whom she felt such antipathy, bordering on revulsion? Was she hoping against hope that they would find each other again in their lovemaking? And now she lay, perfectly still like an animal on the alert, waiting for something that she didn't know what was, as though she feared that a single movement would bring catastrophe.

She lay there a moment longer, then slowly, soundlessly, she put her slip back on.

Frida was almost asleep when she sensed the room grow lighter. Her eyelids fluttered open, just in time to see Damien taking long strides towards the bed. He threw off the covers, pulled off his dressing gown in two swift movements, and in a fraction of a second had turned her on her back and was thrusting his erect penis into her. She was too surprised to make a sound, but managed to twist to one side, hoping to evade him. He grabbed hold of her arm and shoved her roughly onto her back again; she tried to fight back but he pinned her arms down and put his entire weight on her. Then he was inside her, moving, slamming violently against her. She felt pain and cried out, struggling to twist her body to the side. She screamed at him to get off her. He grabbed a pillow and shoved it over her face, pinning the sides down with his hands as he thrust into her. Terror gripped her. She moved her head frantically to the side, finding a small stream of air that came from beneath the pillow. Finally she heard him groan and give one last shudder. His body went limp, she felt him collapse on top of her and release his grip on the pillow. She tore it off, and slammed it at his face. He rose quickly; she kicked at him but he was out of reach. She was still too stunned by what had happened to think rationally; she reached for the duvet to cover herself. He looked at her for a moment longer with an expression of something bordering on hatred, then turned and left the room.

In the morning, he was gone.

~~

She woke up with a lingering feeling of horror and disgust, a trembling deep in her bones.

There was a word for what had happened last night, but she couldn't bring herself to say it, even to herself.

She had seen a side to Damien that she had never seen before. He had been a selfish bastard for most of their time together, she could acknowledge that now, despite the overwhelming temptation to project onto him a character of her own construction. But he had never done anything like this.

Frida went through the day feeling numb and disconnected from everything. Kristín the housekeeper came – they chatted amiably and through concerted effort Frida was able to maintain an upbeat facade. As soon as Kristín was gone, however, she fell back into deep disconcertment. She knew that she needed to get out of here – to move to her own place, preferably far away. Then she'd have to look for work, or go to school, or do whatever it took to stand on her own two feet.

To stand on her own two feet. It both astonished and appalled her that she had relied on Damien for so many things for so long. She'd handed over to him control of her life, allowed the boundaries to blur to such an extent that she felt weak without him. She remembered what her mother had said to her the night she died – they had been in the kitchen putting things away after dinner: "I wonder what you'll have to fall back on if it doesn't work out," or something to that effect. Frida had been angry and indignant that she would even suggest such a thing. Now here she was, smack dab in the place her mother had warned her about. And the only person she could be angry with was herself, for having sleepwalked through her life.

Should have listened.

She shrugged as though trying to rid herself of the past. *Never mind*, she thought and set her jaw. She was awake now, and determined to take back her life.

But it wouldn't be easy. Damien would not exactly be thrilled by her request for a divorce. Knowing him and his proprietary ways, he'd probably try to make it as difficult for her as he could. She might be forced to walk away with nothing, save for the nominal sum that had been the proceeds from the sale of her mother's flat. She didn't even know what housing prices were like in Reykjavík, but she'd heard that they were not cheap.

Perhaps there would be some rentals listed online.

Her laptop was still in the vestibule where she had left it the day before. It had not seen much action over the previous five weeks – in fact, Frida had used it only to load in pictures from her camera. She pulled it out of its case and flicked it open, then saw it briefly search for the Internet connection it had been disengaged from for so long before a message flashed on the screen that the battery was almost empty and that it would shut down in sixty seconds. Goddamn! She rummaged through the bag for the charger, but found it empty. Shit. Shit shit shit. She'd put the charger away in the sideboard up at the house in Fagrifjördur, and in a flash now realized that it was still there.

Shutting the laptop, she thought for a moment. Damien had the same model. With any luck he wouldn't have taken the charger with him. And even if he had, she'd be able to use the desktop in his office.

Climbing the stairs, her heart suddenly began thumping. She stopped and leaned against the banister. Her breath was coming in spurts. What was happening? Anxiety attack? She sat down on the stairs and put her forehead to her knees. Slowly her heart rate stabilized and her breathing returned to normal.

She got to her feet. The door to Damien's study was closed. She pressed down on the handle. It was locked.

She felt a surge of defiance, a strange kind of determination. Anger, almost.

She needed to get in there.

Damien sometimes kept the key to the door in the pocket of his dressing gown. The dressing gown was in the master bathroom. Moving quickly, she went in there and fumbled in the pocket. Bingo.

Stale air rushed out of the study to greet her. Dark wood, antique desk, bookshelf and wardrobe, a thick rug, the sensation of dust in her nostrils. She could feel Damien in the room, though by now he would be thousands of miles away. Frida cast around for the charger, but didn't see it. Her eyes fell on

Damien's computer. She hesitated, then moved slowly behind his desk. She was filled with curious apprehension, as though someone might come in there at any moment and catch her. As though she had no right to be there. And maybe she didn't. After all, this was Damien's private space, the one to which he retreated when he wanted to get away.

From her.

She stopped, astonished at how easily the thought had articulated itself.

That was precisely it. He locked himself up in his study in order to get away from her and from their marriage.

What did he do in here?

Thoughts, questions, rushing towards her at breakneck speed. She swirled around in the chair. As she did, she noticed the antique wardrobe in the corner. It was a part of Damien's office ensemble that he insisted on taking with him wherever they went.

For the first time ever, she saw that the door was ajar.

There was a key in the lock, but the door was open.

She stared at it, unmoving. There was something repellent about that wardrobe, like an invisible barrier between her and it. She recognized now that it had always been there. Another thing that she had blindly accepted, without question.

She stood up and slowly put her arm out, touching the door with the tips of her fingers. She swung it open.

Then she stood perfectly still.

Pasted on the inside of one door were pictures of women, cut out of fashion magazines. Inside the wardrobe there were women's clothes.

She frowned, taking in the contents.

Dresses on hangers. Three of them.

One: fire engine red, form fitting, long, gathered up one side.

Two: emerald green, long, decorated with sequins, a slit up the side.

Three: a little black cocktail dress.

Lingerie.

A red satin teddy with black lace trim.

A sheer black mesh teddy with white and gold lace.

Three bras. Matching panties, slung over hangers.

Two pairs of shoes: black patent leather pumps and sling-backed stilettos made of red satin. Both very large.

A wooden box. A plastic bag filled with something.

A full-length mirror on the inside of the other door.

Frida had no idea how long she stood there, a strange mixture of horror and hilarity gathering inside her. It was like being in a bad movie, with a bizarre set and gaudy props. She felt like crazy Vaudeville music should be starting up behind her.

Cautiously she lifted the lid of the box that was on the floor of the wardrobe. It contained shiny things. Jewelry.

Lying at the top of the pile was an earring exactly like the one she had found on the floor nearly two months before.

Slowly she replaced the lid.

Next she carefully removed the plastic bag next to the box. Perching on the chair, she opened it and looked inside.

Her breath caught in her throat as she stared in disbelief.

It couldn't be. *It could not be.*

Those were her clothes. *Hers.* That she had donated to the Salvation Army, at least two years earlier.

Two blouses and a skirt. A low-cut red wraparound dress and a lace camisole.

Damien had taken them for her. He'd had some things that he needed to get rid of as well, or so he had said.

So he had said.

Her mind was working overtime, struggling to compute the connections she was now making. *Yes*, she thought. *Yes. Yes. Yes.* It all made sense. It made so, so much sense.

There was nothing wrong with her even if her husband didn't want her, even if he spent hours locked in his study every evening.

Her husband wanted something else.

He wanted to dress in women's clothes.

He wanted to dress in women's clothes and masturbate behind closed doors.

He liked to dress …

she stopped, almost unable to finish the thought.

… he liked to dress in *her* clothes.

She leaned back in the chair and put her hand to her forehead. She laughed, incredulously. Then she stopped. Then she laughed again.

Thoughts raced through her mind, colliding and crashing, some stopping dead in the midst of mayhem to formulate a coherent idea.

That earring, it was not to do with his infidelity.

Unless this counted as infidelity.

Did it?

All that lingerie he had bought for her – he had really been buying it for himself, hadn't he?

She sifted through her mind for any information related to cross-dressing. She remembered reading that men who liked to cross-dress weren't always gay. That they could actually have normal sexual relations with women.

That was about the extent of her knowledge.

Something in the furthest corner the wardrobe caught her eye. She stood again and pushed one of the dresses aside. A metallic box. She lifted the lid. It was filled with makeup. Foundation, several lipsticks, rouge, eye shadow, mascara. The bottom lifted up, and underneath Frida found a cut-off nylon stocking. Reaching further, she fumbled in the space next to the box and found a wig.

Standing there, holding a fake head of hair in her hand, Frida suddenly experienced the most intense feeling of release. It was like a huge, dark cloud was being lifted from her, and she could finally see. That intangible *something* that had stood between her and Damien, that had made him so indifferent to her. His obsessive need for control. His daily withdrawals. His objectification of her. None of it had anything to do with her, and everything to do with him. It was all about *his* shame, and here it was. Stuffed away inside this wardrobe.

And yet ... something did not quite compute.

Only then did she look again at the pictures that were pasted on the inside of the wardrobe door. In the midst of making the discovery she had noticed only peripherally that there was something very strange about them.

All of them showed the women's bodies only. Without their heads.

Whoever had cut the pictures from the magazines had cut off the heads at the neck.

A feeling of dread welled up in her.

She glanced up. At the top of the wardrobe there was a shelf, and on that shelf there was something shiny, like a box. She put her hand up now and touched it. No – it was not a box, but a large binder. She took hold of it and pulled it down, placing it on the desk. She opened it apprehensively. It was filled with plastic A4 envelopes, which in turn were filled with the same types of pictures as were pasted on the inside of the wardrobe.

Women in stylish clothes with their heads cut off.

She stood up abruptly and walked out into the hall, breathing rapidly, as though the study had suddenly become devoid of air. There she stopped, then went back inside, taking one more look at the evidence laid so blatantly before her, as if needing to satisfy herself that it was really and truly there, that it wasn't just a dream.

She stood there for several minutes, feeling a strange sense of anger and empowerment gathering inside of her. Then she went downstairs and got her camera.

~~

The week passed in a haze. The discovery in Damien's study came and went in Frida's awareness; sometimes it was like it had been obliterated from her consciousness, and she would be thinking of Damien like she always had in the past ... but then she'd suddenly realize that everything about that past had changed.

She went for long walks, hands tucked deep into the pockets of her parka, so immersed in her own thoughts that she barely noticed the people who would pass by her and utter casual greetings. Her own contrived worldview, which she had once considered so solid, had shattered, and now she was picking up the fragments and piecing them together into an entirely new reality. It was exhausting, yet also liberating, and with each new piece put into place she felt stronger and more grounded. She noticed it the very next day. When she went to the shop to buy a new laptop charger she looked the clerk right in the eye with a new kind of strength – the strength that comes from no longer denying the truth.

Caught up as she was in her own inner refurbishment, she had only a vague sense of what was happening in the society around her. Still, she did grasp that the whole banking thing showed no signs of abating; on the contrary, it was turning into more of a mess than anyone had been expecting. She got a sick feeling in her gut at the sight of Prime Minister Geir Haarde on the news, looking sallow and haggard, claiming everything was under control. It was like her bullshit meter had been activated and was running on overtime to make up for all the years in which it had been dormant. He was lying. She was sure of it.

On Monday morning, almost a week after she had returned from the West Fjords, she woke up feeling like hell. She had slept late – it was ten-thirty am, and she was normally out of bed by nine. She felt like she was coming down with something and attributed it to the strain of the last few days. They had clearly taken their toll.

Downstairs in the kitchen she found Kristín leaning against the counter and speaking into her cellphone. As soon as Kristín saw her, she said something to the person on the other end and flicked off her phone.

"You didn't have to finish on my account," Frida said, heading for the fridge.

Kristín was a petite woman who looked younger than her sixty-three years. She had an efficient manner and a kind face, and Frida often found herself comparing her to Mrs. Kelly and being grateful for the pronounced difference between them. Kristín did not have a hint of that perpetual sullenness that enveloped Mrs. Kelly like a haze. She was pleasant and straightforward, and carried herself with quiet dignity. Frida sometimes thought about the cultural difference – in Iceland there was a decided absence of the servant-master dichotomy that underpinned so many relationships back in the UK. To her, she and Kristín were equals, even as they acted out different roles in relation to one another. It seemed to her that this was Kristín's understanding as well, and it gave her comfort.

"I was finished," Kristín said. "It was just my daughter, needing to talk. These are strange times."

"Is there anything new?" Frida said, opening the refrigerator and looking in. She had little appetite, and examined its contents more out of habit than hunger.

"Geir Haarde has announced that he'll address the nation today at four o'clock."

Frida shut the refrigerator door.

"Oh?" she said.

One look at Kristín and she knew that this did not bode well.

"What's it about?" she asked, concern creeping into her voice.

Kristín shook her head. "I don't know. None of us do. Well, except the people who have been rushing in and out of the ministerial meeting place all weekend. The bank owners and their crew. Members of the cabinet. Labor union leaders. People like that. They clearly know something that the rest of us don't."

"Do you think the other banks will collapse?"

"I think that's what everyone is afraid of."

Frida shifted her weight, suddenly anxious.

"What happens if they do?"

"I have no idea. I hope we find out later today." Kristín hesitated. "Does your husband ... does he have any information?"

Frida quickly looked away to hide her discomfort, not wanting to admit that she and Damien had barely spoken since her return.

"He hasn't told me anything," she said, her voice sounding just a little bit insincere. Still, it wasn't a lie.

Kristín nodded. "This uncertainty is the worst. Some people say the country could go bankrupt."

"Bankrupt?"

"That's what some people are saying."

"My God." She paused. "What happens if a country goes bankrupt?"

"I don't know. I'm most afraid that everything will stop. That the wheels of the economy will stop turning. If things grind to a halt – no one spends, businesses start going bankrupt, and the whole social infrastructure comes crashing down." She paused, then added with a buoyancy that she did not seem to feel: "But maybe we'll be all right. We'll see what Geir says this afternoon."

Frida waited anxiously for the broadcast to begin at four. She could not recall the prime minister ever making a TV address like this, where he summoned the entire nation, apart from the annual new year's address. It had to be serious.

At five minutes to four she was seated on the sofa in front of the TV. No doubt most of the nation was in front of one screen or another, she thought, waiting for the broadcast that she expected would determine the country's fate. Involuntarily, she thought of Baldur. Was he also in front of a screen now? Was he scared and anxious like her – or did he know exactly what Geir was going to say?

And what about Damien? How much did he know?

It struck her that she had thought of Baldur first, as though her bond was first and foremost with him, not with Damien. Was it because he was an Icelander – someone whose loyalties were to this land, someone who was kin?

And if her country was in trouble, serious trouble, would she be able to pack up and leave? It would be easy to do. Just pack her things into a few boxes and hightail it out of here to the safety of a country with a stable economy that was not in danger of going *bankrupt*.

It was just too crazy to comprehend.

She felt her heart swell with love for her country. No. If Iceland really and truly was in crisis, it would *not* be easy to leave. She belonged here. It was her home.

Geir Haarde was on the screen before her, looking grave, his skin pasty. "*Góđir Íslendingar*" – he began, "Good Icelanders. I have requested an opportunity to address you at this time, as the Icelandic nation is facing great difficulties. The world is currently a experiencing a serious financial crisis, so serious that its effect on the global banking system is catastrophic …"

Frida listened, her eyes glued to the screen. The Icelandic banks had not been exempt from this predicament, Geir was saying, and their situation was now very serious. They had expanded rapidly and were now many times larger than the national economy. A bailout was out of the question: "There is a real danger, good Icelanders, that the Icelandic economy would, if all took a turn for the worse, be sucked into a whirlpool along with the banks, and the result would be national bankruptcy."

There it was. That word. But what did that mean, really?

Apocalyptic images flashed through her mind: decaying buildings, people in rags, crying children, desolation, despair, hopelessness.

Now Geir seemed to be outlining some sort of plan to help save what could be saved, some sort of emergency law that would allow the government to go into the banks and take them over. And then what? What about the people, their savings, the normal functioning of society? What about the schools, the hospitals; what about imports: food, gas, medical supplies? What about people's jobs?

Why the fuck can't he talk about the things that matter?

The intensity of her feelings surprised her. She stared hard at the TV screen, as though she wanted to penetrate through Geir Haarde's skull, through to his thoughts, to see if he was really telling the truth, to see what he was really thinking.

"God bless Iceland."

The broadcast ended. Those last words hung in the air. *God bless Iceland.* Well, what the fuck was that supposed to mean? Angrily she flicked off the television and threw the remote control to one side. She got to her feet and walked into the next room, then back again. A film started playing in her head. She could see it now. Things would start running out in the shops. Fresh fruit and vegetables would go first. Then other food. People would start hoarding. In fact, they had probably started already. Soon the petrol would be gone, so no cars could drive. Things would start to break down, and no parts would be available to fix things. People would leave in droves. She and Damien would go back to the UK. Their money was safe – silently she thanked her stars for having transferred the proceeds from the sale of her mother's flat out of Iceland a decade before. She had wanted to move it into that Icelandic bank they'd opened up in the UK – Icesave, they called it. It was an online venture, and despite existing only in cyberspace it had been a tremendous success. Iceland's very own Landsbanki had stormed onto the UK market by offering the highest rates of interest at any given time. Their marketing campaign had consisted of idyllic pictures of the pure, pristine Icelandic landscapes, and regularly there had been reports in the news of all the millions of pounds that were pouring in. Frida had been filled with patriotic pride and had been *this close* to transferring her savings into it, but Damien had stopped her. He wasn't buying the hype – those high interest rates came at a price, he said, and the price was higher risk. She'd been indignant; these were her countrymen, how dare he suggest that they did not abide by the highest standards. Icesave was a branch of Landsbanki, after all, and Landsbanki had been around since the 1800s. Indeed, it been Iceland's central bank until the mid-twentieth century. A more solid banking institution was scarcely found in Europe. Damien reminded her that the bank had been privatized since then, and the owners were dubious – there was some talk about their ties to the Russian mafia, and one of them had been convicted in Iceland for fraud. "I don't know why the Icelandic government would consent to sell to such shady characters," Damien had remarked, at which Frida had ended the conversation, deeply offended. In the end, she had decided to do a bit more research, but other things had got in the way, and eventually she had forgotten about it.

Her cellphone rang, and she jumped. Scooping up the phone, she saw that it was Damien. Her heart started pounding. They hadn't spoken since their last grisly encounter, and all that she now knew about him ... could she keep it together enough to seem normal?

"Hello Damien."

Yes, she could. Her voice was steady and clear. Years of rehearsal in saying the right thing had delivered results.

"Hello my dear. How are you?"

My dear. She felt sick. "I've been better."

"Did you see Haarde's address?"

She could hear people in the background. He wasn't alone.

"Of course."

"And what did you think?"

"I don't really know what to think."

"We had an interpreter here."

There was a brief silence, in which Frida registered his reproach.

"Oh. Good that you were able to find someone," she said, keeping her voice even. "So what did *you* think?"

"He skirted the real issues very nicely."

"You think there are things that he's not saying?"

"Oh, of course. He was being deliberately vague. Surely you noticed that."

That old derision again.

"Of course I noticed that," she said, annoyed by the irritability in her own voice.

"There was one thing we weren't quite clear about, though," he continued after a brief pause. "Did he say anything about the government stepping in to guarantee deposits?"

"He said that deposits were safe."

"Did he mention anything about foreign accounts?"

"I don't think so. Why?"

"It's important for us to know."

Ah. So he had an ulterior motive for this phone call. He wasn't just calling to see how she was. But then again, she should have known that.

"Didn't the interpreter say?" she asked with deliberate sweetness in her voice.

"No. She wasn't clear. And we wanted to double check. I have to go now, my dear. I fly in on the afternoon flight tomorrow."

Frida ended the call and tossed the phone receiver onto the sofa like it was toxic.

He was coming back tomorrow. And everything had changed. Everything.

She felt pressure building inside of her. Their marriage had been a lie. *His* lie. She had been young and pliable and without family, and she had provided him with the perfect smokescreen to hide behind. And his intention was to break her – that was surely what the episode in the bedroom had been about. He was asserting his power over her.

She considered her options. She could move to a hotel. The problem was that she would have to square payment for that with Damien, and that couldn't be done without her first announcing her intention to leave him permanently. She had her own money, but it was tied up in that bank account in the UK, and anyway, she would need it all for when she moved out and got her own place. Hotels in Iceland were astronomically expensive, and her money would be quick to burn up if she had that sort of arrangement for any length of time.

She could go back to the village, ask Egill if she could stay in the house longer. But that would mean being close to Baldur and his ... situation, and in any case, the thought of staying on the West Fjords in the dead of winter, potentially isolated and with no clear purpose, was not appealing. No, it was not an option.

Her best course of action now was probably to tell Damien in no uncertain terms to stay out of their bedroom. If he didn't agree, she was not above resorting to threats.

Her camera now contained all sorts of compromising information.

Meanwhile, she'd continue to work out the best way to walk away from him and this farce of a marriage.

A sound made her freeze. It sounded like the side door opening, the one downstairs. She stood perfectly still. Someone was coming up the stairs, then into the kitchen. There was the sound of movement, then of something clunky being put on the counter.

Frida went to the swinging door that led from the dining room into the kitchen and pushed it open.

It was Kristín, dressed in a thick wool coat. She looked alarmed.

"Oh, I'm so sorry to disturb you – I thought you'd be out. I meant to bring these this morning. It's the flower vases – we used them for the cocktail party at the embassy the week before last."

"You didn't have to bring them – there was no rush."

Her voice sounded distant. Kristín looked concerned.

"Are you all right?"

Frida opened her mouth to say yes, I am fine, everything is fine, but suddenly she felt dizzy. She put out a hand to steady herself.

Kristín came to her. "Are you all right?" she repeated, looking intently at Frida's face and taking hold of her arm.

"I'm fine. I just feel a little dizzy."

"Here. Come sit down."

Frida was already on her way to a chair.

"I'm sorry," she said, struggling to keep her voice normal. "I don't know what's wrong with me."

I don't know what's wrong with me. The words sounded hollow, and she wondered if Kristín would notice. She had a hunch about what might be wrong with her, but she also knew it was a bit too soon to tell. And anyway, it could be the other thing, too. The same thing that had caused her to faint before.

Kristín went to the sink and poured her a glass of water. "Have you been feeling sick?"

"A little under the weather maybe, that's all."

"Maybe you should see a doctor." Kristín perched on a chair opposite her, still wearing her coat. Frida felt her eyes on her. "I heard about your fainting spell," she said pointedly.

"Oh, that," Frida said, waving her hand dismissively. The last thing she wanted was for Kristín to feel sorry for her. "I saw a doctor about that."

"And what did the doctor say?"

Frida hesitated before answering. "Stress, he thinks."

"And what do you think?"

Frida looked up. It was one of the things she loved about being home – the frankness of the Icelanders. She knew there was no lying to Kristín. She'd know.

"I have a lot on my mind," she said.

"Have you spoken to anyone about that?"

Kristín's voice was calm yet insistent.

Frida hesitated, then shook her head.

"Maybe you should."

"Yes. You're probably right."

"I mean it. You really should."

"Yes."

There was an awkward pause. Then Frida spoke. "Tell me: what's your take on all this? Everything that's happening now, I mean. With the economy, and with what Geir Haarde said?"

Kristín's expression grew dim. "It's not good. My son believes we'll have to go crawling to the International Monetary Fund. He says we should have done so already. We'll wind up in massive debt, and who knows what consequences that will have. But we'll survive; that's what we Icelanders do. We are survivors. They're calling this a disaster, a catastrophe, but it's nothing like what this country has seen in the past. Volcanoes, earthquakes, famine, disease. Sure, some money has been lost, but no one has died. No one's home has been destroyed. We still have energy in the ground, we can heat our homes, we can grow vegetables, and we can fish. We'll be OK."

"I hope you're right," Frida said, sounding less convinced than she wanted to.

"And as for you … well, you can always leave. Your husband has a home and a job in another country. You have nothing keeping you here, do you?"

"Maybe not. But my roots are here. I love this country."

"Of course."

"And I want to stay here if I can."

Their eyes met, and she knew that Kristín understood.

"When does your husband return?"

"Tomorrow."

Kristín reached out and touched her arm, giving her a reassuring smile.

"It will all turn out well. You'll see."

Frida nodded again. Kristín had no idea ... but how comforting it was to have someone look at her and actually see her.

"Thank you," she said.

~~

Damien's return was the first thing on Frida's mind when she woke up. Her limbs felt heavy, almost as though there was a great weight pressing down on her. She lay motionless in bed with the covers pulled up around her neck, and stared up at the ceiling. A tiny crack had begun to form in one corner. She wondered how long or how wide it needed to get before the ceiling fell down.

Damien had not asked Frida to come to the airport to greet him, and she had not offered. The embassy driver would pick him up.

In her mind she had gone through the scenario of their meeting a few dozen times: how she would behave, what they would say, how she would set her boundaries, and ultimately how she would confront him with the knowledge that she now possessed.

By five o'clock she was sitting stiffly in the living room, awaiting his arrival. His plane had got in at four, and it took about an hour to drive into Reykjavík from the airport.

By six, he still wasn't there.

She got up and went into the kitchen to start chopping some vegetables for dinner. Movement was good; it helped to tame her anxiety.

At around six-thirty she heard the front door open and close.

"Hello!"

Wiping her hands on her apron, she glanced at her reflection in the window. She hoped her nervousness would not show.

He was in the front hall, hanging up his coat.

"Hello Frida my dear," he said with an inscrutable smile. "Goodness, what a situation we have on our hands."

Oh, indeed.

He came towards her, looked into her face, took hold of her arms with his hands and kissed her once on each cheek.

She looked into his eyes. He avoided hers.

"I'm making a curry for dinner," she said.

"Splendid."

"I was expecting you a bit sooner."

"I went straight to the embassy. It's been one hell of a day. I'm just here to change, I have to go back." His voice trailed off as he vanished up the stairs.

A few minutes later he joined Frida in the kitchen. He had taken off his jacket and tie. For Damien, that was casual.

She turned to him. "So you have to go back to work?"

She hated how artificial her voice sounded. Why couldn't she just say what she wanted to say: *We need to talk.*

"I do," he said. "I'm sure you know that Landsbanki went into receivership today."

"No, I did not know that." So another bank had gone bankrupt. *Just like he said.*

"Don't you follow the news?"

She turned her back to him and clenched her fists, fighting the urge to lash out. There was a time, not too long ago, when she would have allowed that comment to shame her. But not any more.

"And as I'm also sure you know, the Icelandic banks are not

just confined to Iceland," Damien continued.

She breathed deeply, then turned around. *Stay cool.* "I assume you are talking about the online banks?"

"The online banks, and the physical banks. But it's the online banks that are the problem here. Icesave, more specifically."

"Icesave is operated in the UK ..."

"... Was. It's been closed now."

Frida had been on the verge of saying something else. Now she stopped, allowing the implications of this to sink in. Hundreds of thousands of people in the UK had deposited money into Icesave. Billions of pounds Sterling were tied up in those accounts. The stakes were huge.

"So what's going to happen to those people's savings?"

"When a bank collapses, it is up to the state deposit insurance fund to step in and compensate savers for at least a minimum amount."

"So the British insurance fund ..."

"No. The *Icelandic* insurance fund. Icesave is a branch. Just a regular branch of Landsbanki, no different than a branch in Akureyri, say. Or the west end of Reykjavík."

"Is that legal?"

"Yes," he said. "It's legal. Under the EEA agreement, any company can operate in any other EEA country. Our people have been nervous about this from the start. They've been trying to work out a solution to move Icesave into a subsidiary in the UK, rather than having it as a branch."

She shook her head, uncomprehending. "What's the difference?"

"A subsidiary means that it's like any other British company, subject to British law. As a branch it comes under the Icelandic jurisdiction, and the Icelandic depositors' insurance fund, which is designed for the three-hundred thousand or so people that live here, is not nearly big enough to cover the cost. It would be like pissing into the ocean."

"So it's ...."

"It's a fucking disaster, is what it is. And to make things worse, Alistair Darling had a conversation with your finance minister today. That fuckwit Mathiesen."

"And?"

"He wanted confirmation that the Icelandic authorities would cover the Icesave deposits in full, just like Haarde has promised to cover all Icelandic bank deposits in full."

"What did he say?"

"No."

"He said *no*?"

"Yes, he said no. He told Darling very bluntly that the Icelandic government would not be compensating depositors that were outside of Iceland. Darling reminded him that this was a breach of the EEA directive on deposits ..."

"Wait ... the what?"

"... The European Economic Area agreement stipulates that no member nation may discriminate against the citizens of another member nation. Which is clearly what's happening here. There's no difference between a Jón Jónsson in Akureyri and a John Johnson in London in this case, because Icesave is a branch. We have a country on the verge of going bankrupt, that can't possibly take on a debt like that. And it's our people who are out of pocket. Make no mistake, the British authorities will do everything they can do squeeze them into paying. Those Icelandic imbeciles had their chance to prevent this from happening, and they threw it away because they are incompetent morons."

"So why wouldn't they move those accounts into a subsidiary?"

"They claimed they couldn't fulfill the requirements – they needed to have what's called a liquidity deposit, of two hundred million pounds. But I think it was so they could just funnel the money over here without anyone getting in their way."

"To do what with it here?"

Damien shrugged. "The crooks that own Landsbanki used it to build that megalomaniacal concert hall down on the waterfront, buy themselves expensive toys, and probably stashed the rest away in tax havens. That's what I think."

His cellphone rang. He answered. "Lowe. Ah! Yes."

He left the room. Frida turned back to her pot on the stove, stirring absently. Damien came back a few minutes later, his expression grim. "I'm afraid I have to go. I'm sorry, my dear."

"Do you want to take some with you?"

“Well, yes, all right. If it’s ready.”

Frida scooped some stew into a bowl, feeling a mixture of relief and frustration. Part of her didn’t want the confrontation; part of her did. Part of her wanted to stay steeped in false comfort; another part wanted to break free. And all the while she knew she was living on borrowed time. There was no way this could be sustained.

When she went to bed that night, Damien still wasn’t home. She removed his dressing gown from the master bathroom and hung it on the door of the guest room. She took his toothbrush and other toiletries she knew he would use, and placed them in the bathroom out in the hall. Then she shut the door to their bedroom and locked the door.

CHAPTER NINE

On Wednesday, October 8, 2008, the United Kingdom invoked the Anti-Terrorism, Crime and Security Act 2001 against Iceland, placing the country and its Central Bank on a list of terrorist organizations.

That day, Frida awoke late. She had been in a deep sleep, filled with vibrant dreams in full-blown color, that nonetheless had an undercurrent of the macabre. She had been on her way to hospital, and was greeted there by an entourage of doctors, all lined up in a row, who bowed reverently as she exited her black limousine, the very epitome of glamour. Then she had been sitting in a cinema when suddenly the head of a woman appeared on the screen in front of her, disfigured and grotesque. A red stain began in one corner and spread quickly across the white of the screen, like blood, as the woman's face twisted into a soundless cry.

Her eyes flew open. It was already light, which at this time of the year meant that she had drastically overslept. She jerked her head to one side to look at the alarm clock. Ten-thirty.

The house was strangely quiet. Damien would be long gone by now. She had hardly seen him in the few days since he had been back. When they did meet, the talk was of the economic crisis, which was turning into a more monstrous predicament than anyone could have foreseen, although Damien was mostly mum on any details pertaining to his work. Secrecy was his particular forte, after all. She saw that now.

Frida went down to the kitchen and waited for Kristín to arrive. She needed to speak with her about what was going on with the crisis. Kristín had a point of view that eluded Frida from within the stifling world of the ambassador's spouse. Kristín knew what the real victims of this catastrophe were doing and saying and thinking, and those were the things that were important to Frida.

The clock ticked, yet Kristín did not come. Frida was surprised, and then a little worried: Kristín always came at eleven, and she was never more than a few minutes late. Could something be wrong?

At noon, Frida rang the embassy. Had anyone heard from Kristín?

The receptionist, Íris, sounded a little frantic.

"Yes, she rang this morning to say that she won't be in today. I'm so sorry, I should have let you know. It's just that … the phone hasn't stopped. We're having problems coping. People are really angry. We've just called the police … oh good, they've just arrived. I expect they'll watch the residence too, so don't be surprised."

"What are you talking about?" Frida was confused.

"The anti-terrorist legislation. The British government put Iceland on a list of terrorist organizations this morning. There's been a huge reaction. People are outraged."

"*What?*"

"They're doing it to freeze the assets of Landsbanki, and also the Central Bank. We're on a blacklist now, with a bunch of other terrorists. Like Al-Qaeda."

"Can you put me through to my husband, please?"

"I'm sorry, Damien has gone to a meeting at the Foreign Ministry."

Frida ended the call and went straight to fetch her laptop. She logged on to one Icelandic media outlet after another.

UK invokes terrorism laws against Iceland.

Iceland on list of terrorist organizations in UK.

Blacklisted!

What was happening? Iceland and Britain were NATO allies; they were *friendly* nations. She stood up and paced. This was insane. Either the British were reacting out of panic, or there was something going on about which normal people had no idea.

She picked up her phone and called Damien's mobile. It rang until his voice mail came on. She hung up without leaving a message.

She tried calling him regularly throughout the day, but to no avail. She felt exasperated, then infuriated. At one time, he would have called her back the moment he saw her number. Now, not so much.

He finally arrived home at around seven pm, looking disheveled, his tie loose and askew.

"What's going on, Damien?"

She stood in the middle of the living room floor, hands on her hips.

"Oh, Christ. Not you, too."

"What?"

"Every single Icelander I've met today has been going ballistic over this."

"Well, do you blame them? On a list of terrorist organizations, Damien? *Really*?"

"Oh for fuck's sake! *Yes*, on a list of terrorist organizations, because that is the only sodding way they could stop massive transfer of funds out of England. Those fucking geniuses behind fucking Icesave were draining whatever funds were left out of the bank. Meanwhile, our people can't even access their money. Because their money is on its fucking way to Iceland. What were we going to do? Just let them get on with it?"

She threw up her hands, startled. Damien wasn't used to losing his cool in this way.

"Ok," she said. "Calm down."

He sank into an armchair and covered his face with his hands.

"Everything is coming undone," he said. "It's all going straight to hell."

~~

The country was in a state of chaos. Icelanders who had fallen asleep in one reality woke up in another.

By the end of that same week, Iceland's three commercial

banks, which combined were worth twelve times the size of its economy, had collapsed.

The currency, the Icelandic krona, had become worthless outside of Iceland.

The Icelandic government had shut down all financial transactions in and out of the country, to protect what remained of the currency.

Shop owners who had ordered goods from abroad were unable to pay their suppliers.

Icelanders travelling in foreign countries were unable to receive money from home.

Students studying overseas suddenly saw their student loans devalue by more than half and could not cover basic living expenses. Neither could they receive money from home.

Employers all over Iceland served their employees the compulsory three-month termination notices, since none of them knew whether they would be in business in three months' time.

There were wage cuts in every sector.

The construction industry collapsed.

No one knew how long food would remain in the shops.

Or how long petrol would remain at the pumps.

Unemployment skyrocketed.

Tens of thousands of people who had taken loans or mortgages in foreign currencies saw their debts triple or quadruple.

People who had invested their savings in stocks and bonds saw them vanish.

Thousands of households faced imminent bankruptcy and foreclosure.

The government was derided for incompetence and a lack of transparency.

Suspicions of widespread corruption began to surface, and shock gradually transformed into outrage.

~~

Much to Frida's relief, Kristín only missed three days of work before returning. Yet on her first day back, she was visibly haggard, her face etched with worry.

"My husband's company laid off all its twenty-five employees yesterday," she informed Frida without due prompting, just as Frida came into the room.

"Oh. That's terrible." It was impossible to miss the anger in Kristín's voice. No doubt she was as outraged as the tens of thousands of other Icelanders who had signed an online petition denouncing UK chancellor Gordon Brown for his actions. "Where does he work?"

"For a small software company. They've laid everyone off as a precautionary measure because they have to give them three months' notice. In three months' time they might no longer be in operation." She paused and added with what sounded like forced optimism: "If they are, though, I guess they'll hire people back."

"I'm sorry to hear that," Frida said, feeling sickeningly privileged all of a sudden.

Kristín shrugged. "We'll be OK," she said unconvincingly. "We're old enough to take it. I'm worried about my son, though. He has currency basket loans on both his house and car."

"Currency basket?" Frida asked, puzzled.

Kristín straightened up and squared her shoulders. "Currency basket loans. The banks have been pushing them for years."

Frida recalled having read something about them, but she hadn't paid much attention. "What are they, exactly?"

"It's when you borrow in a currency that's not your own. Interest rates have been ridiculously high here because the geniuses who were running this country were trying to cool down the economy. So they just raised interest rates higher and higher, until normal people started looking for alternatives. And the godforsaken banks were all too happy to meet that need and started offering loans in foreign currencies. You could basically pick and choose your own combination, say forty percent Swiss Francs, thirty percent Yen, thirty percent Euro, and that was your loan. You put your currency selection into a basket. Cute little term, right?"

Frida frowned. "But isn't that a bit risky? To be paying for a loan in a currency that is different from the one in which you get your salary?"

"Sure. Everyone knew there was a risk involved – that is, if the krona weakened the loan would increase correspondingly, but also if the krona strengthened, then the loan would decrease. But we're used to those kinds of fluctuations here. My son has an MBA and he was really careful, considered the situation from all sides. He figured the risk was minimal. That's what his bank told him, too. So both he and his sister went ahead and took these loans. No one expected the currency to totally collapse. Now both of them are looking at their loans tripling, at the very least. If nothing changes, my son will lose his house. He can't afford to triple his mortgage premiums even if he's working – and there's no guarantee that he will be. Even if he does manage to keep his job, his salary will be cut by at least thirty percent. It's a given. It's happening everywhere, in every sector. Meanwhile, all the prices are going up because the krona has devalued by about half."

Frida stood and listened to Kristín ramble on about the economic situation, the political landscape, about all the things that were surfacing that no one had known about or realized the extent of. Corruption, cronyism, nepotism, incompetence ... it seemed that Icelandic society was suddenly rife with shadows and dark corners that no one had seen, or had wanted to see, before. Families and cliques that had held all the cards, politicians who had installed their people in the high offices of society and had gradually infiltrated all the positions of power, including the judiciary, the political sector, the media, and the banks. Oligarchs, they were calling them. Just like in Russia.

And now that the veil had been torn from the eyes of the people the anger was rising, though it seemed to Frida that it was both unfocused and random. Outdoor protests had been called but no one really knew what the protesters' demands were or should be. There was a wave of anger towards the former prime minister that was now the central bank director, and which many people viewed as having created the conditions that had led to the meltdown of the economy. There was also a whole lot of hatred towards Britain for their "terrorist" actions. Both the embassy and the residence had been pelted with eggs, and Frida was permanently on edge. She slept badly and had fitful dreams of people storming her house with torches, attempting to set it on fire.

Frida had decided – probably against her own best interests, she knew – to hold off on confronting Damien with their personal issues until the worst had blown over. With all the upheaval and uncertainty sweeping the country, she just couldn't face it. Yet it occupied her mind, and twice she had slipped into his office, feeling furtive as before, and checked to see if the wardrobe was still open. It wasn't. It had been firmly locked, and even one attempt to scout around for the key bore no result. She didn't know what she would do if she found it, or indeed why she was in there at all, creeping around that stupid wardrobe. After all, their issues were far greater and deeper than just Damien's fetish. If that was the name for it.

On a Monday in late October, Kristín told Frida that she had gone, along with her husband and daughter, to a demonstration that past weekend.

"We need those incompetent buffoons who run our country to show some accountability and get out of office. They need to resign. People are finally breaking through the denial in which we've all been living, and starting to demand change," Kristín told her fervently.

"And if they do, who will take over?"

"We need new people in power. Fresh people. Everything has collapsed – and that means we can rebuild. And I'm talking from the ground up. Reconstructing everything. Not just raising the same old power blocks and systems as before. The old guard, the Independence Party and all their ilk, with their cronyism and sick corruption, needs to get the hell out. Those people have brought this country down – and now they want to be the ones to rebuild it. They want to stay in power so they can continue to skim the cream off the top. Well, I don't think so. That's why we need to take to the streets and make ourselves heard."

After Kristín left, Frida sat for a while, reflecting on everything that Kristín had told her. It seemed so implausible. All those things that had been going on right in front of everyone. Why hadn't anyone said or done anything? Could it be that Kristín had it all wrong?

She went to her laptop, which had increasingly become her lifeline to the outside world, and typed in a search for "protests". A whole range of pages opened up. Slowly, she started reading, following one link after another, amazed by what was opening up before her. Blogs, news reports, online editorials. Yes, it was all as Kristín had said, and much worse. The dregs and grime of Icelandic society were being exposed, and the people had decided they would not take it any more.

The past would be cleared away. Once the lies had been exposed and the truth was known. Only then would there be an opportunity to rebuild.

There was power in the fury.

~~

The tension in Icelandic society mounted in tandem with the social chaos. Regular demonstrations were now held in the square in front of the parliament buildings every Saturday afternoon at three pm. They were becoming more structured and organized, with clear objectives and increasing participation. The demonstrators had four specific demands: the resignation of the board of the Central Bank, the resignation of the board of the Financial Supervision Authority, the resignation of the government, and new elections.

The government effectively ignored the demonstrations. Their position was clear: they were in the midst of "rescue operations", they were "putting out fires", and those pesky anarchists needed to pipe down, stat, and let them get on with their work. Unfortunately, the nature of that work remained unclear. Transparency was nil. The government worked behind closed doors and stonewalled anyone attempting to shed light on the situation. This evident absence of accountability and remorse was like throwing gas on the fire when it came to the demonstrations. With each passing Saturday the number of demonstrators grew as speakers made rousing speeches from a mobile stage. People flocked to parliament square to rail against impunity and demand accountability. Respect for the institution of government had gone the way of the dodo, and each demonstration saw the parliament building pelted with eggs, *skyr* – an Icelandic dairy product, and rolls of toilet paper.

Frida heard sounds emanating from the square each Saturday as she paced around the house, wanting to go down there but being afraid to, torn between self-censorship and her own fervent emotions. Come evening she would soak up all reports of the demonstrations from the news, and the following Monday she would pump Kristín – who had attended every single demonstration so far.

"Why don't you go down there and see for yourself?" Kristín said one morning in mid-November, as Frida proceeded to cross-examine her about the events of that past Saturday.

Frida was taken aback. Then she mumbled something incoherent about being an ambassador's wife, and turned away.

When Kristín had gone, she sat motionless in a chair and allowed the question to penetrate. Why *didn't* she go down there and see for herself? Her propensity for self-censorship alarmed her. It was Damien's disapproval she was frightened of, she knew. His disapproval had become indistinguishable from her own will. Yet she also knew that it was up to her to break free. Clichéd as it sounded, it was her life.

Thus it was with trepidation that she headed out just before three pm the following Saturday.

People were already pouring towards parliament square as she drew near, and she allowed herself to be moved along with the crowd. Near the back of the square she stopped, furthest from the stage, where she was least likely to attract attention – though exactly whose attention she didn't know. A man was giving a heated speech on the stage, which was frequently interspersed with shouts and applause from the crowd. Frida moved closer, hoping to hear better. Many people were assembled there, of all ages and from every social stratum, and almost everyone was focused on what was being said on the stage. No one took any notice of her. She moved past well-dressed elderly couples, parents with children on their shoulders, young people holding picket signs, a disabled man in a wheelchair, a couple of adolescents with scarves tied over their faces who were in the process of climbing a statue in the center of the square. She guessed there had to be a few thousand people there.

Just past the statue, she stopped. A young woman had started speaking now. "Our politicians have launched an attack on the fundamental values that our nation's constitution seeks to protect. They have declared war on the people of this country!" she cried, and the crowd applauded and whooped. Frida applauded, too. Her heart beat hard and fast. Standing there, she felt her entire body fill with intense emotion and tears well up in her eyes. She applauded, and felt the thrill and power of every new statement that her instinct recognized as truth. This was it. This was where she belonged. These were her people. She would stand and fight for justice, with them.

The speeches finished and the crowd began to dissipate. Frida wandered slowly back the way she had come. All around her, there was a passionate sense of anarchy, yet also an infectious feeling of hope. It was like everyone saw a new dawn coming. A new Iceland.

Out of the corner of one eye, Frida caught sight of a familiar shape. Tall, lanky, with an easy stride. Instantly her stomach clenched. Putting her head down, she glanced in that direction. No. It was only a stranger. Relief and disappointment collided inside of her.

Suddenly the square felt intensely claustrophobic. She pushed through the crowd and was soon out of the throng. At Tjörnin, she turned right, past city hall, then up along Tjarnargata, feeling better when she was on the other side of the lake.

She turned left and passed over the bridge on Skothúsvegur. From there she could see the embassy at the top of the hill. The light was on in Damien's office. These days he worked incessantly, seventeen-hour days, stopping only to come home for the occasional meal. He was irritable and prickly, and when they talked it was mostly superficial chatter about relations with Icelandic officials, whom Damien considered to be idiots.

As she headed towards the embassy, she saw the light being switched off. Damien was probably on his way home. Almost involuntarily she slowed down, but it was too late – just as she reached the corner she saw him come out of the embassy building.

They had slipped back into the sort of tacit agreement they'd had before – to keep up appearances and pretend. He had not attempted to enter their bedroom after that ugly incident a few weeks earlier. And in any case it was easy to justify him sleeping in the guest room every night given his crazy work situation and hours.

"Hello my dear. Out taking photographs?" he said glibly as

he reached her, giving her a peck on the cheek.

Frida took a deep breath. "I was at the demonstration."

"What demonstration?"

She despised that tone in his voice, that contrived ignorance. He knew damn well that there had been a demonstration – it was impossible *not* to know.

"There was a demonstration today in front of the parliament buildings. Like there has been every Saturday for the past month."

"Oh, that. You mean that bunch of Chavs who get together and throw eggs and toilet paper at the parliament building."

"People need an outlet for their anger."

"Showing up every Saturday to degrade the parliament buildings just to vent their frustrations is completely juvenile and isn't going to change a damn thing. From what I understand they want Davíd Oddsson's head on a stick. Well, everybody needs a villain. If they had any sense they'd be clamoring for the heads of the bankers. Why aren't they going after them? They're the real villains."

"Probably because they've left the country."

They had stepped inside the house. Damien closed the front door behind them. He turned to her with a steely expression in his eyes.

"Be that as it may, I don't find it appropriate for you to be attending demonstrations."

She was incredulous. "I beg your pardon?"

"You are an ambassador's wife, Frida. *My* wife."

"Excuse me, Damien, but I am also a person. I am a citizen of this country."

"I understand that, but it is not your place to participate in political demonstrations."

"Yeah, well, *fuck my place!*"

His mouth curved into a sneer. "Ah. I see. You're just a child too, just like everyone else down there."

"A child?" Her voice was shrill and she was losing control; she hated herself for it, but couldn't stop. "Is it childish to care about your country? To care what is happening outside of your dry, emotionally barren world? Why can't you acknowledge that people are flesh and blood – that *we* are flesh and blood? Why does it have to be about the fucking job *every goddamn time*?"

He looked at her with a haughty, contemptuous smile for a second longer, then turned and left.

She felt sick. At the rear of the vestibule was the guest WC. Nausea welled up and she bolted for the toilet, just managing to lift the seat before she threw up. Dizzy, she straightened her back, turned around and looked at herself in the mirror.

You, who are so concerned with truth. Why won't you acknowledge this?

She shook her head minutely. Then she leaned down and rinsed her face with cold water, turned off the light and went into the living room. Damien was sitting stiffly in an armchair, reading – or pretending to. He looked up at her, and apart from the slightly ashen look on his face there was nothing to suggest that they had been arguing. He was still the master of charades.

"I told Bill and Amy that we would have dinner with them at the Lobster House at eight," he said matter-of-factly.

"I'm not going anywhere tonight."

He looked up with mock concern. "Are you unwell?"

"Oh, come off it, Damien! Don't insult me, or yourself, by pretending that we haven't just had a fight."

"I have no intention to. It's just that you look pale, and it sounded like you were retching in the toilet."

She looked at him. His expression was blank, but in his eyes there was a flicker of ... what? Amusement? Satisfaction?

"I know what you've been hiding, Damien," she said.

It just came out, completely unplanned.

The expression in his eyes faltered just for an instant. A stranger would not have noticed, but she did.

"What are you talking about?"

"I saw what is in your wardrobe upstairs."

His features arranged themselves into a puzzled expression.

"I'm sure I don't understand."

"I found the other earring. The one to match the one I found on your floor."

He smiled vaguely and raised his eyebrows. "I don't have the faintest idea what you're on about, Frida."

"Shall we go upstairs and have a look inside your wardrobe?" It sounded like a threat, but for once she didn't care.

His steely gray eyes bored into hers.

"So you went and broke into my private things," he said coldly after a moment, all the pretense suddenly gone from his voice.

She was stunned, amazed that he wasn't going to try to deny it.

"I didn't break into anything. The wardrobe was open."

"But you were in my study."

"I went in looking for a charger to charge my laptop. You had left the closet open."

"The study was locked."

"And the key was in your dressing gown. I'm sorry, I must have missed the big DO NOT ENTER sign on the door."

He got up abruptly and walked to the window, staring out into the darkness of the evening.

Moments passed. Neither of them moved.

"So is there anything you would like to say?" Frida asked.

He did not turn around, just stared blankly at the dark outside. "No. I have nothing to say to you."

"Have you been engaging in this the whole time we've been married?"

"It's my private life. My private time."

"So you feel it's OK to keep things like this from your wife because they're ... private?"

He turned slowly to face her. His face was twisted into a sneer. "Do you honestly think that most couples are honest about their sexual preferences? Their fantasies, their longings? Even about what they get up to when their partner is not around? If you do, you're even more of a child than I thought."

She stared at him, unflinching, but something turned in her stomach. The pictures of those women with their heads missing flashed into her thoughts.

"Everyone has secrets, Frida. I bet even you have secrets."

Her gaze faltered and she looked away.

"Precisely," he said. "Glass houses, my dear. I know all about that village idiot you've been seeing."

Five steps away there was a lamp. Five steps, and she could grab it and hurl it at his head. She had to physically fight the urge.

"So you had your spies on me, just as I suspected."

He shrugged. "Dramatize it if you must. I simply called some people to make sure you had everything you needed. But obviously you were able to take care of that yourself."

"I want a divorce," she said.

Neither of them spoke. The clock in the hall ticked away the seconds. Finally Damien sighed and lowered himself into a chair.

"Frida ... I'm sorry. I apologize. I shouldn't have said that."

She stared at him. Not for a moment did she consider him sincere.

"It's not about what you just said."

"I know. I know. It's a lot of ... other things."

She was wary now. Uncertain. He seemed meek, but you never could really tell with him.

"When did it start?"

He kept his eyes to the floor. When he finally spoke, he seemed to be having trouble getting the words out. "I don't remember. When I was a teenager I think."

The mood had shifted. It was less antagonistic now.

"Were you ever really attracted to me?"

He raised his head and looked at her. He seemed weary – and genuinely surprised.

"Yes. Yes. You mustn't think … it's not like that."

"Like what?" she said, her voice harsh.

He was struggling to put the words together. "I can be, you know … *normal*. But it always goes back to this. It's an escape from pressure. It helps me relax. I know it's not … right. I'm not proud of it." He paused, then said with finality in his voice: "It would have killed my career, you know."

"Is that why you married me? So you could keep up appearances for the sake of your career? So no one would suspect it?"

"No." He hesitated, staring down at the floor. "I don't know. I don't know myself. I do things I hate." He raised his eyes and looked at her, and for the first time in many, many years she saw something resembling vulnerability. She knew he was referring to the incident in the bedroom, and it made her feel ill. She hated him, too. That was the naked truth. She despised him.

"And all those decapitated women? What about them?"

He blinked. "What are you talking about?"

"You have pictures of decapitated women on the inside of your closet."

He laughed, and just like that she could see that ghost of a sneer return. "Decapitated women? No need to get all dramatic. They're pictures of clothes, that's all."

"Ah, I see. You just prefer that the women's heads be removed when you look at them."

"That's right."

"I want a divorce," she repeated.

"Then you'll have to file it." He paused, and seemed to have regained his composure. "Unfortunately it could get expensive. And alas, I'm pretty sure you won't walk away with much. You have a bit of money from the sale of your mother's flat, I believe? I'm quite sure that will all be gobbled up by legal fees."

"So you're refusing to grant me a divorce?"

"I still think we can work this out."

"I don't want to work this out. I want out of this marriage."

He looked at her. She looked back, evenly. He got up slowly, walked to the window and looked out into the night.

"Look," he said after a long pause. "If that's how you feel ... very well. But please wait until the worst of this has blown over. I can't be going through a divorce right now, Frida. Not with everything, all these demands ... I can't. All eyes are on me now. I can't buckle under the pressure."

So that was the deal. People were watching him. That was his overruling motivation, yet again.

"How long?"

"I don't know exactly how long. Just a bit longer."

"And until then?"

"We continue on as before. We are the loving couple in the eyes of the world."

"And when things have settled you'll be willing to negotiate?"

"Yes."

Moments passed.

"All right," she finally said. "But on one condition. You stay out of my bedroom."

~~

The next morning she awoke with a start. There was a rattling at the door. Someone was trying to get in.

"What?" she called out, suddenly alarmed.

"Open the door. I need some things."

She glanced at the clock on the bedside table. It was just past eight.

Pulling on her robe, she unlocked and opened the door. Damien was standing in the hall, dressed in his Armani suit. His cologne was like a thick cloud around him, filling her nostrils, making her feel nauseous.

He brushed past her. "I'm afraid I'm going to have to leave for London this afternoon for a few days. I need to get some clothes. I'll leave straight from the embassy."

She stood to the side, holding her robe tightly closed, while he took some clothes from the closet. Then he turned to her.

"I'll be back in a few days," he said.

"No rush," she said.

Their eyes met, and a brief sardonic smile flickered across his lips. Then he left.

CHAPTER TEN

Frida exited the ambassadorial residence the following Saturday afternoon with a strange air of defiance. Even though Damien was in London, she could still feel his harsh gaze on her.

It was a crisp, clear day with a hint of frost in the air. The muffled sounds of a speaker system and rounds of applause reached her as she headed towards parliament square. It was just past three pm and the demonstration had started. She inhaled deeply and picked up her pace.

Turning the corner from Lækjargata into Skólabrú, she stopped. The square was packed, the crowd spilling into the side streets. Frida weaved her way through the throng of people to get closer to the stage. She could hear the speaker even before she could see her, and her astonishment grew the nearer she got. Up on the stage was a little girl of about ten, standing on a speaker box to reach the microphone. "I can tell you that we are NOT going to pay for the toilets, petrol, and Range Rovers that those politicians are driving!" she shouted, and the crowd cheered. "And then they go and blame *us* for the crisis, and the minister says the same thing over and over, like a broken record. He thinks we will get tired and stop protesting and give up. Hasn't the time come for the people of this country to rise up, instead of the politicians?!"

She was a sassy little tyke, that was for sure. No doubt she had parents who were politically active and discussed these issues heatedly over dinner. Frida felt a tug of pain. When she had married Damien, that was something she thought they might one day have. A family that had dinner together and discussed things that were important. Love, strength, the ability to pass on good things and values to their children, whom they loved more than anything else in the world. It was a dream that had been doomed from the start, and now it had died.

Grimly and with determination she pushed her way through the crowd. She felt sad and angry, yes, but also inspired and hopeful. Her life was falling apart, yet here she was, participating in something monumental. Her nation's history was being made right here, right now, in this square. She glanced up at the statue of independence hero Jón Sigurdsson on his tall pedestal, staring out across the throng of protesters with lifeless eyes and a stony expression. He and his comrades had fought for Iceland's freedom. No doubt they had experienced the same sorts of feelings that people were experiencing now. Fervent, intense, passionate feelings, beating in the hearts of those who were ready to do whatever it took to secure a better future for their children and for their country, a future built on a new foundation of truth, justice, transparency, equality and respect for every human being.

Her life so far had been a life of little consequence. And yet with the simple act of being here now, she was making a difference.

She closed her eyes and listened.

Even before she opened them again, she could feel him watching her. It was like her entire awareness was being drawn in that direction – not just her mind, but every fiber in her body. She looked up and there he was, to the left of the stage, tall and self-assured, looking at her. He wore a green khaki parka over an Icelandic lopi sweater, and his eyes were burning.

Everything vanished except the two of them.

He moved first. With a determined stride he came towards her, his eyes never leaving her face. Seconds later he stood in front of her. Without speaking he put his arms around her. Frida slipped her arms inside his open parka and pressed him to her, feeling his warmth, breathing it. Holding him, it felt suddenly like all the cares of the world had been suspended, and it was just the two of them there, rocking ever-so gently together. Standing there, in the middle of the frosty square, she had never felt so warm. It felt like she was finally home.

He turned slowly and started moving, keeping one arm around her and gently guiding her through the crowd while she held tightly onto his thick wool sweater, thinking only of not letting go. They walked to the back of the stage. There, with the sound of a revolution in their ears, he pulled her to him. They kissed, lightly at first, then more passionately, hands feverishly clutching at one another.

Then they broke apart and stood there, staring at one another across a chasm of raging feelings.

"*Why didn't you call me*?" she cried under her breath, struggling to keep her voice down so that others wouldn't hear, taken aback by the anger and hurt that threatened to overpower her. She had an urge to pound her fists into him, to physically hurt him, but instead she grabbed his parka and tugged at him, pulling him closer.

"I'm sorry," he whispered. "So much has happened."

"*What* happened? What are you doing here?" Her voice trembled, thick with emotion.

"I'm back in town."

"For how long?"

He took hold of her wrists and looked intently at her face. "Can we go somewhere to talk? Can we go to where I'm staying?"

"Where are you staying?"

"Thingholtsstræti."

She hesitated for just a second. Then she started walking. A moment later they were making their way through the crowd in the direction of Lækjargata. He was a step behind her as they wound their way through. He reached for her hand. She touched it, just the tips of their fingers holding together. It sent an electric shock through her.

When they had passed through the thickest part of the crowd she suddenly felt conspicuous and let go of his fingers. They walked quickly, resolutely, not speaking. She felt as though everyone was watching them, and was acutely aware of her body straining towards him as they walked. A powerful energy drew them together and she had to fight the urge to touch him or to press her body to his.

At the top of Bókhlödustígur they turned right, and then they were standing on the stoop of a house. He opened a door, and they went in. They were in a small entrance hall, beyond which was a narrow hallway and a staircase leading upwards. It was dusky and smelled of singed sheep's heads – a traditional and inexpensive Icelandic food that had lost its ubiquitousness over the past two or three decades but was now experiencing a revival in the face of the *kreppa*, as the Icelanders called the crisis.

At the top of the first flight of stairs Baldur unlocked another door and they went inside. Frida cast around a fairly large room that had a double bed beneath a large window at one end. At the other end was an old two-seater velvet sofa with worn green upholstery, a matching armchair, and a small TV. On one wall was a sink with an old stained mirror above it, and next to that a small table with a hot plate, on which there was a kettle and a small lamp that was lit, casting a warm glow over the room.

He dropped the keys onto a side table and put his arms around her. They stood there for a few minutes holding each other, their coats still on; then he leaned down and lightly, tentatively, touched her lips with his. She responded, her breath coming quickly, all her sensations concentrated into this moment, seeking him out, allowing him to find her, communicating with just the lightest touch of their lips. And then she felt the intensity grow, the passion rise, and then they were clutching each other, kissing desperately, like they had been starving and had found food, debilitated by thirst and had found water.

Then they stopped. Both at once, as though a thought had occurred to them both at the same time.

She took a breathless step backward.

He reached for her again, but she shook her head.

They stood there for a few seconds, looking at each other, an entire unspoken universe between them.

"Should I make some tea?" he finally said, his voice hoarse.

She nodded and swallowed.

He took off his jacket, then went and filled the kettle with water. She perched on the edge of the sofa.

"Whose room is this?" she said at last.

"My friend Rúnar rents it. He's out of town right now."

"When did you get in to Reykjavík?"

"Two days ago."

He came and sat on the armchair. They looked at each other, wary and desperate, holding back through sheer force of will.

"I'm sorry, Frida. I didn't plan on things turning out this way."

"What way?"

"I kept hoping I would see you. I haven't stopped thinking about you."

"Then why didn't you call?" Her words were raw with emotion, barely above a whisper.

"When I came home that night, after we … were together, I told Hafdís we needed to talk."

He paused. She waited.

"Her mother was there, so we went outside. We walked down to the harbor. She was very upset. Her father – Jón – had told her that he'd seen us together." He paused. "I tried to explain that things just weren't working, that it would be best for both of us if we ended our marriage. She kept hammering on about you, asking how long it had been going on, things like that. Just then the manager at the aquaculture plant called me. I pulled out my phone, saw who it was, hesitated for a moment to decide whether or not I should answer it, and before I knew it she had ripped the phone out of my hand and thrown it into the water." He paused. "She thought it was you."

Frida's mouth curved into an involuntary smile. He looked at her, then smiled slightly, too. When he continued, his voice was a little less strained. "When we got back to the house there was a message for me that a net in one of the pens had broken. I had to go. Hafdís seemed all right … she was calmer, and I had a feeling she might be coming around to seeing my point of view."

Frida stared at him. Suddenly she was afraid of what he was going to say.

"When I got back she was lying in bed with an empty pill bottle that she'd downed with about half a liter of her father's vodka."

The kettle boiled and shut off with a click.

"They took her to the hospital in Ísafjördur. I went with her, then her mother came. We were there for three days."

"I'm sorry," Frida said softly.

"I don't think she really wanted to die," he said and pressed his lips together. "She just wanted me to stay. It's harsh to say that, but it's the truth. She risked her life to keep the status quo. It's like she believes she can control things she really has no control over. She just can't let it go."

"And now?"

"She's staying in the psych ward here in Reykjavík. The whole family had to come down to discuss what's going to happen next."

Frida remained motionless, but something sank in her heart. So that's why he was here. He wasn't free. *Any more than I am.*

It was like he had read her thoughts. He looked at her evenly. "I'm not going back. I can't go back."

There was a strange distance in his voice, a curious sense of disconnectedness. Instantly she knew there was still something in his mind and heart that he was fighting. He wasn't done.

"I went to see you as soon as I got back from Ísafjördur, but you were gone," he continued. "I didn't have your number and you weren't in the phone book. And I didn't want to call the embassy to ask for your number. I didn't think they'd give it to me, anyway."

"No, they would not have given it to you." She paused. "All this, out there." She gestured with her head towards parliament square. "You knew it was going to happen, didn't you?"

He nodded. "Yes. But not exactly like this. This is worse than I thought."

"But we have a chance to build a new society now."

"Yes." He stood up abruptly, headed for the kettle. "You're right. This is our chance. Rúnar, my friend who lives here, is one of the people who have organized the demonstrations. They're forming a political movement. If we can push for new elections, we're going to form a new list and stand for office."

"Wow."

"It's a revolution. But not just out there. The real revolution is taking place in the back rooms, in the cafés, at the dinner tables, in the hundreds of conversations between people who want to see a new Iceland. I thought it would be just the banks that went down, but now we have a political crisis, a currency crisis, an economic crisis and an ideological crisis. We're just starting to wake up. It's scary, all this corruption and all those lies that were right in front of us the whole time, we just didn't want to see them. But you're right. This is our chance to build the society we want. But we need new people and a new road map. We need leaders, people with a vision. And they're there. They just have to be given a chance."

He was standing by the kettle, out of reach. She wanted to pull him back, to feel him near her. She wondered if he was doing it on purpose, putting a physical distance between the two of them. The tension of wanting him and not having him was excruciating.

"What does your husband say about the UK putting Iceland on a list of terrorists?" he asked abruptly.

She recoiled inwardly. Damien. Just the very thought of him in this room felt like sacrilege. He was so distant from her that he might as well inhabit another universe.

"He ... says it was done for a good reason."

"And what reason might that be?" Baldur's voice was laced with sarcasm.

"He says there were large-scale transfers of funds out of the UK and invoking this law was the only way to stop it."

"But when Lehman Bros collapsed a few weeks before they had a similar situation, but they didn't put the USA on a terrorist blacklist. But little Iceland … there are no significant interests at stake, so they can beat us up all they want, show their strength to the rest of the world by bullying us. Make us into a scapegoat."

"Why are you saying this to me? I love this country as much as you do. I'm as freaked out about all this as you are. You don't have to convince me that what they did was fucked up."

The air between them was like a coiled spring. They stared at each other, trembling.

Baldur looked away. "Anyway, you're lucky," he said, turning. "You've got a life in the UK that you can go back to. You don't have to stay here in this mess."

"You think I'm going to leave? I'm not. I'm not going back there."

He took a hesitant step towards her and then, suddenly, it was like they were propelled against each other. She leaned against the back of the sofa, his hand was on her lower back, pressing her against him, against his hardness, mouth on hers, their hunger acute and desperate.

"Don't go," he murmured. "Don't go."

"I'm not going."

"I wanted so much to find you."

"And I wanted you."

The air around them was charged with something terrible. Something that had the power to destroy them both.

Love.

Something twisted inside her. A recognition, a realization. She raised herself up, shifted, put her hand on his chest. "We can't do this now."

"Do what?"

"*This*. Not now."

He moved back, his eyes wild and uncomprehending.

"Please. I don't want things to end up spoiled. I don't want our feelings for each other to be tainted."

"Tainted ... why?"

"We're both married. Have you forgotten?"

He stared at her, bewildered, as though this simple fact had eluded him. As though they were not themselves but other people. Which in a sense they were, Frida thought. Other people, outside of this room. Inside this room, she was herself. And he was himself. She knew this with more conviction than she had ever known anything before.

"I still feel the same, you know, as I did the last time we were together," he said urgently. "I feel something with you that I don't understand and can't explain. I don't know what it is."

"I know," she murmured. "I feel it too."

"You move me."

She closed her eyes and exhaled. How she wanted to fall backwards into this bliss, like into a warm ocean that would embrace her and where she could float, free from all the cares of the world. But that wasn't reality. Or was it? What was reality, and what was the play? How did it come to be that everything was turned inside out?

"I'm going to go now," she said.

"Why?"

She pulled away, and stood up, straightening her clothes. Inside, she was on fire.

"It's not right. Not like this."

He stood up too.

"What if things change?"

"Then they change. You have your wife and that whole situation to work out. And I have Damien."

"They *will* change."

She bit her lip. "I hope so," she whispered.

Out in the street Frida blinked back tears. She walked fast with her head down, hurrying away before she could change her mind and turn around. The midwinter darkness shrouded her with its dark hues, and in the distance there was the glow of a lingering sunset. She was upset, she felt pain, yet also a deep sense of wonder at the beauty of her own feelings. Something about Baldur reached deep into her inner core, where there was no artifice, no pretense and no hostility. The feelings he awakened in her were pure and true and strong. Even if she never saw him again, even if he went back to living with his wife, she knew she would have to get back to those feelings, because only by living them would her life be worth anything.

She reached the gate in front of the residence. She hesitated. And then, without warning, she was hit with a wave of nausea.

She put a hand out to steady herself.

Standing there at the gate, the moon casting a glow on the frosty lawn in front of her, she knew there was no denying it any longer. She *knew*.

She was pregnant.

CHAPTER ELEVEN

Two days passed. Frida wrestled with her emotions and racing thoughts, her mind and heart a jumble of wild feelings. At times she felt overwhelmed, swinging violently from one extreme to another, sweet hope to abject despair, and then back again. Different feelings clamored for attention inside of her. Initially after she had taken the test, staring at those two blue lines with a mixture of disbelief and awe, there was exhilarating happiness, an explosion of joy and wonder that went beyond anything she had ever known. But as she began to comprehend the implications a torrent of negative feelings set in: rage, horror, disgust, confusion, anger and terrible, desperate sadness.

One of those two men turned her insides to cold stone. The other made her world iridescent and filled her heart with music. Either one could be the father of her child.

The child she had so passionately wanted, all this time.

Just not like this.

She had wanted to bring a child into her life when she still clung to the romantic notion that Damien was her man and one true husband. How perfectly, ridiculously ironic that as soon as that illusion was shattered, her deepest wish came true.

And now, she was being put to the ultimate test.

Her options were the same as before: stay or leave, only they were now infinitely more complicated.

Stay, and she would have to tell Damien about the baby. She

had no clue as to how he would react. He had never wanted a baby, not even his own – so what would he say to the possibility that she was carrying someone else's child? There was no sense in lying to him about it, even if she wanted to. He knew about Baldur and their ... involvement. He'd figure it out.

Her overriding impulse was to pack her things and leave. But if she did, Damien would refuse to negotiate a divorce settlement. He had made that clear, and she saw no reason to doubt him. Desperate as she was to get away, she also knew that money was an object, even more so now that she was carrying a baby. She might have been able to face being broke for a time on her own, but the thought of struggling financially with a child, with no proper education and no work experience, left her feeling incapacitated and weak.

And what if he is the child's father?

The thought tormented her. The idea of sharing the upbringing of her child with Damien made her shudder deep in her bones. She briefly considered keeping it a secret, moving far, far away to where he would not be able to find her. Then she came to her senses. Sooner or later he would find out. And anyway, what would she tell the child? She would not raise the child in an atmosphere of lies, however justified she felt them to be.

And if it was Baldur – what then? What if he returned to his wife, what if things *didn't* change? Would she tell him; would she want him to be a part of the baby's life? Could she face seeing him, having that emotional involvement with him, if they were doomed to be apart?

So many questions, so many ifs.

And then, out of the darkest recesses of her heart, rose the prospect of the third option.

She could barely bring herself to articulate the thought to herself, but nevertheless it was there, incessant, in the background. It might be easiest for everyone if she terminated the pregnancy. It might be easiest for *her* if she did so. By terminating it she might be able to eradicate the memory of that awful night, the feeling of Damien on top of her and inside of her, pushing the pillow over her head, and the terror, the terror of suffocating ...

NO.

These thoughts were like dark, muddy water, and she was being dragged down, drowning in the same twisted nightmare that had shrouded that awful, soul-crushing night with Damien in the bedroom. *NO.* The word, loud and insistent inside her head, was like a surge of energy that let her kick away the weeds that had laced around her legs and were pulling her down into that dark lake of sorrow and rage and death. And now, she surfaced with a gasp, filling her lungs with the oxygen of reason and love.

Because there was also a chance that this baby had been created during another act, one of exquisite tenderness and beauty. That chance was equally strong, even if a shadow lingered so enduringly over the other.

~~

Frida was sitting in the kitchen looking at baby cribs online when Damien suddenly appeared. He had returned from London earlier that day, briefly said hello, then gone to the embassy to work. It was now ten-thirty pm and she hadn't heard him enter the house.

She slammed the laptop shut.

He appeared not to notice. He looked haggard and tired, his hair uncharacteristically unruly and needing a trim, his shirt wrinkled and open at the neck.

"Hi," he said.

"Hey."

There was an uncomfortable silence.

"You look nice," he said. "Did you have your eyebrows done?"

She ignored the remark. "How was London?"

"Oh, busy. Back-to-back meetings, high-level people demanding to know the situation here. Endless briefings." He seemed to think of something, left the room and returned a moment later with a small package wrapped in blue paper and tied with a ribbon. He handed it to her.

"I got you something. A small token of my appreciation and ... love." He said the last word like an afterthought, then gave a slight smile as though he realized how artificial he had sounded.

"You deserve it," he added quickly.

She unwrapped it. It was a jewelry box. She lifted the lid. Inside was a small pendant on a white gold chain. A sapphire drop in the middle, surrounded by clear stones. Diamonds.

She stared at it. At one time she would have been ecstatic. Now she just felt numb.

"I can't accept this," she said after a brief pause, shutting the lid.

"Why not?"

She looked at him evenly. "Because I want a divorce."

"So does that mean you can't accept a token of my appreciation?"

"Yes. That's what it means."

He sat down opposite her. "Frida, I've had time to think while I was away. I understand why you feel this way. I have not given this relationship what it deserved. I've been too caught up in my own work and … issues. But – honestly – I want to change. I promise you that when the worst is over we will go on holiday – anywhere you want. Just us two." He reached for her hand. "I've given this a lot of thought. I want this to work. I want to make it better."

She pulled her hand away and looked into his eyes.

"You raped me."

A small hint of a sneer appeared at the corner of his mouth. He leaned back in his chair and surveyed her coolly.

"Is that what you call it?"

Her heart was pounding inside her chest and she feared her voice would fail her. "Yes. I call it that because that's what it was."

He rose from the chair. "Well, that's your call. Me, I consider that a tad dramatic."

"And now I'm pregnant."

He froze.

"I see," he said calmly.

He was looking at her with a curious expression. The thought flashed into her mind that maybe, just maybe, he had planned the whole thing. It would have been the perfect ploy, the perfect tool for oppression. Get her pregnant. Then she would never be free.

"I expect there is a bit of confusion as to the paternity of the child?"

She forced herself to sit still. Inside she was shaking with terrible rage, but she knew that if she stood up and slapped him, hard, like she wanted to, he would win.

"So, why in such a hurry to divorce me, then? Doesn't the child need a father?" he said with the ghost of a smile.

He's enjoying this.

"Not *that* much."

"So you really intend to go through with this?"

She rose to her feet. "I intend for *us* to go through with this. I wasn't alone in this marriage."

"I've told you I don't want a divorce."

"You've just come out of the closet as a transsexual …"

"Transvestite. It's not the same thing. Don't confuse the two."

"… and I've just told you I'm pregnant, and it might be by another man. How can you seriously propose that we continue this marriage?"

"Marriages get fixed. People change. And in any case, there is a small chance that the child is mine, is there not?"

"And if it isn't?"

He said nothing, just shrugged as if to say it wouldn't matter.

"You always said you didn't want children."

"Well now that the situation is different, I may have changed my mind."

"And if the baby is not biologically yours? Would you still want to bring it up – as if it was your own?"

"If you decide you want to keep it," he said.

She laughed, a short, incredulous laugh. "*If* I decide I want to keep it? Of course I want to keep it! I have spent years longing for a child. Or have you forgotten? It was you who did not want to have children."

"I didn't want children because I didn't think this sort of life was good for a child. But now that we have this … situation, and if it's between losing you or accepting the child, I choose to accept the child."

"Would you love this child?"

"I would try."

"I don't think you could."

"Why?"

"You're not capable."

He leaned backwards against the counter. "Well, now, that's not very nice, is it?"

"You did not receive love from your own parents. How can you hope to pass on love to a child that may not even be your own?"

"Who says I didn't receive love from my parents?"

"You've told me, more than once. Your father was emotionally cold and unavailable. Your mother died when you were a toddler. You were sent to boarding schools where terrible things happened. All of this you have told me yourself."

"I haven't told you everything."

"Well, what a surprise!"

"My mother didn't die when I was a toddler."

For a moment Frida was speechless.

"My mother raised me, at least to some degree."

She shook her head impatiently, not comprehending.

"Mrs. Kelly was my mother."

Frida opened her mouth to say something, but no sound emerged. Thoughts, memories, images raced through her mind, arranging themselves like pieces of a puzzle. She stared at Damien.

"She's dead. I was called to London because she passed away. I attended her funeral. There were only five people there. Myself, and four friends she'd acquired through the years." He paused. "She had no family."

"Wait ... "

"She died two weeks ago."

He raised his eyes to her face and looked at her. For once, they were not hard and cold but were filled with something approaching bafflement.

"You said nothing," she said. It was an expression of astonishment, as much as a statement of fact.

He nodded. Shrugged.

Frida turned to the window. *Mrs. Kelly Damien's mother*. So that was why their relationship had been so … unusual.

"My mother was … barren," she heard him say. "Mrs. Kelly was their housekeeper. She was young at the time, and she and my father … had a fling. Mrs. Kelly got pregnant. My mother found out about the affair and the pregnancy, and my father and my mother decided to take the child and raise it as their own. That child was me. The arrangement they made with Mrs. Kelly was that she would still work in our household, and that she would look after me. There was also some ... compensation involved. Two years later my mother died. That's the short version."

Frida spun round. "Why do you persist in calling her Mrs. Kelly? Doesn't your mother have a first name?"

"Joanne. Her name was Joanne."

Looking at him now, Frida felt a vague sense of pity. Yet her aversion for him would not leave her.

"When did you find all this out?"

"My father told me just before he died."

"So you've known for years."

"Yes."

"And you didn't tell me."

"I didn't tell anyone."

"And what do you think about the fact that your entire childhood was a lie?"

He shrugged again, and a defensive tone crept into his voice. "I don't look at it that way. It was simply how they chose to do things. It was what they wanted."

"Don't you see anything wrong with that?"

He shrugged. "It was a different era. My father was a peer. A member of the House of Lords. Mrs. Kelly was just a servant."

Just a servant. The woman had been his mother, yet he had not recognized her as such, even after his father's death. Instead he had kept her on as his housekeeper. As his *servant*. And she, the dour Mrs. Kelly, had gone along with it.

What sort of strange sickness afflicted these people; what dark laws and regulations governed their actions?

She turned back to the window. Of course he had no problem continuing their marriage on the terms that he was now proposing. She would give birth to the child, and even if it was not Damien's he would simply pretend that it was – just as his father had pretended that Damien was his wife's son, and Mrs. Kelly "just a servant". Her child would grow up in a home infused with lies. That is, unless they were open about it – but

Damien would never agree to that. Not with his career. Not with his desperate need to keep up appearances. No, he would make another "agreement" with her – that she keep her mouth shut, and play the part of the doting mother and wife. To any outside observer they would be the perfect family. And inside, she would be slowly suffocating.

No. No no no no no.

She turned around. Damien had sat back down and was staring at the floor, elbows on his knees. For the first time in her life she felt pity for him. She wanted to reach out to him, to place a comforting hand on his shoulder, but she couldn't bring herself to touch him. The thought of staying in this room with him a moment longer filled her with an unspeakable dread. Her only thought was to get away.

She moved swiftly. At the door she hesitated and turned around.

"I'm sorry," she said. "I'm sorry for your loss."

By the time he looked up she was gone.

~~

She didn't really think about what she was doing. It was like some kind of force took over, something that bypassed her rational mind, and before she knew it she was outside in the cold November evening, walking quickly, her coat flailing unceremoniously around her. She turned a corner, then another one, and minutes later she was standing on the stoop, ringing a doorbell that she hoped was functional.

A ray of light appeared at the top of the stairs and then she could see him, taking the steps down two at a time, until he was standing in front of her, grinning with a mixture of delight and astonishment. He wore a pair of track pants and a faded t-shirt that looked like it had shrunk in the wash; his hair was a mess and he was barefoot.

He stepped aside to let her in. She went straight up the stairs, heading for the warm glow of the light that emanated out through the door of his room. Suddenly the thought struck her that he might not be alone. She panicked – maybe *she* was there, or even someone else.

She felt him come up behind her and put his hands on her waist. She stepped inside. Yes, he was alone.

The bed was disheveled and the room was in darkness save for a small reading lamp placed on the windowsill. A book lay facedown on the pillow: *The Shock Doctrine* by Naomi Klein.

The door closed behind them. She turned around, and without speaking put her arms around his neck, pulling him close and kissing his mouth. Seconds later she'd thrown off her coat, kicked off her boots and torn off her shirt. Then they fell on the bed, clumsy and awkward. She pulled off his T-shirt, he took off his pants, and then they were naked. Finding each other, they hesitated, almost reverent, amazed at the power of their naked bodies touching, the energy that coursed between them like blood rushing through a single organism. Frida sighed, the entire sum of her sensations concentrated into a single moment. He kissed her face, her neck, her breasts, her belly. Their lovemaking was an underwater dance, slow and sensual, flowing with the tides of their passion, tongues and fingers exploring and finding, deep meditation infused with a sense of being vibrantly, ecstatically alive. It was the most profound and perfect communication she had ever known. Tears welled up when he entered her, tears of new joy and old grief and all her passions bundled into one. With him she was naked. Only with him. Only he knew her, and only she knew him. When they came, together, the heat flowed through her, eradicating that cold serpentine dread that had burrowed its way into her in that stark white kitchen less than an hour before.

Afterwards they lay for a long time, not saying anything, just touching, speaking to each other through the pressure of their fingers, the deft lightness of their caresses.

They fell asleep in each other's arms, and woke only as the gray morning light began to seep through the blinds.

Frida's first thought was one of fear. If it was light out, it meant that it was already mid-morning. Damien would know she hadn't been home.

Does it matter?

Baldur stirred. They lay still for a few moments, then he reached for his cellphone on the windowsill. She glanced at the screen. The display read 9:37.

He turned towards her. "Don't you have to go home?" he asked softly.

He wants me to leave.

She did not respond.

Why did I stay?

"I'm leaving for Fagrifjördur today," he said.

She turned quickly, throwing her legs over the edge of the bed and reaching for her clothes.

He touched her back. "Hey."

She began to dress. "How long are you going for?"

"A couple of weeks."

"Why only a couple of weeks?"

"There are some things with the aquaculture plant that I need to help with. They're in a crisis because of the meltdown. It's all crazy, everybody's panicking, and I need to sit down with them and go through some stuff. Also, Rúnar's coming back today. I have to get out of here for a couple of weeks, until he leaves again."

She hated herself for feeling so raw. Hated herself for her vulnerability. Hated her impulse to scream at him that just a few days ago he said that he'd never go back there.

"So where are you staying while you're there?" she asked as nonchalantly as she could.

"I don't know yet. I'm hoping I can stay with a colleague."

"And if you can't?"

He didn't answer.

She began gathering her things.

"Look at me," he said.

She put on her coat.

He swung out of bed and took hold of her shoulders, spinning her around. She could feel the warmth emanating from his naked body.

He looked intently into her eyes. "I'm going there to help out, and also to settle things. OK?"

She nodded.

"If I call you when I get back, will you answer?"

She nodded again.

He kissed her on the lips, then put his arms around her. They stood, holding each other gently but firmly. Then she slipped out of his embrace, turned, and left, closing the door softly behind her.

CHAPTER TWELVE

Christmas was coming. Reykjavík propped up its tattered heart with seasonal lights – on trees, on light poles, strung across downtown streets. The usual December bustle got underway, though it was noticeably more subdued than usual. The number of protesters at the weekly demonstrations dwindled as people turned to spending time with their nearest and dearest, attending their children's concerts and ballet recitals, and observing all those deeply-rooted traditions that provided such comfort in the midst of crisis. Those who fervently wished for change were fearful that all the force had gone out of the protests – Icelanders had a habit of reacting fiercely to injustice but soon sinking back into the lethargic serfdom that had been conditioned into the nation's soul during centuries of colonial rule and oppression. They despaired that the New Iceland for which they so yearned would ever materialize, afraid that the Icelandic proletariat would simply shuffle onwards with a servile air, snot dripping from their noses, passively submitting to the ruling elite. As ever.

Similarly, a casual onlooker might have surmised that the status quo still prevailed chez Frida Lowe and her husband, His Excellency Damien Lowe. For all intents and purposes it was business as usual for the Lowes. Despite a raw undercurrent of animosity they were civil to each other, addressed practical matters as needed, and even received guests, hosting a Christmas luncheon for the embassy staff and a cocktail party for members of the Icelandic media. Their roles, practiced and polished for over a decade, were flawlessly executed. No one would have suspected that their marriage had already collapsed, nor guessed at the secrets that lay at the heart of the implosion.

Yet quietly and with stealth, new life was pushing up through the wasteland of the old. In Frida's heart, flutterings of new hope sometimes turned to wild excitement, catching her off guard and threatening to compromise her carefully arranged persona. She would go out walking and find herself grinning from ear to ear, until she noticed the strange looks from the people she encountered and swiftly composed her features into something more appropriate. She had already been to see an obstetrician, a vivacious woman with a ready smile who was the first person with whom Frida felt she could share her joy. The obstetrician had wondered why her husband had not accompanied her. Frida had blurted out some excuse, but then stopped and said simply that she and her husband were separating. The obstetrician looked at her sympathetically and continued with the examination, saying nothing more.

Damien had said nothing to Frida about the night she had left and not come home. Indeed, she wondered if he actually knew that she'd been out the entire night, given that they no longer shared a bedroom. Her thoughts returned to that night over and over. Despite her efforts to not think about Baldur she found herself aching for him. It was a deep hunger that went beyond the physical – it was emotional, visceral, profound, and so strong that at times it took her breath away. She had to force herself to stay active, fearful that if she allowed herself to dwell on thoughts of him and all the uncertainty about the future she would lose her mind.

Her main concern was finding a place to live. She had begun looking for available rentals, furtively and on the sly. Alarmingly there seemed to be very few flats available. The Icelandic rental market was difficult at the best of times, since the vast majority of people owned their own property, but at the moment it was virtually nonexistent. Economic upheaval had paralyzed the nation, and by extension the housing market. No one was making any major life decisions in such uncertain times, and no one moved house unless they absolutely had to. Frida was beginning to panic. The thought of being trapped under the same roof as Damien for months, even until the end of her pregnancy, filled her with dread. Such thoughts, too, she had to make a concerted effort to push aside. Things *would* work out. She had to focus on that, and believe it.

Early one evening, Damien had just come in from work and was flipping through his unopened mail. Without looking up, he said: "I had Rósa check on flights today and I thought the seventeenth might be a good day to fly back to London. We can have a few days there, then come back in time for New Year's like we'd planned."

Frida had been scrolling through rental ads online, but now stopped what she was doing and looked at him. He stood there, perfectly composed in his tailored suit and silk tie, and not for the first time she marveled at his ability to act as though reality did not exist outside of his own mind. His refusal to acknowledge what had passed between them these past few weeks was astonishing to her.

"I'm not going to England for Christmas. I thought you knew that." Her voice was calm, but inside she was shaking. To her surprise she realized that he still had that power over her.

He did not look up. "So you'll stay here by yourself?"

"Yes," she said.

He looked up and for a moment their eyes met. His were blank.

"Suit yourself," he said. Then he turned and headed up the stairs.

~

The day Damien left for London, Frida experienced a curious feeling of desolation. He had left in the morning without saying goodbye, and much as she had been averse to going to England with him, she also feared spending Christmas alone in the residence. It had never felt like home, and now it felt more cold and forbidding than ever. She wandered through the empty rooms, feeling displaced and wretched, allowing herself the brief luxury of wallowing in self-pity.

By mid-afternoon she'd had enough of that, and decided that the best way to get over her antipathy for the house would be to leave it. She bundled up and headed out, walking up the hill towards Hallgrímskirkja church. She made a left towards Laugavegur, the main downtown shopping street that was perpetually festive in the advent to Christmas. She longed now to feel the Christmas spirit she remembered from her childhood, when she had escaped in the midwinter darkness from the desolation of home to the excitement of Laugavegur, with its bustle of people laden with parcels, heading home to their families to revel in the joy and warmth of the yuletide season.

Lost as she was in thought, she almost collided with a large bookshelf that a young couple was about to load into a parked van that almost blocked the sidewalk. Glancing up, she muttered an apology, and was about to cross over to the other side when the woman called after her.

"Frida?"

It took Frida a moment to register. Could it be? "Anna!"

They had been in the same class in primary school. In those years Frida's mother had been almost perpetually drunk and Frida carried her shame with her to school each day, like a deadweight in her school bag. Twice Anna had shared her lunch with Frida when there had been nothing at home to eat and Frida was desperately hungry. Those two acts of kindness were forever etched in Frida's memory. They had met again a few years later in upper secondary school, and had become friends.

Anna lowered her end of the bookshelf into the back of the van, leaving her co-carrier to manoeuver it into place. She came towards Frida, grinning from ear to ear. "What an incredible surprise! It's so great to see you."

She embraced Frida warmly.

"How long has it been?"

"So how have you ...?"

"What have you been ...?"

They both stopped, then laughed.

"You first," said Frida.

"Gosh. It must be, what, fifteen years? Where to start? Let's see, after graduation I went to Denmark for university, finished, got married – this is my husband, Lars – Lars, this is Frida, my good friend from school … it so crazy that we should lose touch, really, it's ridiculous … anyway, we moved back to Iceland about five years ago, but we're leaving again. We're going back to Denmark … Lars just lost his job and with everything that's happening and this country going straight down the toilet …" she shook her head and raised her eyebrows, then grinned her infectious grin that Frida remembered so well from school. It was a grin that almost always managed to put her in a good mood.

"Well, it's fantastic that you have the option to leave, at least. That's more than a lot of people have."

"Yeah. I know."

"I can't tell you how great it is to see you," Frida gushed, and meant it. Oh how she had needed to see a friendly face – and then Anna appeared. Gratitude welled up inside her.

"And you! You look fantastic – tell me what you've been up to! Oh …" she glanced at her husband, "we have to be somewhere in about ten minutes … Lars, can you get the two boxes while I talk to Frida for a couple of minutes?"

Lars disappeared inside, and Anna gave Frida another spontaneous hug. "How *are* you?"

"I'm … good. Basically good. Except … well, my marriage is breaking down and I'm about to leave my husband."

She hadn't expected to say that, but oh how good it was to tell someone.

"Oh no!" Anna's smile evaporated. "I'm so sorry. I mean – I didn't even know you were married. We have so much catching up to do. Maybe we can meet for coffee before we leave?"

"When is that?"

"After Christmas. In about ten days. We were going to leave sooner but we ran into a problem with our place – we can't sell it, so we're going to have to rent it, but the way things are now, everything's frozen, nobody is moving anywhere. They're even saying people can't divorce now because they can't afford to go anywhere because of the crisis – they can't sell their homes, and …" she stopped abruptly, suddenly realizing. "Oh God, I'm sorry. How thoughtless of me."

She shook her head. "Don't worry. It's nothing like that with us. Except …" she was suddenly struck by the obvious. "You're renting your place? For how long?"

"Well, like I said, we planned to sell it, but …" suddenly the same thought seemed to occur to Anna. "You think you'd be interested?"

She nodded quickly. "Yes. Yes I do."

Anna smiled. She gestured with her head. "Well come upstairs and I'll show you the place."

The flat was on the third floor of a walk-up, and the moment she walked in, Frida knew that it was home. Something magical surrounded her as she stood in the tiny entrance hall, looking at a small kitchen on her left and a living room with a door leading out to a deck on her right. Straight ahead was a short hallway with three doors, and through the one directly ahead of her she could see a bathroom sink. Frida felt giddy. There was such a sense of lightness in the air, like the universe was winking at her, as if to say: "See? I've got it sussed. All you have to do is have the courage to walk through these doors I've thrown wide open for you ..."

"It's perfect," Frida said.

"Do you think you'd want to take it?"

She hesitated for just a brief second. It would mean opposing Damien. It would mean financial difficulty. It would mean starting her life over from scratch.

It would mean freedom.

"Absolutely."

Anna turned to her husband and they had a brief exchange, deciding that Lars would go and deliver the bookshelf on his own and pick Anna up a little later.

"We've got a few pieces of furniture still here, the old sofa, kitchen table and chairs ... we were going to put them in storage for a while, but if you think you can use them I'd be happy to leave them for you. They're not all that great, but they're in pretty good shape, and ..."

"I'd love to have it. Whatever you can spare."

"We're taking our bed, but there's a small one in the girls' room …"

"Don't worry. There's always IKEA."

For the next hour, they sat in the kitchen and talked about what had transpired in their lives since they last met. Frida told

Anna – in fairly general terms – what had happened recently: that her marriage to Damien had broken down, that she had met someone else, that she was now pregnant, that she was uncertain of the paternity. The last point brought on an deluge of shame, but Anna listened and cooed her sympathy without judgment, and Frida felt a sense of calm come over her. How wonderful it was to talk to someone who knew her as Frida, and not merely as Damien's wife. Such relief.

As they were leaving, Anna turned to her and said: "How amazing that you took exactly this street today, at exactly this time. Surely it was meant to be."

Frida laughed. "Well, yes. Either that – or it's just Reykjavík. It's a such small world. Literally."

"True. I tend to forget how small it is when I've lived abroad for a while. But seriously, this saves us completely. I'm worried about you, though. Who do you know here, that you can get support from?"

Frida shook her head. "No one, really. It's my own fault for not keeping in touch with anybody. But I know I'll be OK. I'll make sure I don't become a social reject."

Anna looked thoughtful. "Maybe we can arrange to get together with a few of the girls from school before I leave. What do you think?"

Frida shook her head doubtfully. "I don't know. I'm not sure we'd have that much in common. I don't feel like I fit in – you know? I feel like I've been away too long."

"Do you mean the small-town, provincial mentality?"

A memory of the cocktail party at George and Patricia's four months earlier flashed into Frida's mind. It had marked the official beginning of her private meltdown, although the lead-up to it had been much longer. "Small minds are everywhere, even in places where you'd least expect to find them. I haven't especially associated that with Iceland."

"Oh, that completely got to me when I lived here. All the gossiping, and negativity, and hating on people who were making something of their lives. It was such a relief to get away from all that when I went to Denmark. But coming back – especially with Lars, who doesn't conform to that whole mentality – was different. You see through it, and you pick the people you want in your life."

"And how many of our old crew do you hang out with now?"

Anna was silent for a moment. Then they both burst out laughing.

"I'm just so sorry you're leaving," Frida said, looking affectionately at her friend.

"Me too. Because I would totally have hung out with you."

"Well, at least you'll have me living in your place."

"Yep, and there's always Skype."

Frida nodded. "There's always Skype."

~~

Five days later, on the twenty-third of December, Frida moved into her new home.

She'd taken most of her clothes from the residence, and the few household items that belonged to her and had sentimental value. Other than that, she had picked up some basic necessities at IKEA, including some pillows, throws, rugs, fairy lights, a couple of plants, and other decorative items that made the flat feel like a home. She had also bought a bed that she was waiting to have delivered.

As for pictures, she had put up only one. It occupied a special place on the refrigerator and it was a very special picture, one she had to stop and look at every time she went past. It had been taken at her first ultrasound, a picture of her tiny baby, showing its head, arms and legs ... that frankly she thought looked alarmingly like a turtle's flippers.

A month had passed since she'd last seen Baldur. A month since he'd gone to Fagrifjördur. He hadn't called, and despite her best intentions she felt crestfallen. No doubt his plans had changed – he and Hafdís had probably reconnected during that period of living together. Or his codependency had got the better of him, and he had not been able to leave her. Or whatever. It didn't matter. She had to stop thinking about it. She had her own life, her own mess to sort through.

Anna had invited her to spend Christmas with her and Lars, their two daughters and her parents, but Frida had gently refused. It had meant a great deal to her, but now that she had her own place, she wanted most of all to be alone, rest, and give herself space to adjust to her new circumstances. She no longer felt anxious and full of fear – instead she felt a quiet excitement, though she was also empty and sad. She would not miss her life with Damien, but it accounted for over a decade of her life, and she knew it was normal to grieve for it.

She had told Kristín that she was spending Christmas with some friends and would not be at the residence. She did not know if she'd notice that Frida had taken some items from the house, but if she did, it didn't matter. She'd know the truth soon enough.

She had not yet told Damien, but she knew she would have to. Today. She owed herself that – to spend Christmas free of the anxiety of knowing she'd have to make that phone call eventually. Best to get it over with.

She dialed his number in London. He picked up on the fourth ring.

"Hi Damien. Am I getting you at a bad time?"

"Hello Frida. No, no – I was just upstairs and the phone was downstairs."

She noted that his usual "hello, my dear" was absent. His tone was a lot more natural and subdued than it normally was. Perhaps he, too, was relieved to be free.

She took a deep breath and launched into the speech she had rehearsed all morning. "I ran into an old friend from school on the street a few days ago – Anna, whom I hadn't seen in years. As it happened, she's moving to Denmark, and was looking to rent out her apartment. I've decided to rent it." She paused. "In fact, I've already moved in."

There was a long pause on the other end. Then: "I see."

"This only happened the day you left. It was completely unplanned," she added quickly.

"Frida ... I'll say it one more time. I don't want this divorce."

His voice was tight with pain. Or was it rage? She couldn't tell.

"Damien. It's no good. We have to let it go."

She waited. Finally he said: "And the child?"

"If the child is yours, I will do everything I can to help you have a relationship with him or her."

"Even if I make it as difficult as I can for you to divorce me?"

She closed her eyes. She felt nothing. No anger, no desire to retaliate, no hatred. There was nothing he could do to her now. She would survive his machinations, and she would end up free. Poor, maybe – but free.

"Knock yourself out, Damien. You can't keep me locked up like a prisoner."

"I expect I'll hear from your lawyer, then. And do let me know when you've determined the paternity of your child, will you?" His voice dripped with scorn.

She took a deep breath.

"Merry Christmas, Damien, and be well," she said. Then she hung up the phone.

~~

Late in the afternoon on Christmas Eve day it started to snow. A white blanket settled over everything as the tranquility of the holy evening began to descend on the city. Traffic slowed as people retreated inside to prepare for the festivities and to be ready to embrace their loved ones when Christmas officially began at the sacred hour of six pm.

Frida lit candles in the kitchen and watched the snow come down outside, wrapping the colored lights on the trees and houses in a magical beauty. She felt raw and vulnerable, but it was a good sensation, like being tender and new with just-opened eyes.

It was ten minutes to six. The radio, which she had on, had gone silent, as it always did these few minutes before the official Christmas celebrations began. It was the only time of the year that it did so, and gave weight to the solemnity of the occasion. It occurred to her that the silence was like a death, a hush in the space before the rebirth that would be announced momentarily with the ringing of bells throughout Iceland, as church bells large and small all chimed at exactly the same moment. She moved silently, afraid of breaking the enchantment that now hung over the city, as tens and thousands of people anticipated the arrival of the most sacred time of the year.

And then it began. The silence was broken by chimes of

jubilation that heralded in joy and hope and love. It came to Frida through the radio on the windowsill, and also from outside, from the Dómkirkjan cathedral down on parliament square. She closed her eyes and let the sound wash over her like water. She had always been an atheist. As a young girl, she was told to believe in God, and like a good little soldier she had gone through the motions dictated by Icelandic society. She went to confirmation classes, put on the white tunic and ate the confirmation wafer, recited the verse that officially admitted her into the national church. She had received her confirmation, even though deep down she felt like a fraud. She did not believe in God because God did not believe in her. He had taken her father, and He had given her an alcoholic mother. What the hell had God ever done for her?

But now, standing there with her eyes closed and the bells ringing, she felt something. It was an energy, both inside and all around her. She stood perfectly still, almost afraid to breathe, for fear that she would break the spell. She didn't want this to end. It was amazing – this sense of being connected to all things, of being perfectly calm in the midst of a tremendous force – a force that was kind and good and benign. She felt utterly tranquil, possibly more than she had ever been.

It seemed to her that something flickered. She opened her eyes. On the kitchen table her phone was blinking, as though she had a message. Or was it? She stared at it in astonishment: it had made no sound, yet it was not on silent. And it was not blinking now. She went to the table, picked it up and looked at the screen. No. No message.

She put the phone down. Her mind was playing tricks. Again she leaned against the counter and closed her eyes, hoping to recapture some of what she had felt just a moment before.

And then she heard a beep.

She grabbed the phone. Yes. There it was.

merry christmas. thinking of u. b.

She sat down at the table, holding the phone in her hand like a delicate thing.

Love is the absence of fear. She had read that somewhere.

And right now it seemed to her she had never read a truer statement.

Slowly, she typed back a message.

> Where are you?

The answer came almost instantly.

> home

Her heart sank. Then, a moment later:

> thingholtsstraeti

She leaned back in the chair, staring at the message on the display screen. Would he come if she told him where to find her?

Fingers trembling, she typed the address and the name on the buzzer.

There was no reply. Five minutes passed, then ten. Frida paced from the living room to the kitchen, flushed with emotion.

The phone rang.

She jumped. Breathlessly she answered it, without looking.

"Hello?"

"Hello Frida."

Her heart sank to the floor.

"Damien."

"How are you?"

"Damien, this is not a good time ..."

"It won't take long."

She walked quickly to the kitchen window and looked anxiously down onto the street. White snow glowed in the golden light of the streetlamp.

"I'll get straight to the point. Do you recall when we lived in Berlin? The evening of September 11th?"

"Uh, vaguely."

"The planes flew into the World Trade Centre and you started to speak about children."

"OK. Yes. Maybe."

"And I told you I had never wanted to have a child, and that I never would."

"Damien, I ... can we ..."

He hesitated so long that she began to wonder if he had hung up. She was about to end the call when he spoke.

"That very next week I had a vasectomy."

Silence. She opened her mouth to say something, but nothing came out.

"Merry Christmas."

The phone clicked off.

Frida lowered her arm to her side as a flurry of thoughts sped through her brain.

On the radio, Bach's Christmas Oratorio began to play. Outside the window, flakes of snow drifted gracefully to the ground.

ACKNOWLEDGMENTS

In writing this book I received invaluable help from a group of "beta readers" – volunteers who took it upon themselves to read the raw manuscript and share their thoughts and ideas with me. A big THANK YOU goes out to Tóti Stefánsson, Christopher Condit, Louise Harris, Jennifer Prichard and Quentin Bates. Your input made such a huge difference.

I am also incredibly grateful for the contribution of my husband Erlingur Páll Ingvarsson, who not only read, discussed and deliberated with me at length, but also designed the cover and prepared it for printing. Moreover, he understands the creative process and nurtures me with moral and emotional support as needed. I'm so lucky.

ABOUT THE AUTHOR

Alda Sigmundsdóttir is a writer, journalist, translator and blogger. She was born in Iceland, grew up in Canada, and has lived in the United Kingdom, Cyprus and Germany for longer and shorter periods of time. *Unraveled* is Alda's first novel. She has previously written two books of non-fiction: the acclaimed *The Little Book of the Icelanders*, a humorous take on the quirks and foibles of the Icelandic people, and *Living Inside the Meltdown*, about the effects of Iceland's financial crash in 2008. Her translations from Icelandic to English are extensive and diverse, ranging from advertising copy to published novels and books. Alda is an avid blogger, and for six years wrote Iceland's most popular English-language blog "The Iceland Weather Report". She has also written extensively about Iceland for the international media. You can connect with Alda via her website aldasigmunds.com, or catch up with her on Twitter: @aldakalda.

Made in the USA
Middletown, DE
23 August 2019